Who is the *real* Mich

Sky Matthews: "Mic ever was one. Had me better than everyone else, and look what it got him. Yeah, I was the one who set the cops on him. I say, shoot on sight."

Vanessa Matthews: "Michael is a liar and a thief. That diamond necklace was mine, by rights. But I don't care about that. If he would just get down on his knees and beg my forgiveness—just once!—I'd take him back. Yeah, in a hot second I would."

Bob Taylor: "You know how all your life there's always some guy who's better than you at everything? That's Michael Drayton. But now he's in deep trouble. If everything they say about him is true, he's in for a long, long prison term when they catch him."

Jessie MacAllister: "The man is impossible. He thinks he can take on the world and win, as long as he has right on his side. The cops are after him, and I went after him, too, hoping for that reward money. But now I don't know. Listen, I've always judged a man by how hard he could ride, how well he could rope, but this guy—he's on a whole other level. I...I've really never felt like this about a man before. It scares the hell out of me."

Please address questions and book requests to: Harlequin Reader Service
U.S.: 3010 Walden Ave., P.O. Box 1325, Buffalo, NY 14269
Canadian: P.O. Box 609, Fort Erie, Ont. L2A 5X3

WESTERN *Lovers*™

HELEN CONRAD

DESPERADO

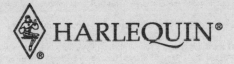

TORONTO • NEW YORK • LONDON
AMSTERDAM • PARIS • SYDNEY • HAMBURG
STOCKHOLM • ATHENS • TOKYO • MILAN • MADRID
PRAGUE • WARSAW • BUDAPEST • AUCKLAND

HARLEQUIN BOOKS
225 Duncan Mill Road, Don Mills,
Ontario, Canada M3B 3K9

ISBN 0-373-30189-8

DESPERADO

Copyright © 1988 by Helen Conrad

This edition published by arrangement with Harlequin Books S.A.

® and TM are trademarks of the publisher. Trademarks indicated with
® are registered in the United States Patent and Trademark Office, the
Canadian Trade Marks Office and in other countries.

Visit us at www.eHarlequin.com

Printed in U.S.A.

PROLOGUE

MICHAEL DRAYTON TOOK a deep breath, then grimaced, reacting to the unpleasant smell of old cigarettes and long-abandoned coffee cups. The room around him boiled with constant motion, constant noise. Telephones chimed, typewriters clacked, the gruff voices of police clerks were answered by shrill denials or surly admissions. Michael had managed to block all that out, making it seem just another part of the hammer that was pounding at his temples. But the smell, Lord, couldn't they air the place out once in a while?

He glanced across the desk at the serious face of Bob Taylor, who sat speaking softly into the telephone. They'd never been friends exactly, but he trusted Bob. They'd gone to prep school together right there in San Francisco, almost twenty years ago. They shared a common thread of experience that held the fabric of their lives in a parallel, if not a common, weave. He'd thought once that Bob had made a bad choice going into police work. Now he almost envied him.

Bob's light hair was thinning on top. Michael's hand went unconsciously to his own abundant dark hair, as though to reassure himself. For just a moment he had a picture in his mind of two young men both running for a soccer ball, sunlight beating down on their heads. He could hardly imagine this Bob doing that now. He wondered if he had changed as much himself.

But of course he had. Looking inward, he remembered the hope and optimism of those days. He'd been a golden boy then. Everything had fallen into place for him. The future had appeared limitless. When had it all begun to go bad?

Michael shifted position in his uncomfortable chair, watching as Bob put the phone back in its cradle and turned slowly toward him. The pale blue eyes were guarded, the face set. Michael stared hard, trying to read something in the man's lack of expression. Whose side was he on?

"No help there," Bob said shortly. Deliberately he set his elbows on the desk and leaned his chin on his folded fingers. "You don't have a heck of a lot for me to go on," he pointed out.

Annoyance flashed through Michael's long, rangy body and he straightened in the chair, his strong hands grasping the armrests as though to keep from doing something else with them. "I went through the warehouses," he said, his voice even and tightly controlled. "I saw abundant evidence of what Sky Matthews is doing. When I confronted him, he didn't deny it. First he offered me a piece of the action, and when I refused, he threatened me."

Bob's face didn't change. "So you decided to come here." Michael nodded.

Bob sighed. "You've got to give me more to go on than that. I mean, after all, the man's been your benefactor. Rumor had it he was the only one who would hire you after you got out. That he was like a second father to you. And you want to turn him in on smuggling charges?" His eyes narrowed. "What's this all about, Drayton?"

Michael's blue eyes crackled with impatience. "I know how this looks. Why do you think I came to you instead of going straight to the FBI? You're a detective on the force. You know me. You know I wouldn't make a charge like this if it wasn't true."

"I know you all right."

Something about Bob's tone sent a warning sizzling through Michael's head, but he didn't stop to analyze it. He leaned forward, his face intent, his manner eager. "Okay, I can accept that you can't run with this on my word alone. There's someone else who knows more about it than I do. His name's Kerry Carter. He was one of Sky's pilots, quit about six months ago. He was close to Sky, was being groomed for upper management...."

"Until you cut him out, as I remember."

Michael's brows drew together. "We had our differences," he acknowledged. "He tried to tell me what was going on at the time he left, but I didn't believe him. Until I saw for myself."

"So where is he?"

Michael hesitated. "That's the hard part. I'm not sure exactly. He was sick to death of civilization when he left, told me he was going to Bisbee, that place in Arizona full of mines, near the Mexican border. He was going to live off the land, do some amateur prospecting, he said. If you could get hold of him…"

Bob's shoulders rose and fell. "Forget it. I've got no grounds, no way I could justify a search for the man."

Michael's mouth thinned. "You've got to move fast on this. Sky's probably covering up as we speak. Hiding the evidence." Michael's hand flexed on the armrest. "Who can you call? What can we do?"

Bob looked down at the paperwork on his desk, shuffling things here and there, before he answered. "Sky Matthews is a powerful man," he said slowly. "You don't go accusing a man like that of felonies without some shred of proof."

Michael felt like a bomb about to explode. He wanted to wipe that guarded expression off Bob's face, wipe his desk clean with a sweep of his arm, yell at him, yell at everyone, get some action. With effort, he controlled his temper and managed to speak calmly. "You'll have the proof if you'll go and take a look in those warehouses of his down by the Embarcadero."

"No judge is going to issue a warrant without some reasonable justification. Your say-so won't do it."

Michael spread his arms wide, then clenched his hands. "I'll go with you to the judge. I'll tell him what I've seen."

A sardonic smile twisted Bob's face. "You're not what I'd call the most credible witness around."

Frustration ripped through Michael. He came up against the same thing everywhere he went, every time he opened his mouth. "I'm telling you the truth," he ground out.

A curious look of satisfaction settled on Bob's face. "You've got to see this from an objective point of view. It's your word against his." He shrugged. "And you've spent time in prison for embezzlement. Who's going to believe you?"

Michael's eyes were hard as flint. "You are," he said coldly, fixing Bob with his steely stare.

For the first time, the other man's gaze flickered uncertainly. He tried to face Michael's glare, couldn't, and glanced down at a paper on the desk in front of him. "Maybe you'd better take a look at this," he murmured, shoving the paper toward Michael. "It came in just before you did."

Michael looked down, taking the form in his hand. "Arrest warrant" was the heading. "Michael Drayton" read the filled-in portion. "Wanted for embezzlement of funds from Matthews Aviation over a period of two years. Wanted for the theft of a valuable heirloom diamond necklace, taken from the Matthews home." Sky Matthews had signed the complaint. His daughter, Vanessa Matthews, had cosigned.

Michael felt the room fall away. The pounding in his head crescendoed. Prison. He wouldn't go back to prison. Nothing…and no one…was going to put him back there.

It took a moment for him to regain control. Dropping the paper, he met Bob's gaze and tried to smile. "Sky works fast," he said, his voice sounding hoarse in his ears. "I was just with him an hour ago."

"You realize what I'm obliged to do."

Michael nodded. "Sure, Inspector." His tone was sarcastic, his gaze fierce. "You going to put the cuffs on me yourself, or are you going to call one of your boys in blue to do it for you?"

The two men stared hard, their gazes each filled with anger, question. Adrenaline was coursing through Michael's veins. Should he make a run for it? Would he get out the door without a bullet in his back? Would he rather go to prison?

"Let me go, Taylor," Michael said softly. "Just give me a chance. For old times' sake."

Bob's face didn't change.

"Come on," Michael urged. "Just give me a few days. Let

me try to get hold of Kerry Carter. Let me talk to him, convince him to come back and tell you what he knows. I'll get this cleared up. I swear it.''

Bob stared back for a long moment, and then his eyes narrowed. ''For old times' sake,'' he murmured. ''I remember old times, Michael. How much do you remember?'' He grimaced. ''Darlene Peterson,'' he went on slowly. ''That was her name. Remember Darlene, Michael?''

Michael's mind spun, trying to dredge up a picture. Blond hair, he thought vaguely. A nervous giggle. Persian Melon lipstick. Prep school. A thousand years ago.

''I was crazy about Darlene Peterson when we were at Oxfield,'' Bob continued. ''She even wore my ring for a while. Until she saw you make the winning touchdown in the Benton Hills game. Remember that?'' He laughed shortly. ''Yeah, you were always making winning touchdowns, weren't you? Darlene saw that, and suddenly I became nothing but a way to meet the great Michael Drayton.''

Michael didn't like the way this conversation was going. ''Bob, listen,'' he began, but Bob was on a tear.

''Winning touchdowns, winning girls, winning state finals with the swim team,'' the other man mused. ''There were times I hated you. And then there were times I wished I *were* you.'' A slow grin crept over his face. ''And then there's now.'' He shook his head. ''Life's funny, isn't it?''

This was obviously a mistake. It had been a mistake from the first. He should have run while he'd had the chance. He should have left town. Bob Taylor had him where he wanted him. Revenge was sweet, they said. Michael wouldn't know. Revenge was being denied him at every turn.

He glanced to the side, quickly judging the distance to the door, and then to the stairs beyond. At the same time he took a survey of how many police officers were milling between him and freedom. Too many. But he would have the advantage of surprise.

Bob was watching him, probably reading his mind, but he couldn't help that. A man could only do what he could do. Michael was tensed, ready to run, when Bob spoke again.

"Want to know something else that's funny?" He leaned back in his chair. "I married Darlene. We've got three kids and a Saint Bernard. And she still talks about you to this day."

Michael met Bob's gaze helplessly. What could he say? To his surprise, Bob grinned and looked pointedly at his watch. "Whoops," he said, "Look at the time. My coffee break." He rose from behind the desk. "I'll be back in about ten minutes. You want me to bring you something?"

Michael stared at him, not yet sure. "What?"

"Don't you go anywhere," Bob said softly. He paused, then chuckled. "You bastard," he murmured. "This one's for Darlene." A moment later he was gone.

It took Michael a few seconds to fully absorb what had happened, but by then he was up and walking swiftly toward the door. Down the stairs, out through the lobby and into his car—it all took under sixty seconds. Turning on the engine, he roared toward the freeway. He didn't have to think about what he would do. It was all laid out in front of him, as though he'd been planning it for weeks.

The salesman at the car showroom wasn't surprised to see him again. He'd been in to look at the new Firebirds the week before.

"I'll take that one," Michael said without preamble. "The black-and-gold."

"You've made a wonderful choice." The man's eyes gleamed. "If you'll step this way, we just need a bit of your time for the paperwork."

"I don't have much time," Michael returned sharply. "I believe you've already checked out my credit references. Anyhow, I've decided to pay cash." He pulled out his checkbook. "Call my bank, if you like. I'll make out a check."

Twenty minutes later the car was his. He parked it next to his old Camaro, glancing around to see if he was being observed. He then removed his tool kit from the trunk, selected a screwdriver and began to remove the cover to the stereo speaker in the new car. Working quickly, he took it apart, laid the cover on the seat, then went back to the Camaro. The car door squeaked as he opened it, but no one looked over. Glancing around once more, he slipped his hand into a slit in the upholstery and pulled out a strand of jewels that sparkled in the afternoon sun. He stuffed them into his pocket and stepped back to the new car, transferring the necklace into the open speaker. It coiled inside the black box like a snake, and he stared at it for just a moment before he clamped the speaker cover back again and began to screw it into place.

Moments later he was testing the power of his new car on the freeway. Destination: Arizona.

CHAPTER ONE

A BLUE NORTHER HAD BEEN BLOWING all day. The winds were finally tapering off, but it was cold, colder than usual, and Jessie had been out seeing to the few head of cattle she had left. She came in the back door of the seedy little truck stop, stomping her boots on the back stoop, pulling off her leather gloves, but keeping on her fleece-lined jacket. She could tell right away Harley hadn't been able to get the furnace going. The only relief from the cold came from what little heat the greasy cookstove could generate. And every time someone came in the door of the Bar None Café, then went out.

One lone customer sat at the counter. He was hunched over his coffee as though it were a camp fire and he needed all the warmth he could get.

Just looking at the man gave Jessie the shivers. There was a curious hardness to his face, as though he'd just been hit and was steeling himself not to flinch. He appeared to be in his late thirties. His dark hair was combed back off his face, emphasizing a distinct and jagged streak of silver that ran from the right temple. His eyes were silver blue, like mountain lakes on a frosty morning, but they were shifty. He spent as much time glancing out the front window to see who was going by on the highway as he did looking down at his coffee cup and eating his day-old Danish.

Jessie saw she didn't know the man, and stayed where she was back in the kitchen. She didn't want to get caught up in a conversation with someone who was just passing through. Tourist, probably, she thought. They asked too many dumb questions. Such as, "Did any of your folks ever know Doc

Holliday down there at Tombstone?'' as though the nineteenth century were last weekend or something.

"Hey, Harley," she said as her father lumbered in to clean the hamburger grease off the griddle. "Cold in here."

He grunted. "Damn furnace" was all he said, not wasting a glance on his only offspring.

Big and raw-boned, Harley MacAllister had fought in Korea and come back fixing to take over his father's little ranch, marry his childhood sweetheart and raise a passel of kids. The marriage worked out okay, but the only kid he got was Jessie, and ranching on a small scale just didn't seem to pay, so he'd tried to get out of that. Only Jessie, more than grown-up now and with a strong will of her own, wouldn't let him.

She poured herself some steaming coffee and wrapped her hands around the hot mug, watching her father work. "Faye didn't come in?" she asked at last, because she knew he was waiting for the question.

"Nope." He turned and fixed her with a glare. "And I sure could have used some help about an hour ago. I had five twelve-wheelers stacked up outside and ten hungry men asking for omelets with their burgers, and me with no one to help in here."

Jessie hid her smile in the coffee mug. You had to boil down everything Harley said, since he had a real knack for embellishment. The truth was probably closer to two pickups and a station wagon, but she knew that didn't diminish his frustration at the fact that his only daughter refused to work the truck stop with him.

Jessie had married young, but it hadn't worked out, and she'd moved back home. Now she and her father lived together in the old ramshackle house Harley's father had built in the twenties, but Harley went to work in the morning, and Jessie rode the range.

The café had been his idea from the start. "Maybe I just wasn't meant to be a cattle rancher, sugar," he'd told Jessie five years earlier. "Ever since your mother died, it's been one disaster after another. I don't have the will to try again. I'm going to open me a nice little restaurant out on the high-way...."

Jessie had hated it. You might as well move to the city as open a restaurant. Serving food to passing truckers had nothing at all to do with ranching. Working with horses and cattle out in the open was all she'd ever wanted to do. She wasn't about to let anyone take that away from her.

"You want a restaurant, you run it," she'd told him. "I'll take care of the ranch."

And that was how things stood. Jessie hired on boys from town to help her, and Harley hired girls from town to help him. Neither venture was much of a success as yet. It all came down to no money.

Harley could have used a nice little nest egg to clean up the café, put in some modern equipment and really make it into a nice place where people would want to stop. Jessic could have used a bankroll to get the herd up to numbers that would be cost-effective. Unless they struck gold on their property, or maybe sunk an oil well, Jessie didn't know where either one of them would get it. Lately it seemed they were both sliding backward. But neither was ready to give up.

"When do you think you'll be able to get the furnace working again?" she asked as he walked past, carrying cardboard boxes of supplies.

He grunted and didn't speak as he arranged the boxes on the shelf. Then he turned and glowered at her. "It's a goner," he said roughly. "I'm gonna need a new one."

She put down the mug, knowing without asking that there was no money for it. "Maybe you'd better pray for an early summer, instead," she said dryly, but her dark eyes were full of sympathy. It was one darn thing after another.

"Maybe...maybe once we get that new sign up, the union truckers will start stopping along with the independents and then we'll have a lot more spending capital...." His voice trailed off and he gestured with his hand, a helpless motion that broke her heart.

She forced herself to look away before her eyes filled with tears and she made a damn fool out of herself. "You've only

got one customer now," she noted, craning to get another look
at the man. At least he'd do for a change in subject. "Who is
he, anyway?"

Harley shrugged, turning away, as embarrassed as his daughter. "Tourist." That was their name for anyone passing through
who wasn't a trucker. He went into the back room to get out
more supplies and Jessie went on looking at the stranger.

Wide shoulders, she noted. But his hands were white and
soft. Well, not soft exactly, but uncallused. She was used to
making a quick appraisal of a man's ability for hard manual
labor because she had to hire men for just that all the time.
This one worked at a desk, she'd wager. And from the look of
his suit and long, dark overcoat, he was straight out of the city.

She glanced out through the front windows, looking for his
car. The black-and-gold vehicle sported California plates, with
San Francisco stamped on the plate holder. She grinned to herself, pleased with her own perceptiveness. But then she looked
back at the man, watching his wariness, his restless unease.
Damned if the guy wasn't scared of something, she thought,
nodding to herself. "Hey, mister," she whispered. "What are
you running from?"

Harley went out and started wiping the counter around the
stranger. "Anything else I can get you?" he asked.

The man shook his head. "No, thanks. But you could tell
me if there's somewhere around here I could camp for the
night," he said.

Harley glanced at the man's suit and overcoat doubtfully.
"There's a motel in town," he said.

"I'd rather camp."

Harley shrugged. "Well, then, you can just about take your
pick, son." He leaned on the counter, and Jessie grinned,
watching him go into his favorite role—local expert and helpful
guide to southern Arizona. "There's plenty of land between
here and Tucson—if that's the way you're headed?"

The stranger nodded.

"As I say, there's ample opportunity and plenty of land,
mine included. In fact, I'd say you could find a likely looking
canyon anywhere along the highway over the next few miles,

and you'd be right on my land. Just go ahead, pull off and find yourself a spot. Ain't nobody going to bother you tonight.''

Jessie grimaced, throwing out what was left of the coffee, which had gone cold. Darn that Harley—he'd give away the ranch if she afforded him half a chance. It was a wonder he didn't give away the food when people stopped by.

Harley talked to the stranger for a few minutes more, then came back into the kitchen and began filling the sink with sudsy water. Jessie lingered. She'd only meant to stop for hot coffee, then be gone, but something about the man at the counter seemed to hold her there. ''Get out of here, mister,'' she whispered. ''Let me get back to work.''

As though he'd heard her, he rose abruptly, throwing money down on the counter and striding for the door. He stopped right in the doorway, looking up and down the highway. Jessie watched. He was taller than she'd expected, filling the opening. There was something dangerous about him, some barely leashed potential for emotion or violence that she couldn't quite put her finger on. It gave her the shivers again. A moment later he was gone.

''You're down to nobody,'' she told her father as the bell sounded and the door closed behind the stranger.

''Good,'' he grunted. ''You want to clear up his mess for me?''

She put the coffee mug down in the sink and grinned as she began to pull on her leather gloves. ''You want to come muck out Smoke's stable for me?'' she asked in return.

The only answer she got was unrepeatable, and she left, laughing.

She was back two hours later, stomping off the mud on the back stoop again and swearing as she came in the door. The place was empty and her father was in the dining area, stretched out on two chairs he'd shoved together, watching a game show on television.

''Harley, will you look at this?'' she grabbed a walkie-talkie unit from its place on the shelf next to the coffee filters and shook it in his face. ''I yelled at you on this thing for ten minutes, and I never got one bit of response.''

Harley took off the glasses he wore for television viewing and looked at the radio in her hand. "You been trying to get ahold of me?" he asked a bit sheepishly.

Jessie let out all her breath in an exasperated sigh, reached over to turn down the blaring television and faced her father. "Yes sir, I have. I thought we got these things so we could use them in cases of emergency! But if you never even pay any attention when the thing is screaming at you…"

Harley looked contrite. "I didn't hear it. Guess I had the TV turned up too loud."

She groaned and put the unit back on the shelf, throwing him an angry look. "Another good idea sabotaged," she grumbled.

Harley never let anything get him down for long. He shrugged away her anger. "What happened, anyway? Somebody throw a shoe or something."

"No," she snapped, plunking down in a chair beside him. "Charlie Cruz got tangled in some barbed wire, cut his leg up real bad. We could have used some paramedics out there, if only you'd been alert enough to call them."

"Oh, my God." Now he was sorry. "Where is the boy? Shall we call them now?"

She pulled off her hat and threw it down on the Formica tabletop, revealing dark blond hair wound tightly in a long braid. "Never mind." She looked sideways at her father's anxious face. She didn't want to let him off the hook too quickly. "Just never mind. It's too late now." She almost smiled at his stricken expression. "The truth is, Norma Mae happened by in her new van and we loaded him in. She's taking him over to Lincoln Memorial right now. I suppose they'll sew him up."

"Oh, good." Harley's sigh was halfway between contentment and relief. His eyes strayed back to the game show.

Jessie sat up straight, demanding attention. "But darn it all, Harley, why can't you keep the walkie-talkie in mind? Last time I was trying to warn you that Aunt Jill was on her way so you could get out of here and hide somewhere, but you didn't pay any attention then, either, and look what happened. She stayed a week."

The crunch of tires on gravel brought both of their heads around.

"Sheriff Jensen," Jessie said, though they could both see who it was. "Wonder what he wants?"

"My last piece of cherry pie, I reckon. That's what he usually wants. And that's what he usually gets."

"Oh, no, he doesn't," she said, jumping up and heading for the kitchen. "Not this time. Where is it? I've had my mind on that pie since breakfast." She rummaged in the bread cabinet and came up with the generous slice that was all that was left of the plump pie she'd seen arrive earlier that day. Grabbing a fork from the silverware drawer, she took a bite, savoring the tartness. Out in the dining room, she heard her father greeting the sheriff.

"How are you doing, Harley?" the sheriff said. "I haven't got time to stop and chat today. Got me this picture came in over the wire service. Some embezzler. Seems he was spotted in Bisbee earlier today. He might just come on through here. Mind if I put the picture up on your bulletin board? You all get a lot of through traffic. Someone might spot this guy."

"Go right ahead, sheriff. Who's the fugitive?"

"Michael Drayton's the name. Took a mess of diamonds from his rich girlfriend and took a mess of money from her daddy's company. Sky Matthews. You remember him? Old war hero from Korea. Started Matthews Aviation, made his millions." The sheriff chuckled. "Say, they've got a reward out for this guy. Maybe you can make yourself a few bucks. You all will keep your eyes open, won't you?"

Jessie forked up the last bite of cherry pie while her father showed the sheriff to the door. Millions. Her lids dropped and she dreamed for a moment. What even a fraction of that amount could do for the ranch and café.

Her father came back in and she got up, slipping her dish into the sink but neglecting to wash it. "Guess I'll get back to work," she said, reaching for her hat. "Still got almost an hour before sundown."

Harley was staring at the picture the sheriff had pinned to the wall. "Come here," he said softly.

"Hmm?"

"Come take a look at this. What do you think?"

Jessie walked over and glanced at the picture. Eyes widening, she looked again. The dark hair with the streak of silver. The lean, hard face. "It's him!" she exclaimed. "That guy who was here earlier. My God, catch the sheriff!"

It was too late. Sheriff Jensen was just disappearing in a cloud of dust. Jessie and Harley looked at each other, then back at the picture.

"'Five thousand dollars reward for information leading to the apprehension and conviction…?'" she read out loud. She turned to her father, excitement surging in her. "We could get that money," she cried.

Harley was doubtful. He rubbed his high forehead with the palm of his hand. "How do you figure that?" he asked. "It's been a couple of hours since he was in here. He's halfway to Tucson by now."

"But that's just it! We know he's halfway to Tucson. No one else knows that. When we tell the sheriff—" Her mouth dropped open. "No, wait! He wasn't going to Tucson tonight. Remember? You told him to go ahead and camp on our land."

Now Harley was beginning to believe in the dream, as well. "You're right. I sure did. I told him about Silver Creek Canyon."

She nodded, eyes shining. "Oh, Daddy, this is it. I can feel it. We're going to get that reward money." She hugged him tightly. "And we'll share it, half and half. You'll be able to get new signs painted, buy a new furnace, and I—"

"Wait a minute, wait a minute." He carefully disentangled himself from her excited embrace. "We don't have that money yet. And what if he didn't camp where I told him to? What if he turned around and headed for Mexico?"

"You're right." Jessie bit her lip, thinking hard. "Okay, here's what we do. You stay here and try to get in touch with Sheriff Jensen. I'll take Smoke and ride out to the canyon and see if he's there."

Harley looked at his daughter as though she'd grown horns

before his eyes. "Are you crazy? I won't have you out there with some criminal."

"Oh, Harley, be serious. I'm not going to ride right into his camp and ask him if he's the guy who stole the diamonds." It had been a long time since Jessie had listened to much her father said. She loved him dearly, but for about half her life, ever since she turned fifteen, she'd been the one whose quick thinking and ideas had propelled their little family. And her father's fears weren't about to stop her now.

She pulled open a drawer and rummaged until she came up with a pair of binoculars. "I'll lay low and watch him through these. That way I can keep track of him in case it takes a while to get through to the sheriff. Meanwhile…" She took the walkie-talkie unit off the shelf and thrust it at her father. "Meanwhile we'll keep in touch with this. If you think you can keep the TV off long enough."

Harley didn't rise to the bait. "You know, that just might work." He looked at his daughter wonderingly. She always did manage to surprise him.

"Sure it'll work." She grinned at him. "That way we'll keep tabs on him and get the credit when he gets arrested." She jammed her hat on her head and turned toward the door. "You get busy on the phone. It ought to take me about fifteen minutes to ride out there. I'll call in as soon as I spot him."

Harley went to the door and watched her swing up on to the large gray gelding. "Good luck, honey," he called after her as she urged Smoke into a gallop. She waved and gave a small rebel yell. Harley laughed, shaking his head. Where had that rascal come from, anyway? When she'd been born, he'd expected a peaches-and-cream sort of girl, someone who wore lace and sat on velvet pillows with ribbons in her hair. Instead he got Jessie, wild as any boy in her time, and now at thirty, as hard a ranch worker as any man. "Good luck, honey," he said again, though she was halfway up the hill and nearly hidden by a small stand of cottonwoods. She was the dearest thing he had left. A tremor shook him, a premonition of danger and loss. He frowned, then shook it off, but he watched Jessie until she disappeared over the hill before he turned back into the café and went to the telephone.

CHAPTER TWO

JESSIE COULD ALMOST TASTE that reward money.

She'd left Smoke down the hill and had worked her way to the top of the rise on her belly, looking for the fugitive. He was there all right, the low-down thief. Binoculars raised, she confirmed it.

"Michael Drayton," she whispered. "Gotcha."

He'd pulled his black-and-gold sports car as far off the road as he could to a place where it was hidden by some creosote bushes. A sleeping bag lay spread out on the ground and he'd started a small fire. The man himself was seated on a rock, still dressed in the suit and overcoat, throwing little sticks into the fire the way a kid throws rocks into a pond because there isn't anything better to do.

Twilight was falling and the light would be gone very soon. Jessie watched him for a moment, listening to the noise of cars speeding by on the nearby highway. It was the moment between the tag-end of day and the leading edge of nightfall when all the desert world seemed to be waiting, breath held, to see what would happen next. The rocky soil was still hot from the clear sunlight of day, and the wind had pretty much died down. Jessie watched the city man look miserable for a little longer, then she wiggled back down out of sight and pulled out her walkie-talkie.

"Harley?" she said hoarsely, cupping her hands to hold in the sound of her voice. "Harley? Come in, Harley."

"I'm here." Her father's voice was oddly reassuring as it crackled through the evening air. Jessie realized suddenly she'd been more tense than she'd let herself know. "You okay?"

"Of course I'm okay. He's here, just waiting to be arrested. Where's the sheriff?"

"Can't get hold of him."

"What do you mean, you can't get hold of him?"

"His line's still busy. If that dang fool would only get off the phone, I'd have him out there. Say, who do you think he's talking to all this time?"

"Liz Clark, most likely." Jessie sighed impatiently. The sheriff had been head over heels for Liz for years and she held him off like a cat playing with a mouse. She swore she'd been a widow for too long to consider marrying again, so she held out, and the sheriff held on. "Look, Daddy, get the operator to break in. Tell her it's an emergency."

"I already tried that," he replied in a tone of injured pride. "No one will answer at the operator's number. The whole dang phone company's been out to lunch since they broke up the monopoly—"

"Keep trying." She clicked off and shimmied her way to the top of the rise again. Michael Drayton was pacing around the area, looking caged, and unhappy about it.

"Watch out, Mister Jewel Thief," she whispered. "You'll ruin your Italian leather shoes."

That didn't seem to concern him at the moment. As she watched, he stopped, took careful aim and kicked the side of a boulder.

Jessie jumped. "Ouch," she whispered. He probably said something similar, but she couldn't hear him. He jumped around for a moment, holding his foot, and though she couldn't make out the words, she knew he was swearing at himself.

"I could have told you not to do that," she muttered.

Then he did a strange thing. Dropping to his knees, he began to roll up the sleeping bag. Jessie sat up, staring through the binoculars, but she didn't wait long to come to a conclusion. He wasn't going to stay. The stranger was moving on.

Hardly caring any longer what noise she made, she scrambled back down out of his view and called her father on the walkie-talkie.

"Did you get the sheriff yet?" she demanded.

"No, I—"

"Listen. He's packing up! I think he's moving on!"

"What?"

"I'm going down there. One way or another, I've got to stop him."

"Jessica." Harley hadn't used that tone since she was a child. "You're not going down there. He might have a gun."

"Don't worry. I won't do anything stupid. He won't know who I am. I don't think he saw me at the café. I'll just wander down there. He can't be so desperate he'd shoot any female who wandered into his camp."

"We don't know that, Jessica. You listen to me, girl—"

Time was running out and she couldn't waste it arguing. She clicked off the walkie-talkie and set it behind a rock, then ran down to where Smoke was waiting.

"You go on home, big boy. You've got oats waiting," she whispered, rubbing his nose before she went to tie the reins to the saddle horn. "Git." She gave him a swat and he started off complacently, never even looking back. She headed back up the rise. Her heart was thumping in her throat. Everyone had always called her brave. She'd never been so sure she was that. Now she was finally putting it to the test.

BRAVERY WAS AN ISSUE Michael didn't want to think about. Actually, he'd never given it much thought. He was the sort of man who did what had to be done and didn't waste a lot of time on analysis. He'd taken care of himself in many an awkward situation—including prison. Even though it had been a minimum-security prison, he'd had a few run-ins where he'd held his own. He'd done high-rise construction work as a part-time job during his college years, and he'd put in enough solo flying time to get his private pilot's license. Brave? No. Just unwilling to let danger keep him from doing what he wanted to do.

But this was different. He glanced around at the gathering shadows and felt a tremor of unease he didn't like to admit to. This place, this wild and lonely desert, didn't even give you the odds of an average crapshoot. Someone else was holding all the cards here, and Michael didn't even get to look at his own hand.

Running impatient fingers through his thick hair, he let out a sigh of surrender. He had to get some sleep. He'd grabbed two or three hours' worth at a rest stop along the freeway the previous night, but other than that, he'd been on the run since leaving San Francisco the day before. He'd thought he could camp out, that it would be safer than staying in a motel. Stopping at a sporting goods store, he'd bought his first sleeping bag. Then he'd brought it here to Silver Creek Canyon and spread it out on the rocky ground, knowing right away there was no way he was going to sleep in it.

The man at the sporting goods shop had shown him a collection of desert insects molded into clear plastic mounds for use as decorative paperweights. Tarantulas. Scorpions. Ants the size of mice. Lizards. They all lived in the desert. Most of them came out at night.

"You've got to watch your sleeping bag," the man at the store had told him. "Check it every time you get inside. 'Specially for rattlers. They love to curl up in a warm sleeping bag."

And still Michael had thought everything would be all right. Until night fell.

He kicked out the fire and looked around at the darkness. God only knew what was out there. He didn't want to find out. Turning on his heel, he walked quickly to his car, opened the door and slid in behind the wheel, enjoying the smell of well-oiled leather. The engine purred and he backed out from behind the ugly bush where he'd parked. Putting her into first, he started for the highway, his tires crunching over the rocky road.

A sense of relief washed over him as he saw the lights ahead. Danger awaited him there, too, but at least he knew the odds and could work with the territory. He'd find some crummy little motel, he decided. Something on the outskirts of Tucson. He'd made it this far, all the way down to Bisbee, near the Mexican border, where he'd thought he would find Kerry Carter. Now he was traveling north, following a new lead.

Something tumbled into the beam of his headlights and he

jammed on the brakes, twisting the wheel at the same time to avoid hitting it. It was human. He could see that right away.

He jumped from the car. "You all right?" he called out.

The figure rose a bit shakily from the ground. At first he thought it was a boy, but then the hat fell off and he saw that the boots, jeans and leather jacket had been camouflaging a woman—not too tall and wiry, but full grown nonetheless. For some reason that annoyed him. You could pick a teenage boy up, dust him off and send him on his way. But some streak of primordial chivalry deep inside told him you couldn't do that with a woman. You had to make sure she was safe.

"What the hell are you doing jumping out in front of cars like that?" he demanded, stopping just short of where she stood.

Jessie tossed her head, leaned down to grab her hat and stuck it back on her head. "I slipped," she said simply, and it was true. She'd been in such a hurry to stop him she'd forgotten to take care coming down the slope. Her heart was pounding. It was lucky he hadn't hit her.

"What are you doing out here in the middle of nowhere?" The exasperation was plain in his voice.

"Riding." Her eyes narrowed and she held his gaze with her own. The headlights from the car lit the scene with an unearthly white light. He looked like the devil himself with his dark face, black overcoat and the streak of silver in his hair. "Just riding," she repeated, gathering her courage. "What are *you* doing here on my daddy's land?"

"Your daddy's land?" he echoed, eyeing her sharply. "Does your father run that little greasy spoon down the road?"

Her mouth formed a stubborn line. She might hate the place herself, but when threatened, her family had always closed ranks. "It's a restaurant," she said, enunciating every syllable.

He almost grinned, enjoying her defensiveness. But he wasn't here to enjoy himself. He had places to go. So he frowned, instead, as though that would help speed her on her way. "If you're out riding, where's your horse?"

Jessie shifted weight from one leg to the other. "She threw me. That's why I'm walking."

Michael shook his head in derision. "Yeah, well, that's why I always say, never trust an animal that's bigger than you are."

She answered his frown with one of her own. This crook was not only from the city, he was anticountry. She didn't like his sort. Not at all. But she didn't have to like him to collect that reward money. If only the sheriff would get a move on. What was she supposed to do now, chitchat with this criminal until he arrived? She'd never been one for small talk in the first place.

"I've got to get going," he said, almost as though reading her mind. He started toward his car, betraying with a sideways look that he didn't feel comfortable about leaving her there in the dark. "You going to be all right?"

She glanced toward the highway. If there was no way to make him stay, she was going to have to go with him. She didn't like the idea. In fact, her throat went a little dry at the thought. But what else could she do? That damn sheriff…

"No," she said shortly. "But I guess I could hitch a ride from someone. There's plenty of traffic out there." She looked at him defiantly, daring him to abandon her.

He turned reluctantly toward her again. He knew the score as well as she did, but he was going to avoid facing it for as long as he could. "You can't go and stick your thumb out on that highway." He glanced up at the hills she'd come tumbling out of. "I don't suppose there's any way to find that horse of yours."

She shook her head. "He's halfway back to his stable by now."

He sighed, gritting his teeth. "I thought this was your land. Why don't you just walk home?"

"Across these rocky hills in the dark? I'd break my leg for sure."

He watched her for a long moment. He wasn't going to offer. She was going to have to ask. They glared at each other, neither wanting to be the first to give in.

"I don't suppose you could give me a ride into town?" Jessie said stiffly.

He shook his head, grasping at straws. "Nope. I'm heading in the opposite direction."

Jessie threw one last despairing glance toward the highway. That damn sheriff! After all these years of boasting, when he finally got a chance to play the hero, he missed his cue.

She hated the thought of getting into a car with this man. She already knew he was a crook. Lord only knew what else he was. She'd be taking a chance—but what choice did she have? She had to get that reward money.

She looked at him searchingly. "Actually, that's the way I'm going, too. I've got to get to Tucson," she added quickly. "I…I was on my way there when my horse threw me." She wasn't going to let this man out of her sight. She'd have to stick with him and wait for a chance to call the cops.

"You were going to ride to Tucson on horseback tonight?" Even he knew that was impossible. "Come on. Give me a break." His sharp glance swept over her. "Besides, you said you wanted a ride into town."

"I changed my mind."

Skepticism washed across his face. "That's some woman's prerogative you're claiming there."

She took a step toward him. "Look, it's none of your business what I was doing or where I want to go. But I could use a ride. And since you've got an empty seat…" She shrugged. "Why not let me sit in it?"

He hesitated. He didn't want to take her along, but a sudden thought occurred to him. Maybe she was running, too. A kindred spirit in a strange land. He studied her for a moment, interested in spite of himself. The dark brown eyes were cool, unfriendly. He couldn't tell if she was pretty or not, not with the dirt smudged on her cheek and the hair coming loose in a wispy tangle around her face. He'd thought she was young at first, but on closer observation he realized she was probably thirty or more. There was no baby softness to her lean cheeks, no naive uncertainty to the set of her mouth. She appeared tough. Only one thing gave away the fact that she wasn't totally at ease. Her thumbs were hooked into the loops at the belt of her jeans, giving a casual look to her stance, but her other fingers were clenching and unclenching nervously.

"I suppose I could give you a ride," he admitted at last.

"Great." She didn't give him a chance to change his mind, striding quickly to the passenger side of the car and climbing in. "Thanks a lot."

He settled in beside her, casting one long look of reproach before he started the car. "Don't mention it," he said sardonically. He pulled the car out onto the highway and headed toward Tucson, keeping to the speed limit.

CHAPTER THREE

JESSIE UNCLENCHED HER HANDS and tried to relax. At first she thought there must be something wrong with the car's engine, but at last she realized that the thumping she heard was her own heart. She took a deep breath, trying to settle herself. Here she was in a car with a wanted man. She'd have to stay cool, stay calm and think everything out before she made any more moves.

For a fugitive, he didn't seem very nervous. She watched his hands. They were steady on the wheel. He wore no rings, no bracelet. She risked a quick glance at his face. It was totally expressionless, as though he were a million miles away, as though he'd forgotten all about her.

"You're not from around here, are you?" she asked, unable to stand the silence any longer.

He grunted but made no other sign that he'd heard her.

"You on a business trip?"

For all the response she got, he might have been deaf. Jessie couldn't resist a challenge like that. She leaned forward in her seat.

"Where are you headed, anyway?" she asked more loudly, letting him know she wasn't going to give up. "California?"

She got an answer this time. He swung his gaze to her, his eyes piercing. "What's it to you?" he growled.

She blinked, but held her ground. "If you don't want to answer the question, forget it," she snapped. "But you don't have to bite my head off."

He turned back to his driving, but the icy chill lingered. "I don't like questions," he muttered.

She wet her lips, looking around her for another topic. "This is a nice car," she said at last, reaching out to touch the wood of the dashboard.

"I like it," he said, and she hid her grin at his more moderate tone. She'd actually pulled a civil response out of him.

"Does it handle well on the highway?" she asked.

His hands gripped the wheel more tightly, but he answered once again. "Yes."

"Great." She was feeling pretty pleased with herself. He didn't want to talk, but she was making him do it, anyway. He wasn't so tough. "I'll bet you don't have any kids, do you? They sure wouldn't fit in a car this size."

"Listen," he said, throwing her a despairing glance before looking back at the road. "What are you after, the story of my life or something?"

She managed to sound insulted. "I'm just trying to make polite conversation."

"I don't want polite conversation."

She sniffed, letting him know she felt rebuffed. "Sorry."

Michael shook his head. Against his better judgment, he was relenting. Half turning to look at her, he gritted his teeth, then said gruffly, "Okay, you want a conversation? You tell me why you were going to Tucson in the middle of the night on the back of a horse."

"I reckon that's my business, same as your destination's yours," she muttered, turning to stare out the window into the blackness.

"Exactly my point."

They were silent for a moment. Headlights flashed by, cars going in the opposite direction. Cars full of families, friends. And here she was, riding with a thief.

"I know what you're doing," he said a few minutes later, seemingly having changed his mind about talking. "I'll bet you're running from something."

She half smiled. "Not me."

"Oh, no?" He looked over at her, his gaze taking in everything and recording it. "No ring. I'd say you weren't married. But you've got a boyfriend."

She snorted her disdain for his theorizing.

"Sure," he said smoothly, beginning to enjoy this. "His name's Curly. He's a cowboy. But he left you in the lurch, moved to Tucson to found a home for unwed horses, and now you're following him—"

"You city jerks think you're so damn superior!" Jessie's anger erupted suddenly. "Keep your snotty jokes to yourself, mister. I don't need them. Anyway, you're just trying to get around having to tell anything about yourself by pestering me."

Funny, she was thinking all the time she spoke, her sense of humor seemed to have curled up in a corner and died. She didn't usually overreact like this. But something about this man got to her. She just couldn't stand to have him making fun of her, or her way of life.

Michael saw that. For a moment, he was tempted to tease her again, just to see how mad he could get her. But one look at her strained face dissuaded him. "I'm not exactly the Lone Ranger, you know," he said, instead. "You haven't been spilling your guts, either."

She wasn't yet mollified. She nestled back against the door, as far from him as she could get. "You won't even admit you're going to California," she grumbled.

He shook his head. "I'm not headed for California. I've got another destination in mind."

She looked at him sideways, trying to guess where a crook would go. "Las Vegas, maybe? After all, there isn't much else going north."

His sigh of exasperation was audible. "How about Canada?" he suggested icily. "How about the North Pole?"

"It sure looks like you're the one running away from something, mister," she said softly, insinuatingly. "You're either in a hurry to get somewhere or in a hurry to get away from something. Which is it?"

He didn't answer, but she knew he'd heard. She also knew she was cutting much too close to the bone, taking chances. She never had learned when to keep her mouth shut. That was what Beau always used to say.

Beau. Why on earth was she thinking about her ex-husband at a time like this? The marriage had lasted for only eighteen months and had been over for almost ten years now. Hardly anyone even remembered it but her.

She glanced into the back seat of the car, wondering where he'd hidden the gems. In the seats, probably. Or maybe behind the door panels. Did he have the money with him, too? All that money. Some people seemed to get it so easily. All her life she'd scraped and saved and struggled. For just a moment she let her mind dwell on what money like that could do for the ranch and for Harley's restaurant. Stock. Equipment. New hands.

She shuddered again, and frowned. It didn't do anyone a bit of good to go pining after impossibilities. That money belonged to someone. She hated stealing, hated a thief. For once, she was going to do something about it.

Still, she was curious. Where had he hidden his booty? She glanced into the back seat again, but her eye was caught by something through the rear window. About a half mile behind, partly hidden by the traffic, was a flashing red light. The cops. Coming toward them, gaining fast.

She swung around and stared at Michael. His eyes were on the rearview mirror. He'd seen it, too. Her heart began to thump again. If they caught him now, would she get any credit? Probably not. This had to be the highway patrol, not Sheriff Jensen. They were far out of his jurisdiction by now. Damn!

Michael pulled over into the right lane and slowed. Her hands gripped the edge of the seat as she turned around to look. The flashing red light was right behind them and the siren was blaring loudly, filling the car with a scream that hurt her ears. Her breath caught in her throat. The red light flashed through the inside of the car, bathing them both in its garish glare. And then the police car was pulling around them, racing on ahead into the dark night, targeting some other victim.

"Wow," she said when she could breathe again. "I thought he was going to pull you over there for a minute."

"So did I." His voice was low, steady. She looked at him carefully, but could detect no sign of his having been shaken. Still, she knew this must be what he'd gone through all day. Perhaps, all his life. He turned suddenly, and his silver-blue eyes met her gaze and held it, daring her to say something. She kept very still, breathing more easily when he turned back to his driving.

Did he suspect she knew who he was? No. How could he? And yet…he felt something. She could tell. That look he'd just given her had been so aware that she felt very uneasy.

She thought of Beau again, and this time she knew why. Beau had been the football star at her high school. When he'd first asked out Jessie the tomboy, people had snickered. But there'd been a feeling between Beau and her, something so strong, so irresistible, they'd called it love.

Jessie knew better now. It hadn't been love at all. Their ill-fated marriage had proven that. It was something else again, something that had landed her in trouble more than once. And she'd just felt a strong hint of it when Michael's gaze had met hers. Reason enough to steer clear of him.

They rode on in silence. Mile after mile raced beneath the wheels, the road noise monotonous, wearying. They were still thirty miles out of Tucson, when Michael spoke again.

"Sometimes," he muttered, more to himself than at her, "it seems like this desert will never end."

She looked out the window at the vast darkness broken only by the lights from the cars that streamed along the highway. Nothing stood out in the gloom, but she knew what was out there. Saguaro cacti. Ocotillos. Coyotes. Red-tailed hawks. It was home to her and more comforting than city lights could ever be.

"You're just not used to it," she told him a little smugly.

"It's like driving through hell."

The bleakness of his tone cut through her. She stared at him openly, wonderingly. Then she frowned, cutting off the compassion she'd begun to feel, letting anger flare, instead. She wanted him harder, colder, like a criminal should be. She wanted to hate him, not sympathize. Sure, it was probably pretty rough, running from the law. But that certainly wasn't her problem.

"That's silly," she snapped in answer.

Michael was tired. His neck ached and his eyes stung. He'd

driven miles with no one to talk to, and suddenly he felt he needed to talk. She could laugh; she could scorn him. He didn't care. He was going to put the things he'd been feeling into words for another human to hear. Maybe then this whole trip would seem less like a nightmare.

"There's nothing out there," he said softly, his voice low, almost spooky. "Can't you feel it? Nothing. A big lonely nothing." He looked out his side window into the darkness. "Or if there is something, it's bad. Don't you feel it?" he asked again softly. "Evil. Like all the sins and vices of humanity are hovering, waiting, gathering forces...."

Jessie wasn't sure she knew what he was talking about, but a shudder went through her and she wanted him to quit. "You're nuts, mister," she said scathingly. "The way I see it, cities are full of all those things. At least, it sure looks that way, from what I've seen. All those tenements with busted windows, the bums all over the streets. That sure looks more like hell to me. The Sonoran desert is beautiful," she added defensively. "More like God's country, I'd say."

Michael stretched in his seat, a slight smile curling the corners of his mouth. It was working. Somehow he'd sensed she would do this. He'd thrown out some of the crazy thoughts he'd been having and she'd shaken them free of their wrinkles, hung them up to dry and shown him how everyday they really were. He could feel himself relaxing.

"You've got it all wrong about cities," he told her, almost cheerful now. "Sure, there are bad areas. But there are also beautiful homes and opera houses and music centers and fancy stores and libraries...."

She shrugged. "Well, it doesn't matter. I'd never go to any of the big ones, like New York, or Chicago or San Francisco."

"Never?"

"Never."

They were both silent for a long time. Jessie couldn't help but think about how far they were getting from home and safety. Every mile took away a bit more of her security. She wished she knew what she was going to do next, how she was going to get the authorities to him without his knowing about it. And then a chance presented itself.

"Can you recommend a good, low-priced motel to stay at in Tucson?" he asked suddenly. "I'm dead tired. I'm going to have to get some sleep."

She nodded, moving about in the seat. "Sure, I know a good place. We used to stay there when I was a teenager and groups of us would come up for football games and parties."

"I don't need any party hotel."

"No, this is a good, out-of-the-way place. It's not even in Tucson—it's in a little town called Moav. And it's right near where I'm going, so you can just drop me off."

He nodded slowly, rubbing the back of his neck. He would have sold his soul for a good night's sleep in a proper bed. This running was working hell on his physical condition. "Sounds perfect."

She almost smiled. Everything was falling into place. "Yes, I'm sure it will be."

He was almost sorry to think of losing her now. She'd been fairly good company, and he was sick of nothing but his own thoughts to keep him going.

He glanced at her. Oncoming headlights outlined her profile in white light. Involuntarily his gaze slipped down to the open neck of her shirt. Her skin was tanned and smooth, creamy looking in the light. Her jacket had fallen open, and beneath it he could see her breasts straining against the cotton cloth, somehow fuller, softer looking then he'd expected. He felt a stirring he hadn't experienced in a long, long while, and for just a moment, he imagined her in the longed-for bed with him.

Swearing under his breath, he looked away quickly, clenching the wheel and frowning. None of that. He had places to go and things to do, and if anyone knew from experience how getting tangled up with a woman could deter a man from his goals, he ought to. Suddenly he was ready to dump her at the nearest bus stop.

But it wasn't long before the lights of Tucson shone on the horizon like a giant's treasure of scattered diamonds, lighting up the night sky. The lights of Moav, off to the left, were duller, more orange than white. At last Michael turned the car onto the main street and they cruised down it, past the Three Bar Three Motel, the Golden Horseshoe, the Happy Hours Bar.

"There it is." She pointed out the Blue Lagoon Motel. Her heart was beginning to pound again.

He slowed and stopped just before he reached the driveway in front of the row of little bungalows trying to look like a resort motor inn. "Where can I take you?" he asked, looking at her searchingly. "I can't just leave you here on the street."

Anger churned in her again. Why not? A criminal wasn't supposed to care if a woman got safely home or not. What was the matter with this man? He was supposed to be crueler.

"Listen, mister," she said bitingly, reaching for the door handle. "I don't need taking care of." She slipped out of the car and stuck her head in. "Thanks for the ride," she said gruffly. "Goodbye."

He didn't answer, but she didn't wait around, either. She slammed the car door and strode off down the street, listening intently until she heard him pull in toward the motel office. Then she ran back, keeping behind the oleanders that lined the street, and watched. He got out of the car and went to register, returning very quickly and parking in front of the last bungalow. She watched him get out of the car, stretch and yawn, then pull a leather bag from behind the seat and make his way to the door of his room. A moment later, he was inside and the door was closing firmly.

CHAPTER FOUR

JESSIE HAD NOTICED a telephone booth at the corner gas station as they'd driven by. She ran to it now, pulling change from her pockets. She didn't have much, but she had enough for a local call. Hands shaking, she looked up the number of the Moav police.

"I'd like to know if you've got information on a wanted man, a Michael Drayton?" she asked as soon as she was connected with a detective.

"Just a minute," he said, his voice bored and sleepy. When he returned to the telephone, he sounded a little more alert and interested. "Yeah, we do. What do you know about him?"

"I know where he is."

"Great. You just tell me where that is, ma'am, and I'll get right on it."

Jessie sighed with relief. "Not so fast," she said evenly. "There's a reward, isn't there?"

"For information leading to the arrest and conviction of— yes, indeed," he replied, though he didn't sound pleased to know that she was aware of it. "Now if you'll just tell me what you know…"

"How about the reward? How does that work?"

The detective didn't like to be interrupted. "We arrest the alleged perpetrator, and if he's convicted in a court of law of the crimes he's charged with you apply to the Matthews family for the reward. Now come on, lady, we're wasting time here. We'll need some information first. Such as your name, lady. Who are you?"

She hesitated. "Jessica MacAllister," she said slowly, wondering if she was doing the right thing. But what else could she do? The information she had wasn't going to do her any good if she didn't give it to the police.

"And where are you right now, Ms MacAllister?"

"I'm in a phone booth at the corner of Bush and Kramer."

"Good. Okay, now where did you see this Michael Drayton?"

They were asking for her ace in the hole. Jessie's innate wariness took over. "I'll show you when you get here," she said firmly.

The detective was getting real tired of her attitude. "Now come on, lady. What if you're not around when we get there? It would be faster and more efficient if you would just tell us—"

"I'll show you when you get here or not at all," she retorted. She was not about to be bullied by a man just because he wore a badge.

"Take it easy, little lady." His tactics changed. "You'll get that reward. We wouldn't try to put anything over on you."

That was when the realization hit her. The Tucson police force was one thing. The Moav cops were something else. In the days when she'd come here as a teenager they'd had a reputation for dirty deals. It seemed possible that nothing had changed much. Why hadn't she taken Michael Drayton into Tucson? She wanted to bang her head against the wall of the kiosk in pure frustration.

She was caught, though. There wasn't much she could do about it now but go through with her plans and hope for the best. She hung up and stood at the corner, waiting for Moav's finest to arrive, but she felt panicky. If she'd gone through all this for nothing...

The police arrived with sirens blaring and lights flashing— all two cars of them. The inspector got out and came toward her, swaggering a bit. His face was chubby, red.

"Let's have it, lady," he said curtly. "Were's he at?"

Jessie held her ground. "Tell me how we're going to work this."

He grimaced with annoyance. "You tell us where the guy is. We arrest him. Simple as that."

"I want to come along on the arrest."

He shook his head firmly. "It's too dangerous."

"He doesn't have a gun."

"It's against policy." She could see he wasn't going to bend. "After we pick him up we'll come back to get you."

She glared at him, and at the other two officers who'd come up behind him. "What guarantee do I have that you'll ever come back to get me?"

She caught the barely suppressed smiles in the looks they all exchanged. "Why, honey, what do you think? Think we'd try to cheat you out of that money? If you can't trust a lawman, who can you trust?"

Heart sinking, she studied the three men. Could she trust them? She wasn't at all sure. Maybe they had friends they would pretend had fingered Michael. Maybe they had ways of getting the reward for themselves. Or maybe they would just keep her from it for pure spite. She didn't have any leverage here. With her own lawman, in her own town, she was sure of herself. But here...

"Okay," she said shortly. "I'll tell you where he is. He's in the Golden Horseshoe Motel."

All three came alert in a hurry. "What room number?"

"I didn't see the room number," she said quickly. "But he's driving a black sedan. With New Mexico plates. You ought to be able to find him easy enough."

They believed her.

"You wait right here, honey," said the red-faced one. "We'll sure enough be back for you when we get him. Then you can come on down to the station and file your application for that reward."

"You bet," she said dryly. "I won't move an inch."

"Yeah, you do that, sugar." Their grins were wide. "We'll see you soon, okay?"

She watched as they piled into the black-and-white cars and took off down the street, red lights rotating. The moment they rounded the corner, she whirled and ran back to the phone booth, jabbing the button for the operator and putting in a collect call to the Bar None Café.'

"Hello?" Harley's voice sounded strained.

"Hello, Harley? It's me. I'm okay."

"Oh, honey. We've been so worried, me and the boys. Where are you? Are you really all right?"

"I'm fine, but listen. I'm up in Moav. I've got him with me. And I'm bringing him home."

"What?"

"Just listen. I don't have time to talk. I've got him and I'm going to bring him home. Tell the sheriff, and maybe have some of the boys around, too, just in case. But stay out of sight until I get him into the café. We ought to be there in a couple of hours."

"But Jessie…?"

"Bye now."

She flung down the receiver and dashed away, hurrying toward the Blue Lagoon Motel. She'd have to move fast. As soon as the police figured out she'd sent them on a wild-goose chase, they'd be back, and the first thing they'd see would be the big flashing sign for the Blue Lagoon. It wouldn't take a genius to realize she'd likely have called from a phone close to where Michael was staying.

She found the black-and-gold sports car and ran right up to the motel room, banging on the door with her fist. "Michael!" she called. "Open up!"

She saw him looking out from behind the drapes. "Quick!" she urged, and a moment later she heard him sliding back the bolt.

"You've got to get out of here," she said urgently, her gaze skimming over his bare chest. He was dressed in nothing but a towel, and had obviously just had a shower. She was unprepared for how muscular he looked, how hard and smooth. Drops of water still glistened on his shoulders, his eyelashes. Jessie took it all in and stored it away. She had no time to deal with her reaction now.

"Wait a minute, wait a minute," he was saying, grabbing her arm as she tried to charge into his room. "What's going on?"

She pushed past him and looked quickly around the room,

ready to help him pack if need be. "The cops are coming. Come on! Hurry! They'll be here any minute."

He stared at her for seconds, taking in the seriousness of the situation. Then he didn't waste any more time. Turning around, he dropped the towel and quickly pulled on his slacks and shirt, while she gathered the clothes he'd left in a heap on the floor and stuffed them into the suitcase he hadn't even begun to unpack. Throwing down the key on the dresser, he followed her out to the car, tossing the luggage into the back and shrugging into his suit jacket at the same time.

"Come on," she said, looking back over her shoulder at the road. "Hurry."

He never questioned why she jumped into the car with him. Backing out of the parking space, he eased the car out of the lot and onto the main street. "Where are we going?" he asked, his eyes veiled.

"I'll show you," she replied. Adrenaline coursed through her. For some strange reason she suddenly felt invincible. She was actually pulling this off. "Don't go on the freeway. I've got a better way."

She didn't want him to know where she was heading them right away, so she directed him onto a route that would take them through part of Tucson before they doubled back for home. They drove swiftly through the desert for ten minutes, and then they were on the outskirts of the city. Jessie didn't know Tucson like the back of her hand, but she had made enough trips there to have some idea of general directions. She led Michael through a bizarre tangle of side streets guaranteed to turn his sense of direction upside-down, but she kept track of where they were all the time.

If worse came to worst and he realized what she was doing, as he was bound to eventually, she would tell him the truth— that she was taking him home. She'd tell him she was on the run, too, or some such nonsense, and that she planned to shelter him for a while. Would he believe her? What choice did he have?

She glanced at his stony profile, feeling a wave of guilt. She was being a real rat, tricking him like this. Quickly she reminded herself that he was a thief—he'd taken the money and those jewels knowing the consequences.

For a time they drove along silently, except for the directions Jessie gave now and then. She sat with her neck craned, staring out the rear window. "I think we did it," she said at last. "They can't possibly find us now. We got away."

"We did, huh?" He glanced at her sharply as he pulled to a stop before a red light. "Then maybe we have time to take a breath, have a look around and get a few things straight." His voice hardened. "Like, for instance, what made you think the police were coming to get me?"

She swallowed and gazed out the window. It seemed so easy to plan lies, but when it came down to telling them, the words stuck in her throat. She'd done more lying tonight than ever before, and it seemed she was getting worse at it rather than better.

"I...I stopped at a café down the street from the motel and overheard some policemen discussing you. They...they had a tip about your whereabouts and they were planning to come and arrest you right away."

Weak. Very weak. And she knew it. But to her surprise, he didn't say a thing. She closed her eyes and tried to keep her breathing even. Her mind was racing, going nowhere. She couldn't think clearly at all. They drove on for a few more minutes and when he spoke again, she jumped.

"How did you know my name?"

The question hung in the air. "Wh-what?" She searched her mind wildly but couldn't come up with one good reason why she would know his name. She knew as well as he did that they'd never exchanged names. He didn't know hers right now.

The car rolled into the intersection as another light turned from red to green, and he rounded a corner, heading down a main street into heavy traffic.

"It's a simple question," he said quietly, his eyes on the cars around them but his attention firmly on her. "How did you know my name?"

She felt her stomach flop, as though they'd gone over a huge bump in the road. Glancing at him, all she saw was his profile. "I...you must have mentioned it...."

"No." There was a finality to his tone that told her he already had this all figured out. "No, I never mentioned it."

He was quiet again for a moment. Her heart was beating so loudly she was sure he could hear it. Her palms were sweating. She looked down quickly, making sure she knew where the door handle was in case she had to use it fast.

"If there were any cops after me in Moav," he said at last, "you called them. How else would they have known where I was that fast?"

Oh, Lord. He was too smart for her. Why had she ever thought she could outwit him? She must have been crazy! "Maybe someone in a town you've been through called and—"

He went on as though she hadn't spoken. "It's the best explanation I can think of, and I've been thinking about it ever since we left the motel. What I can't figure out is why you changed your mind."

She looked straight ahead and refused to answer him. Her plans were in the dust, that was for sure. Desperately she tried to think of some alternative. If she could only convince him to come back to the café with her... She looked out at the dark landscape, and suddenly saw that they'd left town while she'd been musing and were now heading in exactly the opposite direction they should have been going.

"No," she cried, swinging around toward Michael again. "We're going the wrong way. You should have turned right, not left."

His eyes glittered in the darkness. The road they'd emerged on was empty. No car headlights from oncoming traffic lit their faces. The desert loomed dark and lonely for miles ahead. All of a sudden she realized just how vulnerable she was. And how insane it was of her to have attempted this.

"So you can set me up again?" he asked softly, his voice laced with acid. "No, thanks. "I'll plot my own route. We'll go my way."

The dream was over. The reward was up in smoke. All her

work had been for nothing. And now here she was, riding off toward the horizon with a criminal. "Uh, why don't you let me off right here?" she asked stiffly, her hand moving slowly toward the door handle. "I think I've gone about as far as I want to."

"I'm afraid I can't do that." He sounded sincerely regretful. "We're going to have to stick together for a while, you and me."

She glanced out at the landscape. He was going too fast. She couldn't jump out yet. "That's kidnapping, you know."

"No." He shook his head. "You asked for this ride."

She turned toward him. "I'm not asking for it anymore. I'm asking to be let out."

"Well, I'm afraid I can't do that, because I'm going to need you with me. You represent a little bit of insurance right now. I think maybe you owe me that much."

"I just saved your hide, mister," she said defiantly.

"You're the one who endangered it in the first place."

"No, I'm not," she retorted. "You endangered it when you stole the money and jewels!"

With a squealing of brakes, he jerked the wheel and pulled over to the side of the road, turning to face her in the small car. He appeared bigger suddenly, darker. The silver streak in his hair gleamed with an unearthly light. "Okay, let's have it," he said, his voice hard, sure. "Who are you? What do you know and where did you find it out?"

CHAPTER FIVE

SHE FUMBLED for the door handle, but he moved across the small space with the agility and speed of a cat, his large hand closing over hers before she had a chance to do a thing. Stretched across her, he was much too close, much too threatening, making her feel totally helpless.

"Come on," he said silkily. "The time has come to spill your guts."

She pressed herself back against the seat, trying to put as much distance between them as she could. "I…my name is Jessie MacAllister," she said shakily. "I…I just wanted a ride to Tucson."

He slid his hands beneath her jacket, taking her shoulders in his strong grip, letting her sense how slight and fragile she was if he decided to get rough. His fingertips pressed into her flesh, not hurting her, but exerting just enough pressure to give her warning. "The truth," he said icily, his blue eyes cold and fierce in the gloom.

She felt her strength ebb, and she went limp as a rag doll. He was overpowering her, not so much with his physical superiority, but with the power of his will, his presence.

"The sheriff," she began, her voice husky. "Our local sheriff. He stopped by my father's café a few hours after you left. He had a picture.…"

"And you recognized me?"

She nodded, avoiding his blazing eyes. "I was in the back when you were having coffee."

"So what did the sheriff do, appoint you his official posse?"

She shook her head. "No. He…I decided to see if I could keep you at the canyon until he got there. The reward…"

He stiffened. "Reward?"

She looked into his eyes. "The people you stole from have put out a reward."

To her surprise, everything in him seemed to go slack. "A reward," he muttered, and his mouth twisted into a bitter grin. And then he was laughing.

Jessie stirred uncomfortably. He was still holding her shoulders, though his grip had loosened. "Let me go," she suggested softly.

He looked surprised, as though he'd forgotten for just a moment that she was there. "Sorry, Jessie MacAllister," he said. "I can't do that." The color of his eyes deepened as he looked at her, really seeing her for the first time. "You know what?" he said musingly, reaching up to push some of her tangled hair away from her face. "You're really pretty."

Jessie felt as if a band had tightened across her chest. They were so close that when he spoke she could feel his warm breath against her cheek. An awareness of him filled her suddenly, stirring something deep inside that had been dormant for a long, long time. His wide shoulders, the sensuousness of his mouth, the deep rumble of his voice, his strength—all combined to render her speechless. There was something so irresistibly male about him. And when she looked into his silver-blue eyes, even in the shadows of the night she could see a promise there that frightened her.

"Keep your hands off me," she managed to blurt out.

His smile was rueful, but he backed off. Still, he didn't stop looking at her. "Don't worry," he said softly. "I'm not going to do anything to hurt you. I just want to make sure I get a decent night's sleep without your calling the authorities. And to guarantee that, I'm going to have to keep you with me."

"You're just a real desperado, aren't you?" she accused him scathingly.

"'Desperado.'" He rolled the word around on his tongue, seemed pleased with it. "Why not?" he said, and he started the car again.

Jessie stared into nothing. If things had gone right, she would have been planning what to do with that reward money right now. It was just her luck. She sighed. Every time she dealt with men, somehow she always came out the loser. "Where are we going to spend the night?" she asked, feeling more sulky than frightened now.

He shrugged. "Out here somewhere in the desert."

She looked at him. "You mean we're going to camp? You're going to sleep in your sleeping bag?"

"No." He cast her a sideways glance. "You're going to sleep in the sleeping bag. I'm going to sleep sitting up right here in this car."

"Oh." She turned away again. It was almost funny really. Only she didn't feel like laughing.

THE LIGHT from the Tiffany lamp cast a golden glow over the well-aged cognac Sky Matthews held in his hand. Sunk deep in his leather chair, he turned the glass slowly, watching the golden liquid dance. It was the ingratitude that angered him most, he decided at last. Loyalty was what counted. What was wrong with people these days? Didn't they understand you had to stick with your own to survive?

He glanced over at the framed pictures that hung on one of the walls in the den, pictures of his flight squadron in Korea, of his buddies. Those were the days. The men he'd flown with over there had known all about loyalty. They'd faced a common enemy and had come through alive. What people today didn't realize was that although they couldn't see the enemy, he was still out there. You had to fight for survival today, as well. Only the strong survived.

He took a long sip of his drink, wincing at the rich burn on his throat but enjoying the cognac nevertheless, and tossed his thoughts to Michael. Dammit all. He'd played that wrong. He should have brought him in slowly, as he'd done his father. Winslow Drayton hadn't been easy to convince, either, but he'd come around over the years. Now things were going to be more difficult.

Still, he had no doubt he'd succeed. He always achieved everything he set out to. And he'd chosen Michael to take over the business long ago. Michael was perfect. He was smart, savvy, sure of himself. And he had the aristocratic background Sky wanted to enrich his company with. And his own family. Michael and Vanessa's engagement had been the icing on the cake.

Yes, it was just a matter of time. He'd have Michael back here and he'd reason with him. It was as simple as that.

"Daddy."

Vanessa breezed into the room, switching on an overhead light as she did so. The room was flooded with brightness and his first reaction was annoyance, but one look at her beautiful face and his frown melted.

"What is it, sweetheart?"

She perched on the ottoman in front of him, resting one hand on his knee. Her raven hair with its elfin cut was a contrast to his silver mane, but she looked like him. He could see it in the strength of her jaw, the glint of her green eyes. And every time he saw the resemblance, he felt pride flow in his veins. This was his. All his.

"Have you heard anything about Michael?" she asked now, her face anxious. "Do you know where he is?"

His large hand covered hers. "Not yet, sugar. But don't worry. We'll find him."

"Are...are the police still looking for him?"

Sky nodded. "We've still got a warrant out for his arrest and I've put a reward on him, so the stool pigeons should be crawling out of the woodwork by now. We ought to hear anytime."

Vanessa sighed. "You won't make him stay in jail, will you? He'd hate that."

Sky's face hardened. "A few days in the lockup will be good for him," he said, his voice evidencing the steel beneath the velvet tone reserved for his daughter. "He's hurt me, honey. He's hurt you. He's got to pay for that." His tone softened and he stroked her arm. "Besides, it'll do him good to be reminded of what it's like to be behind bars. Soften him up a little. And then, when I go in and offer him an escape, he'll jump at it."

"Will he?" Vanessa wasn't so sure. She was afraid she

knew Michael a little better than her father did. "He was so angry when he left...."

Sky took a swig of his drink. "He wasn't the only one who was angry," he said with quiet menace.

Vanessa studied her father's face, her heart fluttering. She loved him, but his hardness frightened her at times. He'd never been anything but gentle with her, but she knew from experience he could be otherwise with those around him.

"You...you won't hurt him," she whispered.

Sky's face registered outrage. "Hurt him? Why would I do anything like that? You know me better, sweetheart."

Her smile wavered. She knew her father all too well. Memories flashed through her mind like a newsreel, memories she usually suppressed. Ex-employees who'd disappeared. Old boyfriends who'd suddenly become afraid to see her any longer. And Marty, the tennis instructor she'd fallen in love with when she was seventeen.

"We're getting married, Daddy," she'd insisted in a rush of teenage rebellion.

"Over my dead body!" he roared.

When Marty hadn't shown up for their date that night, she'd gone looking for him at his apartment. He'd come to the door, but he hadn't let her in. His face was a mess, his nose broken, his lip swollen to three times its normal size. "Stay away from me, Vanessa," he'd managed to grate out painfully. "Don't ever come near me again."

Yes, she knew her father all right. "Of course, Daddy," she said hurriedly. "But...I love Michael. I want him back."

Sky cupped her cheek with his hand. "You'll get him back, sweetheart. I promise."

She searched his eyes, wondering if he really meant it. But of course he must. He always got her what she wanted—as long as he wanted it, too. Smiling, she rose and leaned down to kiss the top of his silver head. "Thank you, Daddy. I love you."

Her scent stayed in the air long after she left the room. Sky took another swallow of the cognac and pondered life. Memories haunted him, memories of holidays at the beach with the

Drayton family when Vanessa was about five and Michael already a strong, handsome teenager. He'd decided then that the two of them should marry someday. It was the perfect solution.

The Draytons were old money. Class. A secure position in society. The Matthews were upstarts, rough edged, but with energy and know-how. He and Winslow Drayton would never have been friends if it hadn't been for that flight squadron in Korea. When they'd both moved back to the San Francisco area, Winslow had been a big help in getting Sky the financing he'd needed to start Matthews Aviation.

And then there'd been Winslow's beautiful wife, Pamela. Ah, Pamela. Sky sighed.

The two families had been close for years. But for all their success, the Matthews had never attained the position the Draytons held by virtue of their birth. That still smarted. Having Michael in the family would go a long way toward healing that wound.

"Yes, Vanessa," Sky muttered to himself, "we'll get Michael back. Don't you worry."

CHAPTER SIX

MORNING CAME in the form of purple tentacles against the blackened eastern sky. Michael's eyes felt full of sand and his neck was stiff from sleeping with his head propped against the car door. Watching the sky lighten, he attempted to stretch his arms and legs in the cramped space.

Firebirds were not meant to be slept in, but in the dead of night, anything had seemed preferable to the treacherous desert floor.

"Go ahead," she'd said caustically. "Sleep in the car. Let me have the sleeping bag. I'll be fine out here."

He was the one who had to sleep, he'd told himself defensively. She could sleep while he drove. He couldn't very well sleep while she drove, could he? She'd drive him straight to the police to collect that reward she was so hot to win for herself.

He shifted slightly, grimacing at the chill of the morning, and glanced at the black speaker cover. The diamonds almost seemed to glow from inside. He fantasized for just a moment about holding his hand a few inches away and feeling their fire. Fire and ice. It sure as hell was cold out here at night.

He thought he felt something move against his ankle and he jerked his leg, then felt foolish. It was nothing. His imagination. But at least it proved he could still move those lower extremities. That was something.

He ought to get up and see if she was still there. He'd purposely driven miles out into the desert on a very lonely road before stopping to camp. Even if she tried to walk back to civilization, it would take her enough hours that he'd have time to rest.

What a mess. The last thing he needed was a woman complicating things. At least she was a down-to-earth sort, a type he could deal with. Most of the women he'd known over the years hadn't been like that at all. From his experience, most women were sly manipulators, people with secret agendas and ulterior motives that never really came out in the open. He always felt a vague sense of pity for friends who announced wedding plans.

"That's because you've never really been in love," someone had told him recently.

And he supposed that was true. At this late date, he probably never would fall in love. And he entertained that notion with a certain smug satisfaction.

Something moved again. For real this time. Something long and feathery scuttled across his skin, just under his pants leg.

Revulsion shot through him. "Dammit!" he cried, jerking open the car door and flinging himself out, then shivering and wincing as something black and hairy flew out and disappeared into the sand. An uncontrollable shudder shook his shoulders.

But at least he was up. He glanced over to where Jessie still lay in the sleeping bag. So she hadn't skipped out on him in the night. Mixed feelings warred within him. He stepped closer.

The blue nylon bag was zipped up tight. All he could see was a mass of honey-colored hair. He stared down at it, then got down on one knee close to where she slept. Her breathing was light, rhythmic. He sensed a warmth that seemed to glow in the crisp morning air. Some strange emotion he didn't want to analyze welled up in his chest. Her tangled hair caught the first rays of sunlight and shone like spun gold. He found himself reaching out to touch it. Some yearning, some tenderness deep inside, made him need to touch it, to sink his fingers into the warmth of it, to feel the silkiness of it against his skin, as though that would slake some illogical thirst he had burning inside him.

His fingers were almost there when she turned, and suddenly, instead of a tempting gold, he was faced with the fierce dark brown of her eyes. He pulled his hand away quickly. "You ready for breakfast?" he asked gruffly, embarrassed at having been caught giving in to an impulse. He didn't often let that happen.

She glared at him, not answering, and he shrugged, rose and began putting rocks together for a fire pit. She watched him, blinking away sleep, surprised that she'd slept as well as she had. The night was over. What was she going to do now?

"If it will make you feel any better," he'd told her the previous evening, "I'm not really guilty."

How was that supposed to make her feel better? She wanted him guilty. She wanted him arrested so she could collect the reward. Otherwise, what on earth was she doing there?

But she knew he was trying to allay her fears that he might harm her in some way, and grudgingly she appreciated the gesture. He wasn't going to hurt her unless she did something really stupid. She could see it in his face. He was hard, cold and prepared to do things illegal, possibly immoral. But he wasn't mean.

Once he had a small fire going, he pulled a brand-new saucepan out of the car, along with a bottle of water, a plastic coffee mug and a small jar of instant coffee. Snug in the sleeping bag, she watched him work, trying to balance the pan against a rock and not get himself burned. His hands were long, his movements graceful for a man. There was a sleek, white-collar-job look to him, but she recognized an underlying strength and toughness that surprised her a little. He was, after all, a man, she reminded herself. He was quick and agile and smart. She was going to have to plan her escape carefully.

Reaching down into the depths of the bag, she began to pull on the jeans she's struggled out of the night before. Out of the corner of her eye she could see him watching, but she pretended not to care. Let him imagine all he wanted. That was as close as he'd ever get.

"Coffee?" He held the cup out to her as she emerged from her blue nylon cocoon.

Her hair was a tangled mess, but she left it that way defiantly. She would have loved to turn down his offer with scorn, but the aroma of the dark beverage was irresistible. Without saying a word, she took the cup from him, scalding her lips with a long sip before she handed it back.

"Well, good morning, Miss MacAllister," he said sardonically. "Did you sleep well? I certainly hope so. I'd hate to think neither one of us got a decent night's sleep in this godforsaken place."

She glanced at him, surprised and not sure how to respond. He looked even more rumpled than yesterday. A day's worth of stubble darkened his face, making him appear more rugged than before.

"I slept great," she said, reaching for her boots and shaking out first one, then the other, before pulling them on.

He watched her, his mouth twisted. "No bug bites to disturb you?" he murmured. "My moans of anguish didn't wake you at all?"

She forced herself not to look at him. "Nope," she said shortly.

He moved, chuckling softly. "Well, I'm so pleased," he said. "It's rewarding when a guest has a—"

She whirled, outrage radiating from her body. "I'm no guest, mister," she snapped. "I'm your prisoner, and you and I both know it. So cut out the cute stuff. I hate you and you hate me and this here's no tea party."

His eyebrows rose. "Your candor is refreshing," he said without irony. "It's been a long time since I've heard a woman lay it on the line like that. You should give lessons to others of your sex."

He confused her. She looked down at the cup in his hand. "Is that all there is to breakfast?" she asked. "You don't have anything to eat?"

"Sorry. I ate my last Snickers for dinner last night."

Her stomach rumbled at the mere mention of food, but she shrugged, pretending not to care. Shoving her hands into her jacket pockets, she glanced up at the mountains. "So...what's next?" she asked. "Where do we go from here?"

He poured himself more coffee and put the saucepan on the ground. "You tell me. You hired on as an Arizona tour guide, and even though I haven't had time to check your references, I think you're going to do a marvelous job.''

She shook her head impatiently. "Forget the jokes. What are you planning to do with me?"

He took a long sip of coffee, watching her over the rim of the mug. Scrappy little thing that she was, he couldn't help but admire her a bit. The way she'd come after him in the hills. The way she'd ridden along, called the police, then helped him escape. She had guts. He had to give her that. "That's a very good question. What do you think I should do?"

She tossed her head, pushing back the stray wisps of tangled hair that kept flying in her face. "Take me to the nearest town and give me bus fare home." She watched him to see his reaction, then flushed when he sputtered on his coffee and laughed aloud.

"Bus fare home!" He shook his head, grinning. "I said I wouldn't treat you badly, but that doesn't mean I'm prepared to set you up for life. You must think I'm a real sap.''

"I don't think you're a sap," she said sharply. "I think you're a liar and a thief. And I think that you ought to let me go before they add kidnapping to all the other things they're after you for.''

The humor evaporated from his eyes and he watched her speculatively. Taking her along did mean there would be another charge—something he could ill afford. Scenes of the prison yard flashed through his mind. No, he wouldn't go back. No matter what, he would never go back to prison.

He'd gone charging into Bisbee yesterday, sure that he'd find Kerry right away and that the two of them could clear this mess up. Bisbee—what a crazy place that had turned out to be. He'd driven into a ravine called Mule Pass Gulch to find houses spread up and down the steep sides of the valley, all centered around something called the Copper Queen Lode. It had been almost like stepping into another century. He stopped at a local café and it was just like sauntering into a saloon in a Western— everyone knew everyone, and someone directed him to Kerry's house right away.

A sallow young woman with long, stringy blond hair had

answered his knock. "Kerry Carter?" She'd stared at him blankly. "Yeah, he lived here. But he's gone now."

Michael had glanced inside to where two children were seated at the table, eating sandwiches. There was something squalid about the place. He could hardly imagine the dapper Kerry living with this woman. He'd been one for cuff links and white dinner jackets. For just a moment he wondered if they were both talking about the same man.

"Tall guy, dark blond hair, used to fly planes...?"

The woman nodded. "That's him. He was going to get rich finding minerals with a spade and a pack on his back." She shrugged. "I told him my father and my grandfather before him had died trying to catch hold of that dream, but he wouldn't listen. Went out every day into the hills. Came home every night madder than the night before. Drank himself to sleep. And woke up meaner than a skunk." She shook her head. "But I guess he was smarter than the men in my family, after all, cuz he gave up after only a few months."

Michael could see why. "Do you have any idea where he went?"

"No." She shrugged again. "Sorry. He just packed up and took off a few weeks ago. I don't expect he'll be back any time soon."

Michael hesitated. He was disappointed, but more than that, he was unsure of what to do next. The woman appeared so pitiful and the poverty she was living in was obvious. He felt he should give her some money or something, but he didn't know how to do it.

He looked inside at the children again. "Have you got a man around here?" he asked awkwardly.

She brightened before his eyes. "No, sir," she said. "You need a place to stay?"

He took a step backward. "Oh, no, I didn't mean that. I just..." The hell with it. He reached into his pocket and took out a twenty-dollar bill. "Here you go," he said, shoving it into her hand. "Thanks for the information." Turning, he started quickly for his car.

The woman called after him. "Hey, mister, I just remembered something. Kerry had a brother in Phoenix. He said something about visiting him. He might still be there.''

Michael swung around. "Do you remember his name?''

She thought for a moment. ''Chester. Yeah, that was it. Chester Carter.''

Michael had sighed. Phoenix. Another long drive. But at least it was something to go on. ''Thanks,'' he called back, and got into his car. A few hours later he'd shown up at Harley MacAllister's café.

And this cowgirl had landed in his lap. He hoped Kerry was in Phoenix. If he could get hold of him today, this could be all over by nightfall, and he could rid himself of this woman. If he could keep her with him just that long.

''Come on,'' he said abruptly, moving to kick out the fire. ''We're getting out of here.''

''Where are we going?''

''You'll see when we get there.''

Jessie began rolling up the sleeping bag. He picked up the jar of instant coffee, then bent to pick up the saucepan he'd left lying in the coarse sand. Suddenly she heard him yelp with pain. Whirling, she saw him rear back and fling something from his hand, his face contorted. Without thinking, she ran to his side, just in time to see a long brown scorpion scuttle under a rock.

''I'll get him,'' she said fiercely, lifting the rock. The insect was about eight inches long, its coiled tail held high, its lobsterlike pincers ready. Without a qualm, she smashed down the rock, flattening the scorpion with the methodical calm of one used to doing such things.

Behind her, Michael sank to the ground with a thump, holding one hand with the other. His face was white. ''That was a scorpion,'' he said, his voice hollow. ''It stung me. Aren't they poisonous?''

She sighed in exasperation. Only a tenderfoot would let himself get stung so easily. The man needed a keeper. ''Yes, they're sort of poisonous,'' she began, about to launch into an explanation of the difference between the dangerous bark scorpion and the others, whose stings were painful, but not fatal.

But before the words were out, she stopped. Wait. He didn't know anything about scorpions. Like most city dwellers, he thought scorpions and tarantulas were the monsters the movies portrayed them as. As far as he knew, he was about to die if he didn't get help.

"Yes," she said again, more firmly, her dark eyes alight with hope. "We'd better get you to a doctor fast."

He rose unsteadily to his feet. She had to suppress the urge to help him. He looked pale, but not panicked. That was good. It was a little cruel to trick him this way, but she needed an advantage if she was going to get away.

"Come on," she said gruffly. "Get in the car. I'll drive."

Her heart began to beat quickly. Yes, she would drive...she would drive them wherever she pleased. He would be a helpless baby in her control. Look at him now, scared to death of having been bitten by a scorpion. He was putty in her hands.

CHAPTER SEVEN

SHE WALKED OVER and yanked open the car door on the passenger's side, but in her euphoria, she misjudged and cracked the door hard against her shin.

"Ouch," she said, wincing and bending over.

He was right beside her, his own injury forgotten for the moment. "Are you okay?" he asked, taking her arm, steadying her.

She looked up at him, shocked, surprised at his concern. What was the matter with the man? He was supposed to be self-absorbed right now, not worrying about her. "Yes," she muttered, pulling away, resentful of his kindness. "It's nothing."

They got in and drove along the dirt track in silence, Jessie at the wheel, Michael watching everything with eyes that seemed to see more than she wanted him to. The sun was up now, a huge ball of fiery life that had made its appearance over the serrated rim of the mountains to the east. Its color reminded Jessie of the huge glass of orange juice she usually had for breakfast. One long sip of o.j. would go great right now.

The car handled like a dream, even on this rutted dirt road. She'd never driven anything like it before. The leather steering wheel cover felt good beneath her hands. She glanced at Michael.

His silver-blue eyes met hers and he nodded. "Okay," he said shortly. "Go ahead, give me the sordid details. Just exactly what is going to happen to me?"

She took a deep breath, feeling guilty. "Nothing if we get you to a doctor on time."

"But we don't know where a doctor is, do we? Finding one

might take hours." He moved restlessly, holding up his sore hand with his good one. "In the meantime, what can I expect? I'd like to be prepared." When she didn't answer right away, he went on. "Am I going to go into some kind of shock? Lose consciousness? Lose motor control?" Still she didn't answer. "Hey, come on, Jessie," he said, his voice soft and coaxing. "I can take it. Tell me the truth. Is my hand going to go numb? Turn black? Fall off?"

Her throat felt tight and dry. She glanced sideways at him. He didn't look scared, just concerned. He was a logical man. He wanted a logical explanation, a logical plan of action. His peace of mind was in her hands. What was she going to do with it?

"Every…every case is different. Sometimes the victim gets abdominal cramps. Sometimes he loses consciousness." She glanced at him, biting her lip. "How does it feel?" she asked.

"Painful. My whole hand's swollen. It's sort of numb, tingling, yet painful." His laugh was short and humorless. "In other words, I don't like it much."

She nodded quickly, her eyes on the road. "I'm sorry it happened."

"Are you?"

"Sure."

The silence echoed painfully before he spoke again. "This might be just the break you need," he said softly. "I might black out, you could drive me straight to the police."

She felt color creeping up her cheeks and she swore under her breath.

"Did you think I hadn't thought of that? Come on, Jessie. Getting stung hasn't affected my brain. Not yet, anyway."

She took a shivering breath. "But you still let me drive."

"Sure. I don't see much of an alternative here. The only other thing I could have done was swallow the keys and pass out in the sand. I would have died in the sun and you would have begun the long, perhaps fruitless trek, to find water."

That nightmare scenario, city slicker cliché that it was, was vivid for only a moment. Up ahead, the highway came into view. "Look," she said, feeling irrational relief. "Other cars."

She wasn't completely sure if his groan was real or mocking. "I guess it's too late to swallow the keys," he said. "You'll just have to hope for the best."

She glanced at him, then back at the highway. "The best?"

His voice was low and silky. "That I lose consciousness, so you can haul me in. But if I die before, they might not fork over the reward. You never know. People are likely to grasp at any opening where saving money is concerned."

"You're not going to die."

"I certainly hope not. I've got things to do before I go. Scores to settle."

Jessie turned the car onto the highway. There wasn't much traffic, but a highway meant food and gas and a telephone somewhere along the line. Michael was sitting very still. She looked at him anxiously. His face appeared strained. He was obviously in pain. Not to mention the agony of wondering...

"Oh, hell!" she cried at last, jerking the car to the side of the road, then turning off the engine and leaning forward, her arms folded over the steering wheel. "I can't do it. I can't keep lying to you."

Michael stared at her. "What are you talking about?"

She turned slowly and met his clear gaze. "You know that scorpion that bit you? No big deal. He's practically harmless."

He stared at her for a long moment, then suddenly he threw back his head and laughed.

She gazed at him in bemused frustration. What was the matter with this turkey, anyway? Most of the men she knew wouldn't have taken kindly to her playing such a trick. Men like Beau would have reacted with violence. That was one of the many reasons he was now her ex-husband.

Michael was different. He had strength, a taut, stubborn core that wouldn't bend. But it didn't manifest itself in bluster or bashing. For all that, he scared her in ways other men never could.

"Then I don't need a doctor?"

She shook her head. "No," she murmured. "Not unless you show signs of some kind of allergic reaction."

He looked down at his swollen hand. "Funny. Now that you've told me that, it doesn't hurt as much."

"The pain should fade in the next hour or so."

He laughed again. "You keep driving," he said. "Let's get out of here. I need a good cup of coffee after that. Let's go have breakfast somewhere."

That was just fine with her, but she was surprised he would want to go into a public place again. "You're not afraid of being recognized?"

His sigh was heartfelt. "I'll risk it. This is far enough off the beaten track to be pretty safe, I think. And after the night I had, I need resuscitation."

She took off, a cloud of dust flaring behind the black-and-gold car. Michael found himself grinning as he watched her. Lord, you'd almost think you could trust her. But, no...the grin faded quickly. He couldn't go that far. Every woman he'd ever put his faith in had let him down, and he wasn't about to try again with this skinny desert rat.

Sometime later they cruised into the small dusty town of Jericho, nosing the car in behind the coffee shop, out of sight of the highway.

When Jessie got out of the car, Michael had already exited and was waiting for her. This was the first time she'd stood beside him on pavement, and she suddenly felt almost shy. He was tall. He still held his hand as though it hurt him. She stared up into his eyes for just a moment. Was she still his prisoner?

"I want to go to the ladies' room," she said stiffly.

His expression didn't change. "I don't know how you're going to manage that," he said. "You know I can't let you out of my sight."

Frustration swelled in her throat, choking her. She turned sharply and began to march toward the entrance to the restaurant. Across the street at a small, two-pump gas station, there was some sort of commotion, and she glanced over as she walked, attracted by the shouting, though her mind was mostly on the man behind her.

"Get out of here, kid," a voice was calling. "We don't want your kind in our town."

Jessie paused, curious. A small, dark-haired boy of about eleven or twelve with the face of a street urchin was standing in the dirt at the side of the road. Two larger boys were laughing at him belligerently.

"I'll leave," the younger boy said quietly, holding out his hand. "Give me back my bag, then I'll go."

"Your bag?" The red headed boy tossed something made of blue canvas to his blond friend. "This old thing? He says this is his bag, Jason. What do you think?"

"Finders, keepers, I always say," Jason crowed, throwing the bag back to the redhead, just out of the dark-haired boy's reach. "Losers, weepers." He crackled. "You're a loser, boy," he taunted. "Let's see you weep if you want it back so bad."

Jessie's hands balled into fists at her sides. She hated this sort of thing. Two adults were also watching, two men in their thirties with baseball caps pulled low over their eyes, leaning on an old car in the station. They were laughing, seemingly getting a kick out of the situation. She hesitated. Surely one of them would do something to help the younger boy.

"Please give me back my bag." The small face was set, stoic. Only the dark eyes betrayed any emotion at all. "It's all I have. Please. I need it."

"Yeah, but maybe Jason needs it, too," the redhead jeered. "Here, Jason." He threw it again. "Take a look inside. See if you need anything in there."

"No!" the younger boy cried, lunging at Jason.

The bag was forgotten now that the bigger boys had the excuse they needed. Both began to flail at the smaller boy, and to Jessie's horror, the two men watching began to cheer as though they were at a prize fight.

Fury moved her halfway across the street before she realized Michael had beaten her to it. He grabbed the two older boys by the scruff of the neck, as though they were puppies. The smaller boy wasted no time, darting in beneath them to grab his bag, and then began to back away.

"You okay, kid?" Michael asked him, ignoring the shouts and kicks of the other two.

The dark-eyed boy nodded, still backing away.

"You go on then," Michael said.

He nodded again, then turned and began to run down the street, his bag slung over his shoulder.

The two men had rushed over, but something in Michael's hard gaze seemed to keep them from getting involved. They hung back a few feet.

"Hey, you, let those boys go," one of them called. "They ain't done nothin' to you."

Michael turned slowly, his hands still gripping the boys' necks. "These yours?" he asked with deceptive blandness.

"You let them go. They were just playin' with the kid. Damn field gypsy, that's all he was. Probably just didn't want my boy to see into his bag cuz it was full of all the stuff he stole in town already."

Michael glanced down to the end of the street. The boy had disappeared around the corner. He released the other boys, watching their fathers, his mouth a thin, hard line. "Sorry, fellows," he said coldly. "Didn't mean to spoil your fun. In some places, I hear they raise pit bulls to fight each other for entertainment. I guess here you people just raise your own sons for the same purpose."

Jessie waited, tensed. His tone of voice had been menacing, daring the others to challenge his insult. He stood and waited, but the boys went straight to their fathers, and the fathers turned away. There was a lot of muttering and black looks, but the fight was over.

Jessie let out a long sigh of relief. "Is your hand okay?" she asked anxiously.

"Yeah. More numb than sore now." Suddenly Michael's arm was around her shoulders, leading her toward the restaurant, and she didn't feel the need to shrug it away. They climbed the steps and entered the building together before he released her. Michael asked for a table for two, then turned to look at her.

"Go ahead and use the ladies' room," he said. "But, hey." He touched her arm, holding her back for just a moment, looking deep into her dark eyes. "Don't run out on me, okay? I'm counting on you."

Counting on her! The nerve of the guy!

She thought about it as she gazed long and hard at her reflection in the cracked mirror of the washroom. Logic dictated a quick escape. She should be climbing out the window right now. Or scrawling a message on the mirror. Or waiting here for someone else to come in, then asking them to call the police. Anything except what she was actually doing. She was washing her hands and face and preparing to go right back out to join him.

At least she wouldn't try to pretty herself up. Her mouth hardened and she glared at herself in the mirror. Her hands went to her hair, raking through its thickness and pulling it into plaits. Nope, she wasn't about to fall into the trap of making herself pretty for a man, just because he was good-looking, just because his eyes seemed to search for a beauty in her. She was who she was, and proud of it.

A picture flitted into her mind and she remembered how his hand had almost touched her hair, how she'd found him so close when she'd woken up that morning. Something seemed to shiver down her spine, but she ignored it, yanking harder at her hair to ward off that warm, mushy feeling she so dreaded.

Maybe she was going out to join him again, but that didn't mean anything. She was just biding her time, awaiting her opportunity. She put on her hat and pushed her braids up under it, then stared at her own tough image. "Just biding my time," she repeated firmly before she turned to leave.

She sauntered out of the ladies' room, and immediately caught his gaze from across the restaurant. There was no emotion in his face at all, but she couldn't help but flush, and she took her time getting to him, hoping the color would fade.

He didn't say a word about her staying. She slid into the bench seat across from him and picked up the plastic menu. But she could feel his gaze still on her, and that made it very difficult to concentrate on reading.

Finally he spoke. "Do you always do this, or is it just for my benefit?"

She looked up, startled. "Do what?"

He gestured toward her, his eyes amused. "Do your

damnedest to look like a teenage boy. Wear that hat jammed down over your eyes and your hair all shoved into it, and that shirt and those pants. Come on. Do you always dress this way? Do you ever wear a dress? Or something soft?''

The flush was back, no matter how hard she cursed it. "No," she said shortly, staring unseeingly at the menu. He was only teasing, and he was right on the money, but still, his words hurt, and she wasn't sure why.

He didn't seem to notice he'd upset her. "Why not?" he persisted.

Her eyes flashed as she looked up. "You want the truth? I don't want to look 'feminine,' the way you mean. That kind of woman gets pushed around too much, mostly by men. I won't be one of those patsies."

She stared at the menu again, so she didn't see the hard expression come over Michael's face. "Women as victims?" he said softly. "That's a laugh. In my experience it's been just the other way around."

He thought of his mother, and coldness filled him. Even Vanessa, though hardly of the black widow variety, had been prepared to use him in her own way. He wouldn't be used. Not by anyone.

He looked at Jessie again and the frost melted. Jessie wasn't a user, he decided suddenly. She had too much pride for that.

"I'll have two eggs, sunny-side up, and a side of hash browns," she was saying firmly.

Ignoring her statement, he put down his menu and leaned across the table to her. "Anyway, I know a secret about you, Jessie," he said, his voice a tantalizing whisper that forced her to face him, her dark eyes blinking as though she were afraid of what was coming next.

He smiled and said softly, "You don't resent being a woman nearly as much as you pretend. You know how I know that?"

She didn't respond. He reached out and took off her hat, too quickly for her to stop him.

"Hey!" she protested, reaching for it, her braids tumbling down over her chest.

He set the hat behind him, out of her reach, then leaned

across to her again, his silver-blue eyes laughing. "You know how I know?" he repeated, and suddenly he was holding one of her braids. "If you really hated being feminine so much, you wouldn't hang on to your beautiful hair the way you do." He gave her braid a gentle tug. "Would you?"

Her attention was riveted to the hand on her hair. Painfully she forced herself to meet his gaze again, and glared at him. Those mushy feelings were coming back, and she refused to give in to them.

"Mister," she said firmly, only the slightest quaver revealing how he was affecting her, "I dress this way because I have to. You see, I work on a ranch. That's my life. That's how I make my living." She turned her hands up so that he could see the calluses, the work-roughened skin, the short, cracked nails. "I don't waste my time getting gorgeous for some man's benefit. I have work to do, and I do it. And I don't beg off because it would ruin my makeup, or my manicure, or I might get grass stains on my dress. I'm a rancher. And that's all I care about."

She was almost embarrassed by the ring of passion in her voice toward the end of her speech. But she meant every word.

To her surprise, he didn't laugh at her. Instead he frowned, and suddenly he was looking out the plate-glass window at the desert that spread toward the mountains on the other side of the highway from where the little town lay. The morning sun had tipped the mountains Navaho red, and the valley was shimmering with gold.

"Funny. The desert seems almost beautiful today," he mused. Then he looked back at her. "I'll bet it's clean out there on your ranch, isn't it?" he said, his voice eerie. "I'll bet you know just what's right and what's wrong, and where the men you hire stand. If they're behind you or against you. If you can trust them." His mouth twisted. "I envy you."

The waitress came to take their orders. Michael asked for an omelet and Jessie repeated what she wanted. When the waitress had gone, he turned back to her and asked abruptly, "What exactly were you planning to do with that reward money, Jessie MacAllister? Get yourself a house in town? Buy yourself some pretty dresses? Make a down payment on a sports car?"

Her glance was scathing. This wasn't a topic of conversation that she relished, but she wouldn't back away from anything. "Not on your life. I was going to get more stock for the ranch. That, and maybe a furnace for Harley, my dad. And help him fix up the café a little."

"Your dad?" His eyes darkened, and he looked puzzled. "You would have given that money to him?"

Jessie took a long sip from the cup of coffee the waitress had left. "Sure. Didn't you notice how run-down the place was?"

Michael appeared skeptical. "You'd take care of your father before you'd buy yourself something?"

She frowned. What was he getting at? "Of course."

His eyes were full of wonder. "Sometimes," he said slowly, shaking his head, "sometimes I'm almost glad I kidnapped you, Jessie MacAllister."

The food arrived, and he grinned, still watching her. "Almost," he repeated. "But not quite."

She found herself grinning back, though she couldn't for the life of her have said why.

The food was delicious. They were so hungry they ate until there wasn't a morsel left, and then Michael asked for more toast.

Jessie watched his humor improve before her eyes, and knew that she, too, was growing more relaxed. The food, the new feeling of—what? Companionship? Well, something close to that. He teased her, told her stories, told her jokes, and she found herself laughing.

They'd finished their meal and Michael was digging out money to pay the check, when he leaned close again, looking worried. "The waitress," he said urgently, watching the woman from the corner of his eye. "I think she's recognized me. She keeps giving me this look...."

Jessie turned to see what he was talking about. The woman was looking, all right. But instead of getting alarmed, Jessie struggled to hide a grin. "I wouldn't really worry about that if I were you," she said nonchalantly.

"Why not?"

"Those looks she's throwing your way?" She bit her lip to keep from laughing. "They don't get many handsome men in these parts, Michael Drayton," she said. "She's just enjoying you while she can."

Michael started to say something, then for once he had the decency to look a bit abashed, and he closed his mouth. "Let's go," he growled, instead. Sliding out of the seat, he headed for the cashier.

Jessie rose and followed him, but her steps were slower. *Let's go,* he'd said, but what did that mean?

"What now?" she asked as they stepped out into the sunshine. She twisted the silver bracelet she wore on one arm in a characteristic gesture. "Are you going to let me go home?"

Both eyebrows rose. "What on earth gave you a silly idea like that?" he said. "I can't let you out of my sight."

She shrugged. "I wouldn't tell anyone." Her voice was gruff and she avoided his eyes. "I could just get on a bus, and you'd never have to worry about me again."

She held her breath as she waited for his answer to her suggestion, twisting the bracelet again and again. She didn't know whether she was afraid he would say no...or afraid he would say yes.

He looked at her for a long time. The fingers of his good hand rubbed across his day-old growth of beard. She waited. This was it. This would decide things, decide a future's worth of things. Her heart was beating very fast.

"I can't do it," he said at last, regret evident in his frown. "I just can't take that chance, Jessie." He brushed her cheek. "I'm sorry."

She felt choked up, as though she might cry. Turning away quickly, she muttered, "I'll have to go back in and call my dad. He's going to be worried."

"Sure," he said, but he came right along with her, and she knew he wasn't going to risk her telling Harley too much.

The telephone was on the wall near the kitchen. Jessie glanced around the restaurant as she passed through, and as she did, she saw something she hadn't noticed before. "Look!"

she whispered to Michael, coming to a stop and grabbing his arm. "Look there."

A customer was reading the morning paper, holding it up so that the front page was visible to anyone in the room who cared to look. "*Man on the Run*," the headline screamed. "Suspect takes local woman hostage," the smaller print said. "Last seen in Tucson area."

They could see that the article contained two pictures, one of Michael and Jessie's high-school graduation shot.

Michael swore softly, holding her hand tightly in his. It was a wonder the whole place hadn't recognized them. "We'd better get out of here," he murmured. She nodded, and the two of them started for the door again, just steps away from freedom.

"Hey, mister! Hold on. Stop right where you are."

The voice of the waitress froze them both. There was ice in Jessie's veins and the breath stopped in her throat. Slowly they both turned to face the woman.

CHAPTER EIGHT

SHE WAS COMING TOWARD THEM with a determined look on her face, one hand behind her back. Jessie glanced at Michael. He was cool, calm, but she could see the pulse throbbing at his temple. Should they run for it? His hand slipped around hers and held hard.

"Hey, mister, you know what?" the waitress was saying, a flirtatious expression on her face. "You forgot something." She whipped her hand around from behind her back for both of them to see. "Your hat!" She held it out.

Jessie's knees threatened to buckle. Relief filled her and she wanted to laugh. The woman smiled at Michael, and he took Jessie's hat from her. "Thanks," he managed to grate out.

"Anytime." The waitress was obviously smitten, but Michael didn't notice. He held Jessie's hand even more tightly as they went out the door.

"Where are we going?" she asked as they hurried for the car, trying to look casual.

"North," he told her shortly when they reached the Firebird. "Fasten your seat belt. We're going to make tracks."

She did as he told her, then leaned back in the seat as he took off toward the highway. For all intents and purposes, she was with him now. She mulled over that fact, slightly in awe of it. She was with him now. But just where were they going?

"What will happen if they catch you? To you, I mean."

His gaze didn't waver from the highway and his answer when it came was another question. "Have you ever been locked up, Jessie?" he asked softly. "Have you ever felt like a caged rat, a desperate, lost thing about ready to beat itself to death against the bars of the cage rather than go on living that way?'' His steely eyes glances sideways to see her reaction. ''Have you?''

The softness of his tone belied the intensity in his voice, but she still felt chilled. For some crazy reason a picture of Beau flashed through her mind again. Then she realized why. The imprisonment Michael had described fit how she'd felt married to Beau. Trapped. Panicky. But she didn't tell him about that. She didn't say anything at all.

''I won't go to jail.'' Now his voice was rock hard, ice cold. ''That's not even an option here. I won't be locked behind prison walls. Not ever again.''

She nodded, more because she believed in his conviction than because she believed in his future. So he'd been in prison. Was that what had tempered that steel in him?

A boy she'd known in high school had gone to prison for killing a man in a knife fight. He'd been a wild boy, an uncontrollable force that cut a swath across the peaceable landscape like a cyclone. She couldn't believe Michael had ever been like that. Still, he must have done something awfully wrong to end up in prison.

She needed something, some shred of evidence to cling to. She was a black-and-white person; she could either be for or against, but not neutral. She needed something, and she needed it fast.

''You said…last night you said you weren't guilty.''

''I'm not.''

''Well, I'm going to need more than that. Why are they after you if you're not guilty?''

He glanced over at her, knowing she was right and that she deserved an explanation. Still, it made him angry to have to prove anything to anyone. ''I've been framed,'' he said shortly. ''There's a man named Kerry Carter who can help clear me. I'm going to find him.''

She nodded. Okay. That was all she needed. ''Where are we going?''

He shrugged. ''North.''

''How far north? Canada? The North Pole?''

He glanced at her. What was the use of trying to hide his

destination now? They'd be there in two hours. "Phoenix," he replied. "The man I'm looking for has a brother in Phoenix and I'm hoping he's there."

"Okay." Phoenix. "If you'd told me last night we could have been there a lot sooner. That was some detour we took out into the desert last night."

"I know. Last night was a nightmare. Sometimes I feel I still haven't woken up."

Jessie had mixed feelings. Sometimes nightmares could turn out to be daydreams, after all. Just then Michael pulled into a rest area along the side of the highway. She looked at him questioningly.

"You still haven't called your father," he reminded her.

"Oh." Funny he would think of it, she'd forgotten. "Right."

She got out of the car and started for the telephone booth. He was right beside her. So he still didn't trust her. She pushed her hat down low over her eyes and glared at him. "You going to tell me what to say, or are you going to leave that to me?" she asked, her voice dripping sarcasm.

He leaned against the side of the kiosk, his grin crooked. "You can say anything you want, as long as you don't tell him where we are."

She lifted the receiver.

"Or where we're headed."

She put a coin into the slot.

"And get off fast, just in case the cops are monitoring your father's phone. Don't give them time to run a trace."

She dialed the number, then put in the additional money the operator asked for.

"Hello."

Hearing Harley's voice made her knees a little weak all of a sudden, which surprised her. "It's me, Jessie."

"Jessie, baby." His voice was rough with emotion. "Where are you, honey? Are you okay?"

"I'm fine, Daddy, honest. Listen now, I'm going to tell you this quick. I'm okay and I'm going somewhere with Michael. He's going to prove he's innocent and I'm going to help him."

"No, Jessie—"

"Yes, Daddy. I'll call you again when I can."

"What's he done to you?"

"Nothing."

"Nothing? You don't sound the same. You haven't called me 'Daddy' since you were nine years old. What's this man done to you?"

With horror Jessie realized she was blushing. "Nothing Da—Harley. I just wanted to tell you I'm all right. I'm going to hang up now."

"Where are you, girl?"

"Don't worry about me."

"Are you in California? That's it, isn't it? California."

"Oh, Daddy." She put down the receiver with a snap, glared at Michael and began to march back to the car. Neither of them said a word as they both got inside and Michael headed for the highway. Jessie felt as though her lungs were pushing against her heart. She looked out the window at the painted desert and tried to figure out why.

Michael stole a glance at her now and then. She intrigued him, there was no denying it. She was such a bundle of contradictions. In a strange way he enjoyed having her along.

Funny. Women had always been trouble in his life, from his mother, Pamela, right on through to Vanessa.

Vanessa. She'd disappointed him. But he had to admit that was his own fault. He'd known Vanessa all his life and had never bothered to take a really good look at her.

As the miles rolled by, he allowed himself to think about her. The disillusion of that final scene would be with him for a long time. Their families had assumed the two of them were betrothed from the beginning. It had started as a joke, but later it was taken seriously. Even when he'd dated other women, he'd known in the back of his mind that Vanessa was waiting for him.

The idea had never been an unpleasant one. Probably if some great passion had shocked him out of his lethargy, he would have forgotten all about Vanessa. But that never happened.

Vanessa was beautiful and pleasant and fun. Besides that,

she was familiar. Marrying her would have been the comfortable thing to do. It would have made the families happy, and while his father had been alive, that was important to him. By the time his father had passed away, the die had been cast and he'd seen little reason to make a change. Until the day he'd walked into that warehouse and seen with his own eyes what Sky was up to.

When he'd gone to Vanessa after confronting Sky, she'd laughed at his naïveté. Suddenly he had seen the real Vanessa, a selfish, greedy woman completely devoid of anything remotely resembling a conscience.

"Are you trying to make me believe you had no idea what Daddy was up to?" she'd scoffed.

He'd realized then that he wasn't really surprised. Somewhere in the back of his mind he'd known there was something about Sky that wasn't on the up-and-up. Sky and his father had been friends. Looking back, that friendship was a little hard to understand. He'd always known the connection went back to the Korean War, and when he'd been a child, he'd accepted what seemed natural. But as an adult, he'd often wondered what made these two men, so dissimilar in tastes and outlook, stay friends. Pieces of the puzzle were finally falling into shape and he didn't like the picture they portrayed.

"I'm going to the police," he'd told her. "I just want you to be prepared."

Her beautiful face had crumbled. "You can't do that," she cried out to him. "You'll ruin everything. Don't you see that?"

"Vanessa, my dear," he said almost sadly. "That's exactly my goal. Don't *you* see *that*?"

Huge tears had begun a slow progression down her powdered cheeks. "Oh, Michael," she sobbed, hanging on to him. "I love you so much. Please, for me, don't do this. Talk to Daddy. Listen to what he has to say. He's had his reasons. Besides, everyone else is doing these things. I'm sure he'll be able to convince you—"

"Vanessa, I'm sorry, but I can't. What your father is doing is more than illegal. I can't condone it, much less join in."

He'd gently untangled himself from her. "I'm going to the police. Nothing you can do or say will stop me."

"But it's so senseless. What do you care how Daddy gets the money? He hasn't ever been caught. That's what counts, isn't it?"

Michael shook his head, staring at her. "Who are you?" he whispered. "I feel I don't even know you."

Vanessa had blinked back her tears. "Don't you see?" she moaned. "You'll be dragging your own family into the mud right along with us. Your father was deeply involved in things Sky did. And your mother…" She stopped, a light flashing in her eyes. "Ah, yes, your mother. Come along with me. I have something to show you." She strode to a wall safe, opened it and pulled out a diamond necklace. "Recognize these?"

He'd recognized them all right. The Drayton diamonds. The same diamonds that now resided snugly in the speaker of his car. He glanced at the speaker, as if checking to make sure they were still safely hidden. He should never have grabbed them from Vanessa the way he had. But it was too late now. He was stuck with them.

Jessie yawned, drawing his attention away from his thoughts. He liked watching her, whatever she was doing. She moved like a child, unconscious of how she appeared to others. And that was odd, because she looked damn good. She was as different from the women he was used to as night was from day. She was so real it almost hurt to look at her.

They stopped for gas at a station with a convenience store. Jessie got out of the car when Michael did.

"Give me some money," she said evenly. "I'll go get us food for the rest of the day." His hesitation pricked her pride. "Why don't you try trusting me?" she asked.

He didn't smile, but he did hand her the money.

"Get a paper," he called after her. "We can read all about ourselves."

She nodded and went into the little store, picking out sliced meat, bread and cheese, along with a quart of milk, some soda pop and snacks.

She caught sight of herself in the big round mirror that was supposed to give the clerk a good look at every corner of the store. From what she'd seen in that paper at the restaurant the police had her high-school graduation picture to go on for identification. With her hair short and curly and a strained smile plastered on her face, that girl didn't look a thing like the lean, work-hardened woman she saw in the mirror. She felt her shoulders relax. Now if only there were some way to make Michael less conspicuous....

"I got food," she told him as she slid back into the car. "And something else." She grinned at him. "Go down the road about a mile and then find someplace to turn off."

"What?"

She lifted her chin challengingly. "Just do what I say. It's for your own good."

His unreadable gaze held hers and she waited, holding her breath. He didn't smile. He still didn't really trust her. His wariness reminded her that this was no game they were playing. The consequences were too real for that.

Finally he looked away, started the engine and cruised out onto the road, soon coming to a gully lined with scrub brush. Moving carefully, he maneuvered the car across the sand to a spot where it couldn't be seen from the road.

Switching off the engine, he turned to her, one eyebrow raised in question. She reached down into the brown paper bag of groceries and produced a bottle of hair dye.

Michael's handsome head jerked back. "Oh, no, you don't," he exploded.

"Keep calm," she said, unscrewing the top. "I'm not going after your whole head. Just that silver streak."

He actually looked worried. "I like my silver streak."

So did she, but she would never admit it. "It brands you, Mr. Fugitive. They won't even need pictures to identify you." She took a tissue and poured some of the dark brown dye onto it. "Hold still now. This won't hurt a bit."

His hand on her wrist was surprisingly strong. "Wait a minute," he ordered. "How do I know I won't end up with some god-awful green streak?"

She hesitated, looking into his silver-blue eyes, and suddenly she was aware of him in a physical way that quickened her heartbeat. Something flickered in his gaze. He felt it, too. She was much too close to him. His eyelashes were thick and dark. She hadn't noticed that before.

"It's…it's the wash-out kind of dye," she managed to say in almost normal tones. "If you don't like it, you can get rid of it."

His hand still held her wrist and his gaze still held her eyes. "Just wash it out?" he asked softly.

She nodded, swallowing. Her attention dropped to his mouth, but she quickly looked back into his eyes, trying to force back the flush she could feel threatening. She would not reveal her weakness to him. Gritting her teeth, she tugged at his arm.

He let go, though he seemed reluctant. "Be careful," he growled.

"Oh, I will," she retorted, meaning more than just the hair dye, and they both knew it.

She worked quickly. The silver streak that looked so intriguing came from a crescent-shaped birthmark just above the hairline, she discovered. "And here I thought you were a junior werewolf or something," she murmured.

He didn't smile. Covering up the silver streak was a good idea. He should have thought of it himself. It did make him look unusual enough to be noticed. But taking the time to do it was holding them back once again. He was a man who liked to go for the target, single-mindedly thrashing through the underbrush, but ever since he'd been tangled up with Jessie, the underbrush seemed to be ensnarling him.

The man-woman thing was there, strong and true. She puzzled him, fascinated him. The way she was leaning toward him made her shirt gape open and he could see her smooth tanned neck fade to skin untouched by the elements. She was lean and strong. Every inch of her body was ready to efficiently carry out her duties as she saw them, nothing more, nothing less. Michael had a deep, warm temptation to show her something else she could do with it. She was as taut and ready as a racehorse at the starting gate, her body tensed, her round, firm breasts as tight as her nerves seemed to be strung. Under her work shirt she wore a white no-nonsense bra. No laces and bows for Jessie. He smiled, and she noticed.

"What are you grinning at?" she asked defensively. "I'm doing fine. I haven't spilled any on your face yet."

He didn't answer, but the smile faded. He was noticing the fresh, womanly scent of her. Just thinking of it stirred him. He had an impulse to take her hand and press the inside of her wrist to his lips. He could already sense that her heart was beating quickly, more quickly than normal. It would be so easy to reach over and touch her, push aside the utilitarian bra, expose her vulnerability, stroke the dark nipples until she cried out with pleasure. Something told him she would ignite like a bundle of kindling.

But that would only be another distraction, delaying them further. He had to find Kerry. Time was as precious as life's blood to him now. Every minute he delayed, he was that much closer to jeopardy.

Impatiently he pulled at her hand. "That's enough," he said gruffly. "Let's get out of here."

She drew back and he took a look in the rearview mirror. His silver streak was now a muddy brown. "Great," he said caustically. "What an improvement."

She began to tidy up. "At least from a distance you won't be so recognizable," she said.

He grunted. "Get that bottle put away so we can move. We've wasted enough time this morning."

Her motions became slow and deliberate. "What's that you say?" she trilled. "Why, you're very welcome, of course, but you don't have to thank me, Mr. Michael Drayton. I'm pleased to do anything I can to help a friend." She pushed the bag under the seat. "No thanks are necessary, I'm sure," she said, her face turned up toward him.

"Thank you, Jessie," he said with exaggerated politeness. And then it happened. He hadn't meant to do it. He didn't even know for sure how it happened. But suddenly that upturned face was so close beneath his, and his hand was cupping her chin and his lips were grazing hers, finding a sweet intoxication he never would have expected.

CHAPTER NINE

JESSIE RETREATED, wiping the back of her hand across her mouth, her eyes huge. "Don't," she said, her voice quivering.

He looked at her, at a loss. A part of him wanted to apologize; another part wanted to kiss her again. "I was just saying thank you," he noted stiffly.

"Words will do," she said. This time her voice was strong and steady and her eyes flashed fire. "I can understand them better."

What was it, he wondered. Did she find him repulsive? No, he'd met her gaze often enough to know that wasn't it. Did she find sexual attraction repulsive? Or frightening? What kind of fool man would have put that kind of fear into her? He had an impulse to pull her to him, to hold her against his chest and stroke her hair and calm her. But that was silly. He didn't have time for this. "Let's go," he said abruptly, turning on the engine again. "I want to get out of here."

Jessie sat very still, wishing she could take back the past few moments of her life. He thought she was a silly prude. She could tell. And maybe she was. After all, he hadn't done anything very threatening. It was just a simple thank-you kiss. She wished there were some way she could tell him she was sorry. But she wasn't used to telling men that, and she didn't know how to make that first move. So she sat and looked out the window as Arizona flew by.

"Hey," he said at last. "Did you pick up that newspaper I told you to get?"

"Oh." She reached down in front of her seat. "I did." Spreading it open, she studied their pictures on the front page.

Police are still looking for fugitive Michael Drayton, accused of embezzling funds from Matthews Aviation in San Francisco and stealing a diamond necklace from the daughter of the company's founding president, Sky Matthews. Last seen in the Tucson area, Drayton is believed to have taken Jessica MacAllister, a southern Arizona rancher, as a hostage. The aviation firm has offered a reward in the amount of five thousand dollars for information leading to the arrest and conviction of Michael Drayton.

She looked up from the paper. "That's all," she said. "Pretty skimpy. Not much background here, is there?"

He shrugged. "Local papers," he said, but something about the way he said it gave her the idea that he was relieved.

They drove through a lonely, dusty town and then were in the desert again. Here and there they passed hitchhikers, usually grubby men with all their possessions tied to their backs. But as they went by one short person with his thumb out, Jessie realized the face was young...and familiar.

"Stop!" she yelled, swinging around to look behind them.

Michael jammed on the brakes and pulled the car to the side of the road. "What?" he demanded. "What's the matter?"

"Back up."

"What?"

"That kid from the town. The one you saved from the bullies. I think that was him."

Michael glanced back at the boy, who was trudging toward the car and groaned. "Oh, no. Listen, we already saved him once."

"Oh, come on. You've got to give him a ride." Jessie looked at the young boy. He'd recognized them, too, but there was no smile. "Look at that sweet face. How can you leave that on the road?"

"Very easily. Give him a couple of bucks and let's get out of here."

"No." She wasn't sure why, but she couldn't leave the boy behind. "Think of it this way. We need him."

Michael's gaze was skeptical.

"They're looking for you and me, not a family group," she reasoned. "If we take him along, that's what we'll be."

She had a very good point. Michael hesitated, then shrugged resignedly. She opened the car door. "Come on," she called to the boy. "Get in."

He got in as though he were reluctant to take the ride, pulling his bag in beside him. Michael didn't waste any time getting under way again.

"What's your name?" Jessie asked the boy, twisting in the seat so that she could look him in the face.

"Joey." He settled in the back seat and met her gaze with a mixture of shyness and bravado.

"Hi, Joey. I'm Jessie and this here's Michael. Where are you headed?"

His dark eyes went from Jessie to the back of Michael's head. "Where are you going?"

She grinned at him. "I asked you first."

His eyes were hooded. He didn't look scared exactly, just careful. "Bullhead City," he said at last.

She turned to Michael. "It's in our direction. He can get another ride from Phoenix."

He nodded grudgingly, glancing at Joey in the rearview mirror. The kid was probably okay. It wouldn't hurt to have him along for a little while.

Jessie was examining him, too, as she chewed on her lower lip. He was awfully young, eleven or twelve. What kind of a mother would let a boy this age wander all over creation on his own?

"Where are your parents?" she asked.

The look he flashed her was just this side of resentful. Then his face hardened and he met her gaze with his chin high. "I'm trying to find my mom. She should be waiting for me in Bullhead City." He pursed his lips and Jessie could see she wasn't going to get another fact out of him if he could help it.

"What happened? How did you get separated?"

He avoided her gaze and shrugged.

She looked at the stained, callused hands. "Your people are

migrant workers, aren't they?'' she said, recognizing the signs. "Did she go on ahead to cover a new crop?''

He nodded.

She turned away, biting her lip again, cursing the woman, whoever she was. This boy thought he was tough, but he needed taking care of. He was still a child. She'd hired boys barely older than him on her ranch. Some of them had been tough, hardened. And some of them had been a little thick. But this boy was neither. His bright, dark intelligent eyes told her that.

He didn't want to talk. She knew she should leave him alone. But she kept remembering how he'd looked confronting those bullies in the town, that brave face, the resignation in his eyes, and she couldn't stop. Turning, she smiled at him again.

"Is Bullhead City where you live most of the time?'' she asked.

His expression said, *Here she goes again*, but his mouth said, "Uh-uh.''

"Where do you live?''

He avoided her eyes. "Around.''

Around. In the dusty camps that usually didn't even have real structures for the people to live in. Poor kid.

Michael looked back at the boy and almost grinned. In a way he envied him. He was young to be on his own, but what Michael wouldn't have given to have had that kind of freedom when he was a boy. Lucky kid. "Leave him alone,'' he advised Jessie. "If he doesn't want to talk don't make him.''

Jessie turned and sat straight in her seat, but she was seething. It took her a few minutes to calm down. Leaning forward, she turned on the radio, fidgeting with the dial until she found a country-and-western ballad of love lost. She hummed along with it until another sound caught her attention. Every time the singer hit a high note, something rattled in the speaker. Opening the glove compartment, she discovered a small tool set, removed a screwdriver and started for the speaker.

"Hey!'' Michael's hand shot out, stopping her, and the car nearly swerved off the road. "What are you doing?''

She grabbed the side of her seat, surprised. "There's a noise in the speaker. I was just going to remove the cover and take a look.''

"No. Don't go anywhere near that speaker."

The harshness of his tone surprised her once more. She was going to show off her expertise with tools and he wasn't going to let her. "Fine." She put the tools away, snapping the glove compartment shut. "Whatever you say. You're the boss."

The edginess between them was back full force, making Jessie wonder what she was doing there when she should be home, seeing to her ranch. Michael was as infuriating as he was attractive.

Attractive! Was that what was keeping her with him? She sighed with self-disgust. If she was really letting herself fall into that old trap she was a bigger fool than she'd ever been before, and she didn't want to think about it. Abruptly she picked up the brown paper bag and dug out a snack. "Want some peanuts?" she asked, turning to offer them to Joey.

He shook his head, but she could tell by the way he looked at them that he was hungry.

"Come on." She tried to hand him some.

He shook his head again, looking out the window.

"Hey, come on," she coaxed. "You've got to eat these. You'll be doing me a favor. If you don't eat them, I will. And then I'll get fat. And then I won't be able to ride my horses anymore." She blew out her cheeks, pretending to be fat, and there was the ghost of a smile in his eyes when he glanced at her, then looked away again.

"Please," she said softly.

He looked back, his gaze uncertain. "Okay," he muttered at last, holding out a hand to take the peanuts from her.

A feeling of triumph welled up in her as she passed the food back, but she hid it from the boy. She couldn't resist a haughty look at Michael, though. To her surprise, when her eyes met his he started laughing.

"Don't I get any?" he teased. "Or am I in the doghouse?"

She handed him a few, and when her eyes met his this time, heat shot through her like brandy and she looked quickly away.

The small country road they'd been traveling on widened, and all of a sudden they were on a major thoroughfare.

"Phoenix looks a lot like Los Angeles," Michael said disapprovingly as the freeway brought them closer to the city. "Do you know your way around?"

Jessie shook her head. "Not like I do Tucson," she said. "I guess I'll just take an off ramp and hope for the best."

They found themselves in a sleepy looking suburb. Michael pulled into the parking lot of a small shopping mall, right in front of a telephone booth, making sure the car was not visible from the highway. Customers were few and far between. The ongoing carnival in a nearby field was probably the reason.

"I'm going to have to make quite a few calls," Michael said, counting out his change. "Why don't the two of you stretch your legs?"

Jessie looked at him, one eyebrow raised. "You trust me?" she asked, only half teasing.

He started to reach for her, an involuntary gesture he couldn't analyze. It seemed natural, as though they were lovers and touching was part of their relationship. But it wasn't, and they weren't. He had to remind himself of that. "I trust you," he said softly, his eyes shining in the sunlight.

She'd noticed everything, and even though she wasn't sure what it all meant, she responded emotionally. She smiled, pure happiness shimmering through her.

He shook his head, grinned and ducked out of the car. "See you all in a few minutes," he said, heading for the telephone.

Jessie tingled, but she shook the feeling away. "Come on, Joey," she said. "Let's you and me get us a couple of ice-cream cones."

Joey got out of the car to follow her, and she noticed he had his bag along. "What are you bringing that thing for?" she asked casually, unprepared for the way he was hugging it to his chest.

"I...I guess I'd better get another ride here," he said, but he looked her full in the face as though waiting for something.

Jessie felt her heart contract. "No," she said quickly. She couldn't bear to think of him standing alongside the highway with his thumb out again. "No, wait until Michael makes his calls. Maybe we'll be able to phone your mother."

"No." He shook his head vehemently. "She doesn't have a phone."

"Oh." But he didn't say anything more about leaving them, and neither did she.

She bought him a double chocolate fudge supreme and got herself a lemon custard. They walked back slowly, licking their cones and gazing in store windows. The sporting goods store caught Jessie's eye. "What's your favorite sport, Joey?" she asked, looking over the footballs displayed in the window. But Joey didn't answer. Turning around, she found he'd stopped in front of the furniture store next door. Curious to see what had captured his attention, she went back to stand beside him. What she saw was a perfectly ordinary maple dining-room set.

"Do you have a table like that at your house?" Joey asked.

"I guess what we have might have looked like that about twenty years ago," she said cheerfully, then felt a shiver of dismay. She'd been going to ask Joey what kind his mother had, but what if she didn't have one? Migrant workers often spent years moving from tent cities to shacks along the highway, following the crops as they were harvested. She'd never thought about it before, but suddenly she was angry. Those people worked hard. They deserved a decent standard of living. Paying them more would mean higher food prices, but maybe that was the only fair thing to do.

As she stood there mulling over the plight of the migrant workers, Michael emerged from the telephone booth. "Did you find him?" she asked when he got back to her. The look on his face told her that the answer was no.

"I've got one more number to call. They told me to phone back in about half an hour." He shrugged and looked around him. "Want to go over and check out the carnival?"

Joey's face lit up and they both laughed. A moment later the three of them were strolling toward the noise and music. A Ferris wheel flashed in the sunlight. The raucous sounds of a calliope split the air. Children walked by with huge cones of cotton candy, and a monkey on a chain chattered at them as they passed.

Jessie noticed people turn to look twice as their little group went by. She guessed it was because of the odd combination they made, she in her boots and cowboy hat, Michael in his rumpled business suit and the little dark-eyed boy in ragged jeans and a faded blue sweatshirt, clutching a canvas bag to his chest. It made her smile. She kind of liked it.

Joey rode on the merry-go-round, with Jessie and Michael cheering him on from the sides. He actually grinned at them as he passed. Then he wanted to go on a roller coaster, and Michael talked Jessie into coming along.

Actually, she loved roller coasters, but she was a little nervous about being jammed up hard against Michael as the three of them shared a seat. The car started to roll and his arm came around her, and she found herself bracing herself against him, more excited by the sense of his strength than the speed of the ride. When the car finally came to a stop, his arm lingered. She turned to look at him, her heart beating wildly. He gazed at her for a long moment.

"Come on, you guys," Joey said impatiently, his original reticence forgotten now. "Let's go on the Boomerang."

The two of them drew apart reluctantly, and Jessie wondered what was wrong with her. After all these years, all the experience she'd had in avoiding romance, this was no time to lose perspective. Clenching her teeth as they left the ride, she vowed to remember that from now on. Michael was poison. And she'd better not forget it.

Something about "pony races" came over the public address system and Joey stopped, listening intently.

"What is it?" Jessie asked him.

He looked around. "Where's the track?" he said. "They're having pony races."

They found the quarter-mile track easily. The man with the microphone was exhorting all boys and girls under the age of thirteen to sign up for the races. "A twenty-five-dollar prize to the winner," he said.

Joey's face was set as he turned to Jessie. "Will you hold my bag?" he asked.

She took it from him automatically. "Are you going to ride?" she asked, delighted at first, then skeptical. This was a child of migrant workers, not of ranchers. "How well do you ride, Joey? Do you know what you're doing?"

He nodded.

She chewed her lip, wondering what his mother would want for him. "Don't you have to have your own horse?"

He pointed toward the sign for the event. "They provide horses. You can use your own if you want to, but mostly they provide them."

Jessie shook her head. "I don't think you should do it."

He was hitching up his pants, his mouth a thin line of determination. "I need that money," he said solemnly.

Jessie looked quickly at Michael for help, then back at the boy. "Joey, have you ever been on a horse before?"

"Once. On my uncle's farm in Mexico."

Jessie frowned. "That's not enough, Joey. The other boys are experienced riders. It could be dangerous."

But he wasn't listening. He walked toward the announcer and Jessie turned to Michael. "He could get hurt. And he sure won't win anything against these boys who've probably grown up on ranches." The clear implication was that Michael should do something fast.

Michael looked at her and shrugged. "What do you want me to do? Forbid him?" His tone suggested he thought she was being overcautious, but Jessie had seen inexperienced riders hurt in this sort of thing before.

Suddenly Joey was back waving a sheet of white paper. "I need you to sign," he told Jessie, handing it to her, his dark eyes huge and hopeful.

She scanned it. It was a parental consent form. "You need your parent or guardian to sign," she told him. "I'm neither. I can't sign this." She handed it back to him, relieved. "I guess you won't be able to race after all."

His face held no resentment, but he sighed and handed the form to Michael. "Could you sign it?" he asked.

Michael looked at the boy, then at Jessie. One pair of eyes pleaded for help; the other demanded he refuse. He swallowed and wished he could offer to take the ride himself. Life had certainly gotten complicated since he'd hooked up with Jessie MacAllister.

But there was a place for feminine caution, and there was a place for bold adventuring. He was ready to vote for the latter right now. "Sure, kid," he said, taking the paper from Joey. "I'll sign for you."

"Michael!"

He shrugged, his expression that of resignation. "A boy's gotta do what a boy's gotta do," he informed her sadly, reaching for a pen.

Jessie was outraged. "You can't," she snapped, looking around quickly to see if they were being overheard. "That's like forgery. It's illegal."

Paying no attention, Michael signed the paper with a flourish. "Just add it to my list of transgressions. I'm going for a record." He grinned at Joey, who grinned back for a moment.

"Thanks, Michael," the boy said before loping off to join the other boys preparing to ride.

"You shouldn't have done that," Jessie grumbled.

"Probably not." His eyes met hers. "I've been doing a lot of things I shouldn't lately."

Something quivered in his gaze, and she blinked, then looked quickly away. "Isn't it time you got back to your phone call?" she reminded him gruffly.

He hesitated. "Right after the race," he told her. "I want to see Joey ride."

Jessie shivered. She didn't like this. Joey was such a cute little guy. When she thought of what could happen to him out there... She shivered again and leaned up against the railing that rimmed the track.

Closing her eyes, she took in the atmosphere, the dust of the corral, the smell of horses, the country music playing in the background, and she let herself feel at home. This was her sort of place. Michael probably didn't appreciate it for what it was.

Most probably you had to be born to it. And even then, sometimes the liking didn't take.

That reminded her of Beau, her ex-husband. He'd been born on a ranch just as she had, but he'd never really liked ranching. It was a wonder he'd ever thought he loved her. He was always champing at the bit, talking about moving to Tucson or Phoenix or even Dallas, talking about schemes to make millions, fancy cars, going to parties. What on earth had she ever seen in him? It made you stop and think about how dumb a person could be. Dumb or blind.

She glanced over at Michael and found him staring at her. "What are you looking at?" she asked defensively.

"You." He tucked a stray lock of hair behind her ear. "How is it that you keep looking prettier to me all the time?"

She reached up and shoved her hat down low over her eyes and frowned at him, hoping he wouldn't notice the spots of color that had rushed to her cheeks. "The Arizona sun must have blinded you, mister."

"No." He narrowed his eyes, watching her through the sun-lit blur of his lashes. For some strange reason he was picturing the Drayton diamonds around her tanned neck. And they looked as though they were made for her.

The Drayton diamonds had been in his family for generations. Most recently they'd spent most of their time around his mother's neck. But they didn't really belong to Pamela. They belonged to the Drayton family. To think that she'd handed them over to Sky Matthews brought anger surging through him once again.

His mother. A bitter taste haunted him when he thought of her. She'd never been a real mother to him, more a figurehead. When he conjured up a vision of her now, he always saw her dressed for an evening out, a cigarette in one hand, a bejeweled, gold-plated lighter in the other.

That afternoon in San Francisco, he'd taken the necklace from Vanessa's hands and let the stones slip through his fingers. "Where did you get these?" he'd asked harshly.

"Gambling debts," Vanessa had told him as he'd stared at

the glittering jewels he held. "She gave them to my father in exchange for cash to pay off her gambling debts."

The horrible thing was he'd never doubted that what Vanessa said was true. When he'd been a little boy, he'd loved his mother, loved her all the more because she hardly gave him a thought. He'd been desperate for her attention. All the tricks and antics of his young life had been to attract her eye. He'd had his father's love, a love that was unquestioning, but his mother… Why couldn't she love him? Though for years he'd been too young to understand it, finally he realized that the question had been a constant one in his mind. Why couldn't she love him?

He thought of his sad, graying father, his kind eyes not comprehending the events going wrong in his life, and his heart ached. Pamela had spent less and less time at home over the years. She was always at some party, always traveling. Michael was pretty sure she saw other men, though no one had ever dared lay the proof out before him. But his father had loved his beautiful, brittle mother, too. What a pair of fools they were, he and his dad.

So Sky Matthews had paid off his mother's gambling debts and held the Drayton diamonds in return. Did that mean his mother had been having an affair with Sky? Not necessarily. But something told him it was all too possible. And that might be one reason she refused to come back from Europe these days.

"I can't let you keep these," he'd told Vanessa. "Have Sky let me know how much money he gave my mother. I'll cover it. But I can't let you keep this necklace."

Vanessa had made a grab for them, but he'd pulled away in time. "No," she'd cried, real anguish in her face. "The Drayton necklace is mine now!"

"It doesn't belong to you," he ground out, starting for the door with the diamonds in his hand. "I'll keep it, if you don't mind."

Vanessa had tried to block his way. "Oh, Michael, no, please! I've wanted the diamonds for so long, ever since I was a little girl. They obviously didn't mean a thing to your mother, but they mean everything to me.'' She blinked at him, thinking fast. "They're like a symbol of our commitment.''

He'd thrust her out of his path, the diamonds threaded through his fingers. "Our commitment is over, Vanessa. Surely you can see that.''

Confusion clouded her face. "No! I love you.''

"You don't love me any more than I love you. I'm just another possession to you, Vanessa. A name that adds a certain prestige." He felt almost sad, looking at her. "Take my advice as an old friend. Go out and get yourself a job and an apartment. Make yourself a life. Get away from Sky.''

And then he was gone, out the door and downtown to police headquarters, where he would try to talk sense into Bob Taylor.

Jessie's elbow was making contact with his ribs, bringing him back to the present.

"Here they go," she said.

The kids were mounted and ready to ride. Joey didn't look nervous. But he didn't have the easy confidence the other boys and girls showed, either. While they grinned and laughed and called to one another from astride their ponies, Joey sat very still, his face a dark mask of concentration.

Jessie reached unconsciously for Michael's arm, her fingers circling it as she watched the boy. "Hold tight, honey," she said just under her breath. "Take it easy. Sit back and let the ride flow through you.''

Joey did just the opposite. The starter fired his gun and the horses were off, and Joey was crouched over his pony's neck, his face whipped by the animal's mane.

"He's falling off!" Jessie cried, her fingers digging into Michael's arm.

"Ouch," he said, prying her fingers loose. "He's not falling. He's riding great.''

The dust from the horses' hooves was in her mouth and in her eyes and she wasn't sure what she was seeing. Was Joey really out in front? Out along the backstretch, that was sure what it looked like.

"C'mon, Joey!" she said now, her hands balled into fists. "Go, Joey! Go!"

Michael laughed softly as he watched her. The woman who'd been so against this was suddenly Joey's number one fan, her face alive with excitement. As the riders came around the turn and headed for home, she began to jump up and down, chanting over and over, "Go, Joey. Go, Joey!"

When he won, she whooped and threw herself into Michael's arms. He held her gently, looking down at her tangled hair. She felt good. He wanted to draw her up against his chest and close his eyes and hold her. But she was gone in the next instant, running to help Joey down off the horse. He followed slowly, wondering what it would have been like to know Jessie earlier, before prison, before this headlong race across the countryside had begun. But he remembered that she wouldn't have given him a second glance back then. After all, there'd been no reward posted for him. That made him grin.

CHAPTER TEN

THE LAST CALL HIT the jackpot. The C. Carter did turn out to be Kerry's brother Chester.

"He was here all right," he told Michael on the telephone. "But he left last week. Went to Las Vegas to see some people."

"Las Vegas." Michael thought for a moment. "Do you know where he's staying?"

"Sorry."

Michael had visions of Kerry slipping away from him again. "How about a name, someone he was going to see?"

"He didn't tell me."

And you wouldn't tell me even if he had, Michael realized. What could he do to win this man's trust?

"Listen, Mr. Carter. Kerry and I worked together at Matthews Aviation. Kerry wanted my help in clearing up some illegal activities there, and I wouldn't back him at the time. I thought he was making mountains out of molehills. Now I know better. I've seen evidence that he was right all along. I'd like to help him, but I can't do that unless I find him."

Silence. He held on tensely. "Mr. Carter," he added at last. "If you could just give me some name to go on, someone Kerry might know in Las Vegas...."

"Look, I told you I don't know. I can't help you. If you'd like to leave your number with me, I'll tell Kerry you called when I hear from him."

Michael sighed. "I don't have a number. I'm on the run."

More silence. "Okay, here's what I'll do," Chester Carter said, his voice low and conspiratorial. "I'll give you the name of someone who knows a lot about what's going on in Vegas. If he trusts you, he might help you find Kerry."

Michael's sagging spirits lifted. "Great. Who is he?"

"His name is Nargeant. He runs the Samarkand Hotel and Casino, on the Strip. Look him up when you get to town."

Michael walked back to the car, where he'd arranged to meet Jessie, and slid in behind the steering wheel. Jessie looked at him expectantly. "Well?"

He didn't answer.

"Was he the right guy?" she asked. "Did he tell you where to find this person you're looking for?"

Michael's eyes were cool and hooded. "Yeah, he told me."

She waited, but he didn't go on. "Where? Where is it that we're going?"

He looked at her silently, his mouth a hard line.

Suddenly her face changed. "Oh, of course." Exasperation made her sarcastic. "I should know better than to ask. After all, they just might capture me and torture me until I spill my guts, and then I would scream it out and then they'd know, wouldn't they? You're absolutely right not to tell me. It's for my own good."

He couldn't hold back a sheepish grin. "Jessie…"

"No!" She held a hand up for silence. "Say no more. I understand."

He glanced to where Joey was sitting on a curb, counting out his twenty-five-dollar prize for the tenth time. Turning back to Jessie, he looked at her with mock menace. "If you must know, we're going to Las Vegas," he told her. "But keep it under your hat."

At the same moment he said the words, he used one hand to flick her hat off of her head, while the other grabbed both her wrists and got her quickly under his power. His eyes gleamed with amusement. "You, lady, are getting on my nerves," he told her as she writhed, half laughing, half protesting his dominance. "You've been getting out of hand. In fact, I think I'm going to have to tame you a little."

She went very still, her eyes huge. His face was so very

close to hers. "I don't think you'd like me tame," she heard herself whisper.

His eyes darkened. "I think you're probably right."

He was going to kiss her and she didn't care. Her heart was pounding and her body was very still, like the earth was at dawn, waiting for the sun to rise. His breath was hot and sweet against her lips. In a moment his mouth would touch hers, and then—

"I guess I'll go now." Joey's voice came crashing into the car. "See ya."

Michael straightened, pulling away from Jessie, but his gaze met hers for a second as he did so and she read the promise there. She shivered and pulled herself up in the seat of the car, finally focusing on what Joey had said.

"No, wait a minute." She turned urgently to Michael. "We've got to put him on a bus or something. We can't let him hitch out on the highway." Her face brightened. "Wait a minute. If we're really going, uh, where you said, Bullhead City is right on our way."

For once, Michael agreed. "Get in, kid," he said gruffly. "We'll take you to your mother."

Joey didn't argue. It was becoming apparent he liked being with them.

Michael pulled out a map and studied it, making sure of routes and distances. "I don't know if I want to get there tonight," he said softly to Jessie, frowning. "I don't want to check into a hotel there, and God knows I don't want to sleep on the desert again."

"There's not much else but desert out there," she said, thinking. He'd want to stick to back roads, she figured, since surely the authorities knew what kind of car he was driving. He really should have picked something less glitzy. No one could miss this baby rolling by.

Then an idea came to her. "Listen, I've got an uncle who runs a jojoba ranch ninety miles south of Las Vegas."

"Runs a what?"

"A jojoba ranch. You know, those beans they get the oil from. It was a get-rich-quick scheme that didn't pan out, but he makes a living and he's there, out in the middle of nowhere. Why don't we go?''

Michael's glance was skeptical. "Your father will have called him.''

She chuckled. "No way. They haven't spoken in years.'' She shook her head. "No, they're way out in the country. And unless he's changed a lot, my uncle doesn't believe in modern conveniences like television and telephones. The only way they might have heard about us is if someone drove over specially to tell them about it.''

Michael shrugged. "Sounds perfect.'' Too perfect, maybe. He glanced at her, wondering. Was she setting him up again? Then he was ashamed of the thought. She hadn't done anything all day to make him think that. He was too paranoid.

Jessie settled back against the seat as they headed for the main road. Now that their strategy was all mapped out, she was having second thoughts, not sure at all that her uncle would be pleased to see her.

The last time they'd been together was ten years earlier and there'd been a shouting match between Fred and her father that could have been heard three counties wide. The whole thing had been over a misplaced inheritance from an elderly aunt or something like that. Jessie couldn't remember the details, or even who was supposed to have the money and who ended up with it, though she rather thought it must have been Fred. Harley was no money shark, and Fred was always on the lookout for money-making schemes. The last she'd heard, he'd lost everything but the ranch on some worthless mines in Colorado. But you never knew. Maybe he'd found another way to get rich by now. She would just have to wait and see.

They were soon leaving Phoenix behind, then turning north toward the high country of Flagstaff.

"It would be quicker to go straight out of Kingman,'' she advised Michael.

"Also more obvious.''

"True.''

Her eyes began to droop and soon she she was asleep, not waking until they were near the red rock hills and starting the climb to Flagstaff. As she stirred, she heard Michael and Joey talking. They were discussing baseball scores and players.

She sat very still for a while, her eyes closed, and took in the camaraderie that seemed to have sprung up between them. She liked the sound of Michael's voice. It had a warm rumble to it, and yet it wasn't really deep. His words came quickly, but clearly. As often as not there was a touch of humor to his tone. All in all it fit the man.

As if she really knew what sort of man he was. She stirred uncomfortably at the thought. Some people believed he was an outlaw. Had she really seen anything that would prove them wrong?

And then there was Joey. He'd touched her heart from the moment she'd seen him with the two bullies tormenting him. Opening her eyes, she glanced back at him just as he was in the middle of a story about hitting a ball over a cow pasture fence, and suddenly she knew why. There but for the grace of God and gender went little Jessie MacAllister of years ago.

She'd been lost and lonely after her mother had died. She'd felt the world on her shoulders, and she'd had to grow up fast and take care of Harley and the ranch and everything that went along with it. If she could see back into time and take a look at her own eyes at that age, they would have appeared like his—ready to accept responsibility and at the same time terrified of it.

What was his home life like, she wondered. How much rested on his thin shoulders?

By the time they rolled into Flagstaff, the three of them were getting on like a house on fire. It was long after lunchtime and they were all hungry. Driving on through town, they followed a side road until they found a campground. Michael drove around looking for the most remote campsite, then pulled the car into the underbrush as far as he could. They all piled out.

Jessie breathed deeply of the fresh, pine-scented air and reached into the car for her jacket. "It's beautiful here," she said, looking up at the snow-covered mountains.

Michael nodded, but she could see by the look in his eyes that he had more on his mind than nature. She could forget for long periods of time that they were the hunted ones in a dangerous game, but he couldn't afford to.

"I'll make up some sandwiches," Jessie offered, carrying her brown paper bag to the picnic table.

"Joey and I will go exploring," Michael said. "We'll be back in a minute."

She smiled as she watched the two of them go off together, then got busy with the food fixings. Two sandwiches for Michael, one each for herself and Joey. She put them on napkins and shaded her eyes, looking for them to come back. Minutes passed and she began to worry. Listening intently, she could hear the low muffled buzz of voices from other campsites, but nothing to mark the place Michael might be. A chill ran down her spine. What if something had happened?

She began to walk in the direction they'd gone, hoping to meet them coming back. Ponderosa pines were everywhere, limiting her field of vision. Smoke drifted through the trees from campfires. In no time she was out of sight of the picnic table. Where were they?

She avoided coming close enough to other campers to be seen, staying in the thick of the trees. The sound of a twig snapping stopped her.

"Michael?" she called softly.

There was no answer, but there was a crunch. Jessie held her breath, her heart pounding. The stillness seemed to echo ominously around her.

"Michael?" she whispered.

"Here," he said from behind her, sending her a foot into the air with a shriek.

"Hey." Grinning, he took hold of her. "What are you so jumpy for?"

"Where have you been?" she demanded. "I was going crazy!"

The humor left his face, but he still held her close. "What's the matter? Did you think I'd run away?"

She wasn't sure what she'd thought and she didn't answer. Blinking up into his somber eyes, she tried to pull away, only to find his hold growing stronger.

"Did you think you'd lost your prisoner?" he said softly.

"You're not my prisoner!"

"Sure I am. I'm yours, and you're mine."

She tried harder to pull away from him, but his arms tightened. He had her hips pushed hard against his and there was something just a bit wild in his eyes, as though he'd been breathing the clear, cold mountain air and it had set something free inside him.

"How long's it been since you've really been kissed, Jessie MacAllister?"

Something sharp and hot shot through her chest. "That's none of your business!"

He still held her with one arm, while the other freed itself so that he could brush several stray hairs away from her face.

"Someone ought to kiss you, Jessie," he said softly, his eyes flickering with something deep and untamed. "Someone ought to remind you about how things can be between a man and a woman."

Whipping her head away from his hand, she glared at him. This was exactly what she wanted and she knew it, but that only made her angrier. "I took a shotgun to the last man who tried that," she warned. "So I wouldn't recommend it."

"A shotgun."

What a fool she'd been to think that would scare him off. Instead his eyes glittered with interest.

"I bet he thought it was worth it," he murmured, his face coming closer to hers.

His hunger was raw and basic and evident in his eyes. She was weak, paralyzed, her breath stuck in her throat, her pulse pounding like a jungle drum, horror mixing with excitement in a blur that heightened her senses. She could smell his clean, masculine strength, feel the heat from his body against her wind-chilled skin. Before his mouth had touched hers she could feel it, and her lips parted in anticipation.

His lips moved on hers, smooth and warm and caressing, and his tongue flickered against her lips, and then, when she sighed with guilty pleasure, plunged into her mouth. Now he was hot and demanding. The world spun and fell away. Jessie felt as though she were falling through space. A million emotions whirled through her, excitement, fear, need, wariness, and then an explosion of desire such as she'd never felt before.

He kissed her again and again, short, stroking kisses that made her reach for him, hungry for more, hungry for something deeper, and then her arms were twining around his neck and she was pulling him closer, her body an arch that fit against him, yearning for him.

"Hey, you guys." Joey's distant voice was like a whip cracking between them. "It's cold."

She stared up into Michael's eyes as he hesitated, so close, so far. The kiss had been so much more than she'd bargained for, and her shock was clear on her face. Smiling, he dropped a final kiss on the tip of her nose. "Who asked this kid along, anyway?" he grumbled.

Reluctantly he released her just as Joey emerged from the trees. "It's cold all right," he called to the boy. "Let's get back to the campsite."

She turned, feeling light-headed, and tried to smile at Joey. "I've got sandwiches," she said, hoping no one else noticed how shaky her voice had become. "Come on."

She could tell Michael was looking at her, but she didn't have the courage to meet his gaze. She couldn't believe what had happened. She'd thought she'd been so strong, that she'd been so guarded, and then in one weak moment... She shuddered again, this time, she hoped, with dread.

They walked back together until they found the clearing close to where they'd parked the car.

Joey was a bit ahead of them. "Oh, no!" he cried, turning around and gesturing for them to hurry. "Look what happened!"

They rushed forward to find squirrels covering the picnic table where the food had been.

"You little devils!" Jessie yelled, running at them. Every last one of them took off for the trees, leaving not much more than crumbs behind them.

"I don't believe this," Michael said. "You're the nature girl.

You're supposed to know better than to leave food out where animals can get it.''

Jessie sighed in frustration. ''The cows and horses I deal with usually aren't too interested in sandwiches,'' she retorted. ''Besides, you two are the ones who disappeared and…and…''

They looked at the pitiful mess, then at each other, and the next thing Jessie knew, they were both laughing.

''We'll get hamburgers at a takeout in town,'' Michael said.

She looked at him. ''You want to risk it again?''

He nodded. ''Just a quick hit. We can send Joey in to get the food.''

Jessie glanced at the boy, wondering if he was curious about why they might be wary of populated areas. ''We've been lucky so far,'' she said softly to Michael.

''Yes, we have. Sticking to back roads is paying off. We haven't seen one cop all day.''

''That's right,'' she agreed, and at the same moment heard the crunch of tires on the rough road behind them. They both turned to face the ranger's car as it rolled to a stop in the clearing, blocking the road and any escape route they might have had in mind. The ranger got out slowly, pulling his hat straight and looking around the campsite with a stiff, unsmiling face. Jessie's heart leaped into her throat and she swallowed hard. This surely looked like trouble.

CHAPTER ELEVEN

THE RANGER HITCHED UP his pants and glanced from one questioning face to the other. "Howdy, folks. Where's your vehicle?"

He looked like the suspicious type. He sounded like the suspicious type. Jessie licked her dry lips and Michael answered, "Over there," pointing to where he'd parked the car out of sight of the road. From where the ranger was standing, the license plate was clearly visible. Jessie looked at it nervously, then tried to read the ranger's face. Would he run a check on the car?

The ranger walked over slowly and examined the car. Jessie's heart was beating hard, but she tried consciously to relax so that he wouldn't wonder about the tension. The ranger's steely eyes glinted as he turned around. She held her breath.

Finally he spoke. "You planning to stay all night?"

Jessie shook her head vigorously. "Uh, no. We're just having a quick picnic. We're on our way—"

"To the Grand Canyon," Michael finished for her quickly.

The ranger nodded. "We've got a camping fee here, you know. If you all want to camp..."

"No, no, but we'll pay it for the picnic if you like." He reached for his wallet. "How much is it?"

The ranger watched with interest as he pulled out his wallet, but he turned down the money. "Oh, no, that won't be necessary. Just as long as you all remember to vacate so that someone else can camp here."

Jessie hardly dared to hope. He didn't seem to know who they were or suspect anything.

"Sure. Certainly, Officer."

The man nodded, but he still didn't leave. Instead he wandered over to Joey. Jessie tensed. What if he started asking a lot of questions?

"Hey, kid, how you doin'?"

Joey looked up but didn't answer.

"You belong to these people here?"

Joey's face was impassive, his gaze going from Jessie to Michael and back again. Jessie stepped forward, holding her hands tightly together and hoping the ranger couldn't see how they were shaking. "That's Joey. He's ours. Say hello to the ranger, Joey."

The ranger turned with a frown. "He's yours?" he asked skeptically, obviously noting the boy's Mexican ancestry.

Jessie glanced apologetically at Joey and prayed he wouldn't mind her lying. "Adopted," she said breathlessly. "We adopted him."

"Oh."

The ranger gave her a long look. She waited, trying to smile.

The silence seemed to last forever. Finally the ranger turned and started back to his car. "You all have a nice vacation," he called as he opened the door. "Bye now."

Jessie held her breath until the car was out of sight, then she turned to Michael and met his laughing eyes. "Let's get out of here," they both said in unison, and they did, packing the remnants of their food up quickly and heading back out on the road.

"Joey," Jessie said, turning to look into his dark eyes. "I'm sorry I had to lie about you. Telling that ranger that we adopted you."

He stared into her eyes, his own unreadable. "I don't mind," he said softly. "You can tell anybody you want."

She smiled her thanks. They didn't stop for hamburgers until they were well away from the campground, and then Jessie drove for a few hours to give Michael a chance to sleep. They traded off again as the desert got lonelier.

A lightning storm on a distant mesa caught her attention. The desert seemed to stretch forever, the distant mountains rising like gaunt islands in a sea of coral sand. Now and then they passed through a lonely, dusty Arizona town.

This part of the state was miles away from the luxury condominiums, the high rises and glass buildings of the big cities. Jessie glanced at the town they were passing through now, a typical one, with a few scattered frame houses, a cluster of silver trailers, a horse, a couple of bedraggled yellow dogs, one looking almost wild enough to be a coyote. The little gas station had a big neon sign with the *s* missing from the word *gas*.

Last food or gas for 90 miles, said the sign outside of town. Michael stepped on the accelerator and Jessie looked out at the black shadows the clouds were making on the warm desert floor.

"The shadows are racing us," a little voice behind her said.

She turned to smile at Joey. "Do you ever look out at places like that mesa over there, or those black hills, and think about when the cowboys and Indians used to ride this land?" she asked him.

A small smile twitched at the corners of his mouth. "Sometimes," he said.

"I used to dream about the old days all the time when I was your age and we used to drive through here on our way to my uncle's ranch in Nevada. Even now—" she grinned at him "—even now I can close my eyes and see cowboys on the ridge, searching for a stray, or Apache warriors on pintos with their black hair flying behind them."

He assessed her curiously. "Are you part Indian?" he asked.

Her eyes widened. "No. What gave you that idea?"

He shrugged and looked embarrassed.

"I can see why he asked," Michael said, breaking his silence, which had lasted for miles. "Those braids, your dark eyes, the jewelry you wear."

"What, this?" She held up her arm with the silver-and-turquoise bracelet, and Joey nodded. Quickly she slipped it off and handed it to him to study more closely.

"An old Navaho woman gave it to me years ago when I did her a favor. I've worn it every day ever since. It's part of me now."

"It's neat."

She nodded. "I have a lot of respect for the Indians who roamed the Southwest in the old days. They really knew how to cope with the land, how to adapt their lives and use what nature provided them. It's sad to think it can never be like that again. That way of life is going fast."

Joey looked at her with dark, limitless eyes. "Everything changes," he said calmly. "Nothing stays the same. Not for anybody."

A chill ran through her at the sound of his voice. So young to be so wise—or was it cynical? Something had hurt this boy, hurt him badly. Jessie had never known she had a mothering instinct. Suddenly she wanted to take the boy in her arms and promise him everything would be all right.

"Where's your uncle's ranch?" Joey asked, still examining the bracelet. "Did you have horses there?"

"I have horses on my own ranch, south of Tucson," she told him. "My uncle doesn't have as many horses. He grows things, instead. He owns the Three Bar Cross just outside of Talcum. You know where that is?"

Joey nodded slowly, his eyes bright. "Maybe I'll come out and visit you someday," he said.

The thought touched Jessie's heart. She laughed. "Oh, honey, we won't be there but for the night. Then we'll be gone." The smile faded from her eyes. Never to see the boy again.

She shook her head, getting rid of ridiculous notions. So what? She'd only known the kid a few hours. He was just a kid, like any other.

She glanced at Michael. He looked so right in that business suit he was still wearing. So alien to her world. Turning, he met her gaze, and something flashed between them like a bolt of lightning, making her bite down on her lip.

She'd always measured masculinity by how hard a man could ride, how tough he was, how well he could work a horse. Michael had probably never been on a horse in his life. He worked with his brain for a living, not his hands. And yet there was something about him that affected her senses. He was the sexiest damn thing she'd ever seen.

"What do you do for a living?" she asked him abruptly. "Are you a lawyer or something like that?"

"Not a lawyer," he told her with a quick smile. "A stockbroker of sorts. I've got an MBA from Harvard Business School and I've worked as a financial director of various enterprises, mostly in New York, until a few years ago, when my father needed me to come back to San Francisco and help out his firm. He was a stockbroker for years." He shifted in his seat. "Then I worked for Matthews Aviation. Vice president of financial planning." He glanced at her. "Boring stuff, isn't it?"

She had to agree. "It sure sounds like it. Did you really sit in an office all day?"

He laughed. "Sometimes. Sometimes all night, too."

It sounded like a particularly nasty version of hell to Jessie. She couldn't help but wonder how a man who spent all his time in a musty office ever learned to kiss the way he had. The memory made her cheeks hot again, so she wiped it from her mind.

Time was passing all too quickly, and soon they arrived at the outskirts of the town that sat near the entrance to Lake Mead. The sun had disappeared behind the mountains and dusk was falling, filling the land with elongated shadows and making stark patterns on the sand.

Jessie felt a melancholy twinge. "You'll have to tell us where to drop you off, where your mother is."

"There," he said right away, pointing out a roadside Mexican café.

"Here?" Jessie was dubious as Michael slowed the car and stopped. She opened the door and looked around. The place appeared deserted, but suddenly a small gang of ragged children came running from behind the shack. One of them spotted Joey.

"Hey, guys!" he cried. "It's Joey!"

Joey was out of the car before Jessie had a chance to pull up the seat, dragging his bag behind him. "Thanks a lot," he said, avoiding her gaze. She started to reach for him, but he began to edge away. Tears prickled her eyelids and she smiled, but before she had a chance to say goodbye, he was off, running with the boys.

"Wait," she called after him.

"Hey." Michael put a hand on her shoulder. "What do you think you're doing?"

"Don't you think I ought to talk to his mother or something?"

"Don't be crazy. Any mother who would let a kid run around the state on his own isn't interested in hearing a lecture from you. Come on. We've got places to go. People to see."

She looked back sadly as the Firebird slid out of town and past the sign that said Welcome to Nevada, the Silver State. Michael stole a glance at her, surprised that the crusty tomboy he'd hooked up with had such a soft spot for a ragged kid from nowhere.

"Okay," he said matter-of-factly, hoping to take her mind off Joey. "Give me the lowdown on this uncle of yours. I want to be prepared for all possibilities."

Jessie turned back to face Michael with a sigh. "I haven't seen Fred in over ten years. That was when my father and he stopped speaking."

"What happened?"

"I never really knew for sure. Something about money. It was kind of sad, because I really liked my uncle. But I never could stand his daughters. They were girl cousins, if you know what I mean. We had to come up here every Christmas when I was a kid. Sheri and Cerise and Mandy were all the type to wear red velvet dresses and curl their hair and I was the type to wear my jeans underneath my Christmas skirt just in case I got a chance to get outside and ride a horse."

His grin was crooked. "I can just imagine you in that scene. The cousins offering strawberries and cream, you asking for grits."

She didn't want him getting too cocky. "I don't like grits."

"Chili, then."

She turned back toward the landscape, memories floating

into her mind. Funny how those old days were so remote one minute, so much a part of her the next. "Aunt Florence was his wife. She died about twelve years ago. She was always saying things like 'Now, Jessica, look at the way Cerise is sitting with her ankles neatly crossed. Can't you at least try to sit that way?' As we got older they started having a Christmas dance for the 'young folks.' Real teenage boys came over. My cousins would wear slinky things, with slippers on their feet and ribbons in their hair, and I'd be stuck in some clunky dress two sizes too big and cowboy boots because that was just about all I had, and they would dance and dance and I would wait until no one was looking and sneak out and feed the horses."

She looked at him quickly, aghast that she'd told him so much. He would laugh at her. Or say something snide.

But he didn't. He drove on, and when she didn't continue, he asked, "Did you want ribbons and slinky dresses, too?"

"No, I didn't. I wanted a...oh, a new saddle, maybe." But deep inside she suddenly knew a truth she'd never admitted to herself. She *had* wanted ribbons in her hair. She *had* wanted the boys to ask her to dance. But she didn't want to think about that now.

Michael glanced over and saw her determined face. "So is Fred still mad?" he asked, deliberately changing the subject.

"By all indications, I imagine he is."

"And what makes you think he's going to welcome us on his doorstep?"

"I don't. Time will tell." Her right hand went to her left wrist in an absentminded gesture natural to her. But something was missing. "My bracelet," she muttered, turning and going on her knees to reach into the back seat. Michael switched on the interior light to help her. "Joey must have dropped it back here," she said as she shoved her hand down between the cushions, searching every cranny.

"Nothing?" Michael asked as she slowly sank back into her seat.

She shook her head, her mind going over every possibility— and shying from the obvious. "I just don't understand," she said. "Could it have dropped out of the car when we stopped in Bullhead City?"

He gritted his teeth. For a woman who laid claim to a tough exterior, she sure did have a squishy center. "I don't think so," he said solemnly. "I think the kid has it."

"Oh, no," she said quickly, twisting her braid in her hand. "No, I'm sure he—"

"Do you remember him giving it back after you handed it to him to look at?"

"N-n-no, but…"

"Face it, Jessie. He's got it."

She didn't want to accept that at all. It hurt too much. "Then it must have been an accident."

Michael snorted. "Sure. He just accidentally dropped it into his pocket and forgot to tell you."

"He wouldn't steal from me!"

Michael threw her a dark look. "He got to you good, didn't he?" he noted softly.

Yes. He'd gotten to her good. But that wasn't all. If Joey turned out to be a thief, what did that say about her judgment? About trusting people? About…Michael?

"Let's go back and ask him then, if you're so sure. Let's get his side of the story."

"I'm not about to turn back on this journey, Jessie. You know we can't." He hunched his shoulders uncomfortably. "Anyway, you saw how he ran off. He won't be easy to find. He's probably fencing it right now."

Her face was a battleground of mixed emotions. He looked at her and felt a twist of sympathy. "Hey," he said more gently. "Don't take it so hard. He's a street kid, living off his own smarts. He takes what he can in order to survive. You've got to understand. That bracelet represents a few hot meals for his family."

But to her it represented a lot of other things. And the loss of it hurt. She'd trusted him. She'd developed a genuine affection for the boy and he'd stolen from her, knowing the way she felt. Did that mean that affection, caring, didn't change anything?

She swallowed hard and tried to put her mind on something else, but the question still haunted her. If Joey had turned out to be so untrustworthy, what about the man beside her?

The car roared on through the black night, a lonely light traveling across a barren landscape. Jessie felt cold and alone and thought longingly about her warm bed at home. Hers was a nice life, after all, with nothing to worry about but keeping the stock in shape and getting money to keep on going. At least those problems were real and straightforward. With Michael, she wasn't sure where to step, what was real, what was illusion.

"Turn here," she said as they passed a row of dark cinder cones she recognized. She sat up straighter in the seat as they traveled down a bumpy dirt road. "There it is. My uncle's ranch."

The sign for the Three Bar Cross was hanging by one rusty chain. In the headlights she caught a glimpse of tumbleweeds packed three feet deep against the fence. She licked her lips nervously as Michael pulled the car up before the low ranch house.

Dogs were barking, but they must have been tied up because they didn't appear. Jessie got out of the car carefully, just in case. The front door opened and her uncle stood silhouetted against the light from outside.

"Who's out there?" he called sharply.

"Uncle Fred? It's Jessie. Jessie MacAllister. Do you remember me?" She came closer, into the light from the house, and it was almost as though she were stepping back in time. Only this time everything was different. Michael was with her.

CHAPTER TWELVE

THE MAN WAS GRAYING, heavyset, older than she remembered him. His weathered face stared at her for a moment, then broke into a delighted smile. "Jessie! I haven't seen you since…come here, girl. My, how you've grown up. You look like a rancher's daughter. Indeed you do. I always knew you'd stay true to type."

Emotion surged in her chest. He looked a lot like Harley. "I've got somebody with me." She motioned for Michael to step out of the shadows. "This is Michael, Uncle Fred. We're going to California together."

"Traveling together, huh?" Fred frowned as he looked Michael over. "What are you doing with this city slicker, girl?"

Jessie was glad it was still dark enough that he likely couldn't see her blush. "I…"

"We're getting married, sir," Michael broke in without a glance her way. "In Los Angeles."

Jessie stared at him, caught between confusion and resentment. He didn't have to lie to her uncle. Maybe they didn't have to tell him the whole truth, but she didn't like lying.

Fred grunted. "Having the honeymoon first?" he asked dryly. "What's Harley got to say about this?"

Jessie cleared her throat, but before she could fabricate a plausible answer, Fred shook his head and turned toward the house. "Never mind. I don't want to know. You're a grown woman. I guess you can do what you please. Though God knows why all the females in this family are demented when it comes to choosing men. Come on in the house. Cerise is here. She'll be glad to see you."

Jessie wasn't so sure that was true, but she and Michael

followed him in, anyway. Cerise rose from the worn couch where she'd been sitting listening to pop tunes on the stereo. Her china blue eyes met Jessie's and narrowed immediately.

"Well, well, look who's here. On a peace mission? Or just spying?"

Jessie looked from her blond cousin to her uncle, taken aback by the woman's sarcasm.

"That'll do, Cerise," Fred said shortly. "We'll have none of that. Jessie's getting married and she stopped by to introduce us to her fiancé. This here's Michael."

When Cerise's gaze fell on Michael, she changed before their eyes. A coy expression crossed her face, her hand went to her hair, smoothing it and her eyes widened. "Well, hello," she said sweetly. "Where on earth did Jessie find you?"

Michael smiled as he took her hand in his, and watching, Jessie realized just how devastatingly handsome he really was. Her heart contracted a little as he and Cerise chatted, Cerise flirting, Michael taking it as his due. Women must act like this around him all the time, she told herself. So what?

So everything. Cerise fluffed the full skirt of her sundress and arched her back to make the most of her physical attributes, and it was fifteen years ago again, with Jessie in cowboy boots and Cerise getting the guys.

Cerise invited Michael to sit on the couch beside her. Jessie slumped down into a rattan chair while Fred went to the kitchen to get a round of sodas for everyone. Trying to keep her eyes off the man and woman laughing together in front of her, she gazed around the room, remembering things, noting new items.

The place had a surprisingly run-down air about it. She always thought of Fred as a go-getter, a man who knew how to turn a buck. And hadn't Harley said something a few years ago about Fred's coming into money? If so, he must have found a way to lose it fast. Jessie stared at a broken window pane and wondered.

"Go ahead and gape, Jessie," Cerise's shrill voice cut into her reverie. "Take a good look." Her blue eyes flashed. "Sad, isn't it? And this house used to be so nice."

"It's still very nice," Jessie began, puzzled by her cousin's attitude. They'd never been good friends, but they'd never been enemies before. Why was she acting as though they were? Jessie decided to ignore the situation and pretend all was well. "I see Uncle Fred is allowing stereos into the house now. And a telephone," she added, noting the one that hung on the wall. "In the old days he'd rail against such modern conveniences for hours at a time."

Cerise's face softened a little. "Yes," she said, her mind obviously on memories, too. "I guess he's given up on 'raising us right.' It's too late for that." She frowned. "It's too late for a lot of things around here," she said, staring at Jessie.

Fred returned with the drinks. "Settle down, Cerise," he said mildly. "You know very well just as soon as this jojoba bean thing gets rolling—"

"Oh, you and your old beans!" To Jessie's surprise, tears sparkled in Cerise's eyes and her voice trembled. "Everybody knows you're crazy."

Ignoring her outburst, Fred placidly passed around the glasses of soda. "Yes, sir, these jojoba beans are the thing of the future," he said, directing his statement mainly to Michael. "I've got my entire spread planted with the damn things now. Do you know that a healthy plant will produce up to ten pounds of beans a year? Ten pounds!"

Michael nodded his appreciation of that stunning fact. "Are they good eating?" he asked innocently.

Fred stared at him. "Eating? Heck, no! You don't eat 'em. You get oil from them. Haven't you heard?"

Michael stifled a smile. "I guess not."

"Sure. The oil from jojoba beans is almost exactly like the oil they used to get from sperm whales, only now you're not allowed to get stuff from sperm whales anymore, so this here oil's going to be as precious—"

"As sperm oil used to be, which isn't so very," intoned Cerise. "At least not when every other ranch is growing the stuff."

"You just wait." He shook a finger at his daughter. "You just wait, missy. You're going to see something once this thing gets rolling."

"Dreamer," Cerise scoffed, but her eyes were as full of hopeless affection as they were of exasperation.

"How's your husband?" Jessie asked Cerise, hoping to change the subject. "Paul, wasn't it?"

"It was once," said Cerise, turning her glass in her hands, her blood-red nails gleaming against the liquid. "It is no more. We're divorced."

"Oh." So much for a change in subject. "I'm sorry to hear that."

"No-good louse," Fred grumbled. "Mandy is divorced, too, living in Reno. And that sleazy gambler Sheri married in Las Vegas..."

"Oh, Sam's okay, Daddy."

"He is not okay. If that polecat doesn't work for the Mob, I'll eat my hat."

"Oh, Daddy."

"I don't understand you girls." Fred's worried gaze settled on Jessie. "Why do you keep messing with these city boys when there are good solid ranchers all over the place who'd be happy to have you?"

"Be happy to work you to death, you mean," Cerise muttered.

"You especially, Jessie," he went on, as though he hadn't heard Cerise. "I never ever figured you to fall for that type. Why, you were born to ranch, girl." He turned with a nod to Michael. "No offense, mister, but it's true." His pale eyes were back on Jessie. "I mean, look at him, honey. In his suit, with them pointy little shoes. He's not going to be any good on your ranch, and you know it."

"Oh, Daddy," Cerise groaned, "he might just be so good at other things, Jessie doesn't care about his ranching talent."

Jessie had just about had enough of Cerise. She wasn't sure how to take her, resenting her one moment, feeling sorry for her the next. Something slashed through her whenever the woman smiled at Michael. Jealousy. She knew what it was, but she couldn't admit even to herself just why that should be. And she was too tired to try to figure it all out right now.

"Could we stay here tonight, Uncle Fred?" she asked, her dark eyes imploring him.

"Can't afford a hotel?" Cerise asked acidly. "Las Vegas is only another hour up the road."

"Cerise!" Fred's voice was furious. "I've had enough of that spitefulness. Jessie didn't ever do us any harm. She can't help it if her father..." His voice faded and he shook his head. "We'd be proud to have them, wouldn't we? They can take Mandy's room and Sheri's."

Jessie was more confused than ever, not sure just what her father was supposed to have done to Fred, not really caring. She had other things on her mind. For once Cerise didn't have an answer. They drained their glasses and she meekly helped set up the bedrooms for the two travelers to use.

"No luggage?" she asked at one point while showing Jessie where things were in Mandy's old room and the bathroom that bridged the space to Sheri's room, in which Michael was staying.

"No." Jessie was too tired to make up an excuse.

Cerise hesitated, then pointed to a drawer. "That's full of nightgowns. Go ahead and use one."

Fred and Cerise said good-night and Jessie faced Michael in the hall. His silver-blue eyes were wary, not warming when they met hers.

"So far so good," he said softly, his fingers already unbuttoning his white shirt.

She nodded, her gaze lingering on the smooth, muscular chest he was revealing. "They don't know anything." His hands looked dark and strong against the white fabric. She waited for a moment, remembering the encounter in the woods near Flagstaff and wondering where that passionate man had gone. Michael appeared to be a stranger now. She could feel the distance between them. "What happens tomorrow?" she asked.

"I go on. But I've been thinking, Jessie. You'd better go on home."

A chill swept through her. "I thought I was going to stay with you until—"

"I'm going to leave before dawn tomorrow," he said shortly. "So I guess this is goodbye."

She was stunned. She hadn't allowed herself to think ahead, but if she had, she would never have thought he was going to disappear from her life so suddenly. Irrationally she wanted to reach for him, to say, *No! No, I have to go with you to make sure—*

Make sure of what? That he was going to find the man he was looking for? That he was going to be all right?

"Look at it this way," he was saying. "I trust you now. I know you won't go straight to the cops and turn me in. Even for that reward money."

The reward money. That was what had started this crazy ride across the countryside. The money seemed remote now, hardly worth remembering.

"Goodbye, Jessie," he murmured, but she was still in a daze and hardly understood. "Thanks for everything. I'm sorry I disrupted your life like this."

He hesitated for another moment and still she stood absolutely silent, her eyes wide and uncomprehending. He reached for her and she moved into his arms, and then he was kissing her, softly, lingeringly, breathlessly. Finally he pulled away, something hardening in his face. Swearing, he turned on his heel and disappeared into the bedroom.

Jessie went into the other bedroom. Moving mechanically, she took a hot shower and put on a long white gown she'd found in the drawer. She dried her hair and brushed it out, then slipped into bed with a sigh, more than ready for sleep to come and blot out everything else. But sleep wasn't cooperating tonight. Too many thoughts invaded her head, and soon she was staring at the ceiling.

It was over. The ride on Michael Drayton's roller coaster was finished and it was time to get off. She was free to go back to her sane, sober life on the ranch, free to return to normal.

But she would never see him again. Why was that so impossible for her mind to accept? "I will never see Michael again," she said aloud into the empty room, and something inside her cringed and twisted and refused to come to terms with that concept. She tossed and turned and struggled with acceptance for another half hour before she rose from her bed and padded to the door. As she listened intently, it seemed to her that the entire household was asleep. Gliding as silently as possible, she let herself out the front door and stepped into the dark. Not even the dogs heard her go.

"WELL?" Sky Matthews turned and looked expectantly at the young man who'd just entered his office. "What is it? Where is he?"

The visitor shook his head. "Sorry, Mr. Matthews. There's no news out of Arizona. Nobody knows where he is."

Sky swore harshly and obscenely and the young employee beat a hasty retreat through the office door. Sky rose and stalked to the huge windows that overlooked the glittering lights of San Francisco and the bay beyond.

They'd grown soft, all of them. In the old days he'd have had Michael back here in front of his desk within twenty-four hours. The boys who'd worked for him then had been pros who'd dedicated their lives to the business. Nowadays all you could get were these weaklings who wanted to be home by dinnertime and take vacations at Lake Tahoe. It was no wonder his business was going to pot.

His secretary buzzed. "Call from a Mr. Keel in Las Vegas, Mr. Matthews."

Sky looked at the phone with dread. More bad news. He could feel it. Keel was a gambler who occasionally called in tips for him. "Okay. I'll take the call in here." He lifted the receiver. "What you got for me, Keel?"

"Rumors, Mr. Matthews." The voice was a flinty rasp. "Nothing but rumors. But I thought you'd want to know."

Sky resisted the urge to scream at the man. "Go ahead. Let's have it."

"The buzz is there's someone in town looking for backing to take you down, Mr. Matthews. Someone who used to work for you and says he had the inside scam on some unsavory activities, the nature of which is unspecified at this time."

Sky clutched the receiver so tightly his knuckles turned white. "What's his name?"

"Don't have that yet. Will call when I do."

Sky put down the receiver slowly, his face drawn and pale. This was what happened when you got soft, when you tried to play the game by the rules and do nice by everyone. He should have known better. He should have taken care of Kerry Carter when he'd had the chance. The man had said he was going to live off berries in the desert for the rest of his life, and Sky had let him go. He'd believed him. It was time to get tough. Only the strong survived.

This Michael thing was driving him crazy. Winslow Drayton had been so easy to manipulate. He'd never put up much of a fight at all. Even though he'd disapproved of the things Sky had gotten him involved in, he'd needed only the vaguest kind of threat to keep him in line. And his wife had been even easier. She responded so well to money, a commodity she was always short of. It still made him grin to think of how easily she'd handed over the Drayton diamonds when he'd demanded them after Vanessa had begged him for them. Yes, the elegant Pamela Drayton was never a problem.

But the son was a different story. It might just be that Michael was too different. That Michael was history, in more ways than one.

Vanessa came breezing into his office before his secretary even had time to ring him, which was par for the course. He didn't mind, though. He was always there for his daughter.

"Daddy, you're late. You promised to take me to Top of the Mark tonight."

He couldn't help but smile at her pretty face. "Not tonight, sweetheart. I've got trouble I've got to take care of."

Her expression changed. "Michael?" she asked.

Annoyance flashed across his face. When was she going to get it through her lovely head that she was not to mix in his business affairs? "Never mind what it is. It's going to take up my time." He thought quickly. Maybe it would be best if Vanessa were out of the way. "Tell you what, honey. How would you like a few weeks in Paris on me?"

Joy flushed her face. "Really, Daddy? Margot and Phyllis are there right now. I could surprise them."

"Why not?" He reached out and gave her a bear hug. "I'll have my secretary fix you up with tickets and you can leave in the morning. Your passport is up-to-date, isn't it?"

Vanessa grinned. "Always. You know me. Oh, thank you, Daddy! I really wanted to go, only all this stuff with Michael has had me down."

"I know." He kissed the top of her head. "You go off to Paris and forget all about Michael. Promise?"

Vanessa hesitated for only a moment before her dimples appeared again. "I promise, Daddy. And maybe by the time I get back, you'll have Michael here ready to make up. Won't you?"

Sky's face went very cold, but his daughter didn't notice. "I promise, honey. I'll have the Michael situation in hand by then. Indeed I will."

He waited until she'd left, then called his secretary again. "Betty, I want you to put in a call to Las Vegas for me. Get me Nargeant at the Samarkand Hotel. I've got some business with my old friend."

CHAPTER THIRTEEN

EVERY CELL in Michael's body was crying out for sleep. He dozed for a while, then awoke with a start and lay still, wondering what had disturbed him. This was all he needed—another sleepless night. That ought to put the icing on the cake. He already felt as though he were floundering, not getting to his objective, letting things drift. His luck would only hold out so long.

Actually, he was surprised that they'd made it this far, that the long arm of the law hadn't snatched them up along the way. Finding Kerry was the first imperative. It had to be done, and fast. A part of him was annoyed that he'd let himself get bogged down with Jessie. If it wasn't for her he'd probably be in Las Vegas right now. After all, it was only an hour away. Why had they stopped?

But he knew the answer to that. He'd been reluctant to rid himself of her. Damn fool that he was, he enjoyed having her along.

Women were poison. He knew that. He'd learned his lesson well. But somehow Jessie was different from the women he was familiar with. Honest and straightforward, she reminded him of an ocean breeze, or fresh snow. There was no artifice to Jessie. Despite her elaborate plan to take him into custody, there was no real malice in her. She didn't play games.

He was going to miss her.

Restless, he got up out of bed and went to the window, pulling aside the drapes to look out on the moonlit landscape. The first thing he saw was something in a flowing white gown running toward a stand of shimmering trees, free as a colt that had bolted the corral. He knew without thinking twice that it was Jessie.

He had two choices here. He could ignore her, go back to bed and try to sleep, preparing for an early departure in the morning. Or he could go out to see what she was doing...to see what she was like in the moonlight. His hands gripped the edge of the windowsill while temptation warred with resolve inside him.

JESSIE LIFTED HER FACE to the cool breeze and listened to it stir the cottonwood trees. The desert smelled clean and earthy, like crushed fall leaves and cactus flowers. The folds of the flannel nightgown flattened against her legs and her long, thick hair flew about her face in a golden cloud. Her heart was still hammering from her run across the field.

She'd gone to see the horses first, though there were only two left in the stables and neither was familiar from the old days. Then she'd gone to visit the stand of cottonwoods where she used to hide when she didn't want the others to find her.

A fence stood there now, and she leaned against it, looking toward the hills and thinking about time and how it changed things.

"Jessie."

She whirled. Michael was coming toward her, stepping out of the shadows.

"What are you doing out here?" he asked as he neared her. "It's cold."

"I like it cold." If it had been anyone else, she would have resented the intrusion. Her heart beat quickly again, but not from the exercise this time. He looked darkly handsome with his black hair falling over his forehead.

He stopped just inches from her. She gazed up at him. His silver-blue eyes glistened in the moonlight.

He studied her for a moment, noting the loose hair, the soft white fabric of her gown and the way it clung to her breasts, the glow of her dark eyes. He could hardly believe this was the same woman he'd ridden across Arizona with. The tomboy was gone. She looked soft and seductive and irresistibly touchable.

"You're beautiful," he said at last. "You should have worn this to those Christmas dances. Every boy in town would have wanted to dance with you."

She flushed in the darkness, but his words pleased her. "I doubt it."

"I'm sure of it. I'll show you."

Before she could stop him he'd swept her into his arms and was whirling her around the yard, humming a Strauss waltz. She laughed, resisting a little at first, but then falling into the rhythm and letting him guide her. It was ecstasy to be held in his strong arms, to feel his heat so close.

His hand grazed her breast and an ache started inside her. She wanted to press herself against him, and that embarrassed her. She couldn't remember ever feeling that way about a man before. Her whole life had been measured in incidents of fighting off clumsy attempts to arouse her, giving in occasionally, then regretting it. But this was different. This was something she wanted, and she didn't know why. So she denied it, suppressed it and enjoyed the moment.

He felt her hair whip across his face as they made a turn and he wanted to feel it again, to bury himself in it, in her. A wave of desire washed over him, an impulse so strong it was closer to need than to want. He had to steel himself not to show it, not to pull her against him so that there could be no mistake in her mind....

Abruptly he stopped, pulling away from her and leaning over the fence. She followed him, laughing softly, not yet aware of why he'd drawn back.

"Where did you get these clothes?" she asked, letting her hand flatten against the plaid cotton fabric of his shirt with the familiarity the dance had brought with it.

He shuddered as the heat of her touch burned right through the cloth and into his skin. She removed her hand, puzzled, and he tried to brush his response off with a grin.

"Cerise," he told her. "She gave me some things her ex-husband had left behind."

She nodded, looking at the snug jeans and form-fitting shirt. "Nice," she allowed. "You look different." She grinned at him. "Cerise is so generous. I'm surprised that's all she offered you."

He threw her a cynical smile. "Saying things like that makes you sound like her."

"God forbid!" She groaned.

They lapsed into silence, both leaning against the fence and staring at the blue clouds scudding across the inky sky on the horizon. She shivered and he noticed, but he made no move to protect her.

She felt the excitement that quivered between them, but she wasn't sure he felt it, too. She only knew it was dangerous. She was a little intoxicated by the night air, the moonlight. The desert.

"Listen." She touched his arm, her fingers curling around his biceps. The muscular bulge felt thrillingly masculine. "Hear that coyote howl?"

He didn't answer her question. Staring down at where her hand rested, he said softly, "Do you want to make love?"

She gasped at the directness of his question, yanking her hand away from him. "No!"

"Then don't touch me like that again. Because I do."

She shrank back, but she couldn't pull her gaze away from the burning intensity of his. She was shaking and she wasn't sure if it was from the cold or from the emotions bottled up inside her.

"Are you afraid of me, Jessie?" he whispered.

"Not...not physically."

"I'm afraid of me," he murmured, still staring at her. "I'm afraid of doing something stupid, something that will mess everything else up. Do you know what I mean?"

She nodded slowly. "Yes, I think I do." Her hand pressed against the rough wood of the fence. So he felt it, too, the magic between them. And what did they do now? Deny it? Ignore it? Or let it flower?

She looked at him, trying to read his expression in the darkness. His eyes appeared huge, but clouded, obscure. And yet she felt as though she could talk to him. She'd never felt this way with a man before. In her experience, men played rough games and liked dinner on time and a beer when they were thirsty and a woman when the urge hit them. But they didn't want to hear about feelings.

Come to think of it, she was usually a little that way herself. She didn't like girl talk all that much. She'd taken some pride in the fact that she didn't cry easily, didn't need to talk things to death.

But this was different. She was feeling things she'd never felt before. She had a need to sort them out a bit, talk them through. This man seemed capable of listening. And maybe even understanding. It was worth a try.

She moved closer to him, but leaned against the wood again, staring out across the yard. "I...I kind of feel like I'm crazy, Michael. I don't know who you are or what you're all about. Being with you has been like living in another world."

He leaned on the fence beside her, his eyes half-closed. "I know."

"You're different. I've never known a man like you. I don't know how to read you, what you want."

He was quiet for a moment. "I'm not so different," he finally answered. "I want the same things every man wants—respect, friendship...love."

She half turned toward him and opened her palms to him beseechingly. "But who are you? I don't really know. And I need to know."

He ran a hand through his dark hair. "Are you asking whether you can trust me? I'm not a criminal, Jessie. I'm innocent of the charges they're hunting me on."

"You've told me that before."

"Yes, and I mean it. I'll tell you more now, if you like."

She nodded, folding her arms across her chest and hugging herself to keep warm. "First tell me what you went to prison for."

His head jerked up at her words. "How did you know?" he demanded.

"From what you said this morning about not wanting to be locked up again."

"Oh." His face relaxed and he looked away. "Well, you're right. I was in prison for eighteen months. But that had nothing to do with this."

She studied his profile, set off by a line of silver moonlight. "I want to know, anyway."

He hesitated, then shrugged. "Why not. I was convicted of embezzling funds from clients of my father's stockbrokerage. I served my sentence at Yerba Buena, a minimum security prison in northern California. Eighteen months of pure hell. I found out prison is just as bad as they say it is, and then some. I hated every minute of it." His voice was a monotone as he recounted his past. "So that's it. Now you know all."

"Except for one thing. You weren't guilty then, either. Were you?"

He stared at her. There was a glow around her, a halo effect. She seemed pure, a being from beyond human experience. Or maybe he was just hallucinating. "How did you know that?" he murmured at last.

Something warm was curling inside her. She felt a sureness, a rightness. "Tell me about it."

"I pleaded guilty. Everyone else believed it."

"I don't. Why did you do it?"

He'd never told anyone. At first it had been to protect his father. But after his father had died, it had been his own pride that had stilled him. His own arrogance, perhaps. But he was going to tell her, this woman in white, this angel. And telling her would be like releasing a burden from his soul.

"My father was a kind, honorable man, but he became a stockbroker to please his family, when what he really wanted to do was sculpt."

"Sculpt."

"Yes. He made marvelous animal figures for me when I was a boy. But that wasn't real work, you see. So he had to do something deemed proper for the eldest son of an upper-class family. He tried hard. For years he seemed to pull it off. Finally his business went bad through pure mismanagement."

And other things. Now that he knew more, he understood more, too. Sky Matthews had been involved, he was sure of it. His father had been laundering money for Sky. He'd seen the evidence at the time and he'd ignored it. But now all the pieces fit.

"I'd been working for other companies up till then, in New York. I came home toward the end and tried to help him straighten things out. But it was too late. He'd used money from new clients to cover funds he'd misappropriated from old clients, and finally the whole thing fell apart."

There was no emotion in his voice, but Jessie could detect the emotion in his heart. He'd loved his father. That came through clearly. And what he was telling her hurt a lot.

"He'd cut corners here and there, mostly to make sure my mother had all the things she demanded. And over the years, mistakes added up. The whole thing looked crooked on paper. It looked deliberate. Someone had to pay."

"Why did that someone have to be you?"

He gave her a long look. "It couldn't very well be my father. He was sick. I couldn't stand to think of him disgraced. Locked away. I knew he'd never live through it." He shrugged. "So I took the rap. It was easy enough to do." Easy to do, hard to stand. He'd numbed himself for months, not allowing himself to feel anything. But he'd hated prison with every fiber of his being, and he knew he could never go through that again.

All in all, he was at peace with himself. He knew he'd done the best he could for his father and he was satisfied with the way things had gone. He had no regrets.

But once was enough. Never again would he go to jail for something someone else had done.

"And these new charges?" she asked calmly.

"A man named Sky Matthews, an old family friend, was the only one to offer me a job when I got out. When I realized he was running a smuggling operation, I confronted him, then went to the authorities." He smiled ruefully. "But he got to them before I did, claiming I was the criminal. It came down to the word of an ex-con against a big man in town. Naturally they believed him."

"But you're not guilty."

"No. I'm not guilty."

She nodded. "How about the diamonds? Did you steal the diamonds like they said?"

"Steal the diamonds." If the light had been better she could have seen how bitter his smile was. How could he steal something that already belonged to him? "No, Jessie. I didn't steal them."

That was it, then. She was on the right side. It was a relief to know for sure.

"Now that you know all this, are you still afraid of me, Jessie?"

She met his gaze without a smile. "More than ever."

He loved her honesty. His hand rose and took a strand of her hair, letting its silky length slip between his fingers.

She reached up and stilled his hand, ringing her fingers about his wrist. "I want to go with you tomorrow," she said.

He stared at her. "I shouldn't let you. It could be dangerous."

She smiled at his words. "But you will let me."

His hand slipped into her hair, the palm caressing her cheek. "I may have to," he murmured.

Her hand covered his and she closed her eyes, savoring every moment. His lips touched hers briefly, caressingly....

"Jessie," he whispered, pulling her closer. "This is dangerous, too." His hands slid down her sides. Her slender body felt pliant and feminine beneath the soft fabric of her gown. He felt for her breast, and there it was, round and firm, the nipple a tight, hard protrusion under all that white cloth. Nothing he'd ever touched had aroused him more.

"If you want me to stop, tell me now," he urged huskily very near her ear. "Before it's too late." He drew back and stared down into her wide eyes. "Tell me now, Jessie."

She didn't tell him anything at all. Instead she put her arms around his neck, arching her body into his, offering him everything she had. His hand on her breast had been ecstasy, a pleasure she wanted again. Her impulse was to rub her body against his like a cat, purring and begging for more of his tantalizing touch.

He groaned and began to kiss her, first her mouth, then her neck, then lower, using his hand to push aside cloth so that his lips could find her smooth skin. She helped, pulling open the buttons that held her gown closed in front, until it was open to the waist. He pushed back the sides and exposed her breasts, the nipples dark and tight and more sensitive than she'd ever known them to be.

She gasped as he touched them, first one, then the other, stroking with his thumb, then leaning down to take each in turn into his mouth, tugging and teasing, while his hands moved down to cup her bottom, strong fingers digging into the soft flesh, moving, molding and finally pulling her tightly against the cradle of his hips so that she could feel the growth of his own need for her. Electricity shot through her at each touch. Her hips were already moving with the rhythm of his caresses.

"Hey," he whispered softly, his hands sinking into her thick hair on either side of her head and forcing her to look up into his smoky gaze. "Slow down," he said, his voice husky and slightly slurred. "We've got plenty of time."

She closed her eyes, trying to still her heavy breathing, and he began to kiss her face, letting his tongue outline her brows, dropping soft, slow caresses on her eyelids, nuzzling the hollow at her temple, taking her earlobe into his mouth with a lazy, rhythmic motion that made her shiver. She moaned, searching for his mouth with her own. His tongue traced her lips and she reached for him hungrily, growling when he teased her, almost purring when he finally met her halfway, his hot, intoxicating mouth coming down hard on hers.

She wasn't thinking. It wasn't time to think. She was lost in a mindless swirl of desire. It was time to feel, to set herself free. This was something special, this time, this man. Though she hadn't put it into words, she knew she couldn't let this get away without taking the chance. She might never pass this way again.

He drew back, short of breath himself. Sighing with pleasure, she reached out to open his shirt, flattening her hands against his warm body. His chest hair was concentrated about the flat nipples, so the hard contours of his muscled body were clear. She outlined them with her fingers, tracing lightly and laughing when he shuddered at her touch.

"Come on." Taking her hand, he led her into the cotton-wood grove where they couldn't be seen from the house. She tingled all over everywhere he touched. She felt drunk and she loved it. Gently he lowered her onto a pile of autumn leaves, coming down beside her. "Is this okay?" he asked her.

She nodded, looking up at him, marveling at how he cared about her, asking if she was comfortable. She'd never known a man to do that before.

He kissed her mouth, then sat back to look at her. "You're so beautiful, Jessie." His voice was hoarse, throbbing with some strange emotion. "I…I don't want to hurt you. You do understand that I'll be gone, out of your life very soon. That I can't promise you anything.…"

Reaching up, she pressed her fingers against his lips, stilling him. She understood only too well, and she didn't want to be reminded. It was too dark for him to see the feeling in her eyes, but she lifted his hand and placed it on her breast. "It's getting cold," she murmured. "Make me warmer."

His laugh was low in his throat as he moved closer. "I'll make you boil," he promised.

She closed her eyes and threw back her head and remembered that it had been in this very grove that she had spent hours when she was a girl, dreaming of a special man, a knight on a white charger who would come and sweep her up into a fairy tale. And now her dream was coming true.

He was tugging her gown up, sliding it across her thighs, his hand slipping beneath it to caress her, to stroke again and again, until she cried out, her eyes wild.

"Michael!"

"Yes," he said, his eyes taking on a wildness of their own.

She reached for his belt, but her hands were shaking and he took over, quickly removing his clothing. She held her breath and, when he turned to her, let it out in a rush as she reached for him, so hard, so butter smooth, so real, so beautiful in the moonlight. His breath was rasping now, and when she touched him, his hands clenched her shoulders. Excitement quivered between her legs, demanding fulfillment, demanding his presence now.

"Now," she growled, her eyes wide. "Now, Michael! Oh, please..."

His entrance was like an explosion inside her body and she wanted to scream, wanted to bite down hard on his shoulder, but she resisted and concentrated on him, instead, the sinewy hardness of his body beneath her hands as they rubbed up and down his back and nestled in the hollow at his tailbone.

He moved and she came along, faster and faster, caught up in the whirlwind, thrilled by the ride. They were one, she and he, pleasure and need tightly bound, desire and fulfillment joined in a dance as old as human memory, and the wind drove them higher and higher, until there was nothing around them but clouds and Jessie touched heaven.

CHAPTER FOURTEEN

SUNSHINE CAME STREAMING IN through the bedroom window. One glance and Michael groaned and closed his eyes again. He'd missed his predawn departure, that was certain now. He turned his head and buried his face in Jessie's hair, trying to care that he'd screwed up again.

She sighed and moved, and his hand found her breast, caressing it gently so as not to wake her. Lord, but she was exquisite. Making love to her in the cottonwoods, and then again here on the soft bed, had been like finding a dream lover in the night. He'd almost been convinced she'd disappear by morning. But here she was. All his.

Stroking her hair, he watched her soft breathing, the way her chest rose and fell, the delicate line of her collarbone, and he felt a tenderness he didn't know he was capable of.

And then his mood darkened. He should have been on his way to Las Vegas by now. Once more he was letting a woman into his life and it was diluting his resolve. He should get out while he still had the strength to do so.

Jessie was also awake, listening to his breathing just as he was listening to hers. She felt his hand in her hair. She was deliciously drowsy, as though her veins were filled with honey. She felt protected, appreciated almost—did she really dare to think the word—*loved*.

They'd made beautiful love the night before and for once in her life it hadn't been "sex," physical recreation, a half-reluctant duty that could be sort of pleasant if everything went all right. This time it had been flying without a license, soaring above clouds on a magic carpet made of spun gold, catching a ride on a comet's tail, and a thousand other lovely things that had given her a taste of paradise. Even if it were never to happen again, she would always have the memory of this night to cherish. She hugged that knowledge to herself, secretly happy it was all hers.

"Good morning," she murmured at last, her eyes barely slits. "If you're a wonderful dream, I'm not going to open my eyes, because I just want to keep right on dreaming."

Grinning, he abandoned his doubts and dropped a kiss on her nose. "You're not going to come after me with a shotgun now, are you?" he asked her teasingly.

"A shotgun?" She opened her eyes and stared up at him.

"Like you told me you did with the last fellow who kissed you."

She had only the trace of a smile on her face. "Don't mention that in the same breath as this," she said, starting to pull herself up.

His eyes darkened and he stopped her with a gentle hand. "What happened, Jessie?"

She hesitated a moment, a haunted look in her eyes. Then she shook her head. "I'll tell you sometime. Not now." She yawned, then smiled brightly and said without further preamble, "The first thing we have to do this morning is trade that fancy car of yours to Uncle Fred for his pickup truck."

"My car?" Michael stared at her. "Are you crazy?"

"Every highway patrol officer in the country must have a description of that car by now. The crazy thing would be to keep right on driving it."

Conflicting emotions warred in him once again. He'd been lusting after that car for weeks, before he'd finally bought it. "You're right," he said, his agony reflected on his handsome face. "I know it's necessary. But that doesn't mean I like it." Climbing out of bed, he went to the window and looked at his car in the driveway. His eyes were wistful. "How are you going to get him to trade?" he asked. "He's going to think we're nuts."

"I'll think of something."

She got up out of bed and began to hunt for her clothes, then turned and stopped, watching Michael at the window. For the first time in her life, she understood why they called it making love. *Making love,* she mouthed silently to herself as she watched him. Michael was hers now, for the moment, for the time being, for however long it took to take care of him, to get this thing straightened out. She felt this with a fierceness she had never felt for anything else except her ranch and Harley.

They had a quick breakfast—luckily without Cerise, who was still working hard on her beauty sleep. And then Uncle Fred took Michael out to introduce him to the mighty jojoba bean. Jessie watched them go, watched them stop to look at Michael's Firebird on the way. Michael sure did look good in those snug jeans. She grinned, and he turned and caught sight of her at the window. He didn't smile, but he winked, then turned back to pay close attention to something Fred was saying. That simple gesture broke something free inside Jessie. She felt as though her heart had been cracked open like an eggshell, and out had spilled a hot, sweet, pleasure-pain that scared her at the same time as it thrilled her.

Sometime later, Uncle Fred came in while she was making the bed. She looked up from the hospital corner she was working on to give him a welcoming, but wary smile.

"Jessie, I've got to talk to you for a moment." He flopped down in a chair near the bed. "I don't want you to go away with hurt feelings, now. I know Cerise said some pretty mean things to you last night, and you probably think we're always thinking mean about you, but I want to tell you it's not that way."

She set herself down on the bed and smiled at him. "Uncle Fred, I have no idea what Cerise keeps talking about. I know you and Harley had some kind of fight, but I don't really know what it's about. It has nothing to do with me."

"Don't really know what it's about!" He slapped his knee in disbelief. "Come on, girl. How could you not know?"

Jessie shook her head. "He's never really said anything, except little comments now and then, but nothing specific."

"It's the money, Jess. Just the money."

When Jessie didn't say anything, Fred frowned and went on,

"Old Aunt Jessica's money, of course. The MacAllister fortune. The money Harley got all of and I got none of."

Jessie looked at him as though he were pulling with the wrong oar. "Aunt Jessica didn't leave us any money."

"She sure as heck did!"

"No." She shook her head. "I remember when she died. I didn't give it the attention I should have because I was going through a divorce at the time. But I remember Harley being mad cuz he wasn't asked to attend the reading of the will."

"Harley got every penny of the MacAllister fortune!"

"If he did, he never told me. We've been barely scraping by for years now."

Fred looked purple and began to sputter. "I...I can't believe this."

"What made you think Harley got her fortune?"

He shook his head. "I wasn't told about the reading of the will, either. Why, you were named after Aunt Jessica. And I just assumed...well, I mean, Harley had threatened..."

Jessie remembered now that Aunt Jessica was supposed to have a fortune left to her by her grandfather from the old days of the Comstock Lode.

"I swear to you, Uncle Fred. We never got a cent."

Fred appeared old all of a sudden. "I don't believe it. All this time, I was certain that Harley had gypped me out of the money. He warned me. He threatened." He shook his head wearily. "He came up here and asked me to stake him in some fool idea about starting a restaurant or something. Well, I'd just sunk every last dime into jojoba beans and I had to turn him down. He thought I was holding out on him and got real mad, said he was going to go to Aunt Jessica for the money, and that he was going to make sure I got cut out of the will while he was at it."

"Oh, Lord. And what did you threaten him with, Uncle Fred?"

He had the grace to look a bit sheepish. "Well, of course I said I was going to go to Aunt Jessica and tell her lies about how you'd been badmouthing her and such. But I never meant it, and he knew it."

"Did he? Just like you knew he never really would go to Aunt Jessica and tell her to cut you out of the will."

"Well, he said…"

She sighed. "Uncle Fred, it wasn't until five years ago that Harley finally scraped together enough to start his restaurant. Piecing together things he's said in the past, I now realize that he thought as falsely about you as you did about him. And you're both wrong. Now don't you feel silly?"

Fred harrumphed but didn't answer. His pale eyes looked confused and worried.

"For ten years the two of you have not been speaking because you each thought the other one had all the money. This is the most ridiculous thing I've ever heard."

He nodded slowly. "You're right, girl. It is ridiculous." He sighed. "I'm going to have to go down and see Harley and see if we can get this straightened out."

Jessie laughed softly. "Right. Good idea." She sobered. "Listen, in the meantime, we want to trade cars with you."

"What's that?"

"That Firebird you were out there admiring? How would you like to own it? We'll trade you for that old beat-up Ford pickup you got around in back."

He looked at her as though he wasn't sure of her sanity. "Why would you want to do a fool thing like that?"

"Never mind why. Just say yes or no and get out your pink slip."

He considered for barely a moment. "Well, why not? I could have some fun with that Firebird, drive it around some and then trade it in for two of those pickups if I've a mind to."

"My thinking exactly."

He frowned at her. "So why would you want to get rid of a beautiful car like that?"

She leaned forward and patted his knee. "Call it a present, a hostess gift, to thank you for letting us stay the night."

He was skeptical, but willing. Jessie went outside to let Michael know.

It was a glorious day, the sky china blue, the desert sparkling like gold dust left behind by the miners when they retreated from their gold-strike mines. She took a deep breath and felt like dancing across the yard.

Michael was coming toward her. Restraining herself, she walked sedately to meet him.

"He says okay," she told him as they met, her eyes sparkling. "You'll have to transfer things from the Firebird to the pickup, and then we can get going."

Michael's look was incredulous. "This is crazy, you know," he muttered. His Firebird, left in the desert. He could hardly bear it. He looked at her and his eyes softened. The sunshine made her loose hair gleam. She was wearing jeans again, this time a pair from Cerise's drawer, but there was a softness to her now that hadn't been there the day before. He wanted to make love to her again. Maybe a few hundred times in a row. He smiled at her, glad she was coming with him, even if it was going to be in a rattly old truck. "Let me check the engine out first, though. I'll tinker with it a bit."

"You mean to tell me you know how to work on cars?" she asked, only half teasing.

"Of course I know how to work on cars. I was once an all-American teenager, just like everyone else."

"Really?" Her eyes laughed into his. "I thought maybe you city folk skipped that part of life."

He caught hold of her and kissed her soundly, his mouth hard and hot on hers, his hands strong. "I can tell I'm going to have my hands full just trying to keep you in line," he murmured.

"Nobody's ever managed it before," she told him softly, pressing herself to him and wishing she never had to let go.

"Come on," he whispered, the flat of his hand against the small of her back. "Let's go into the stables. You can introduce me to the horses."

"Since when were you interested in horses."

He nuzzled her temple, breathing in her scent. "Since I heard about all that nice clean hay they keep around them."

JESSIE WAS HUMMING a tune as she went back into the house sometime later, but the look on her uncle's face as he opened the screen door for her stopped the notes in her throat.

"What is it?" she asked anxiously.

"Come on in, honey," he said worriedly. "I've got to talk to you."

She followed him into the living room and sat on the couch behind him, trying to be unobtrusive as she picked bits of hay from her hair, but soon abandoning the effort as she realized how upset her uncle was. He'd looked concerned before, but now he was positively gray. Jessie wondered if it was his health.

He turned to look at her and sighed heavily. "Now you know me, Jessie. You know I don't have much contact with the outside world. That's because I like it that way. But I do get the paper once a week. And I just got out this week's and started reading it."

Jessie knew what was coming. There was no need for him to go on. Furtively she glanced at the door, irrationally planning to run for it.

"This week, lo and behold, what should I find, but you and that Michael guy on the front page. Do you want to explain this to me?"

He spread the paper out in front of her. The pictures were smaller, but they were the same ones she'd seen the day before. The headline read, "*Pair still at large*." She didn't want to read the story.

"Just what the devil are you two up to?" Fred demanded, his voice rising with his concern.

"It's hard to explain." She bit her lip, not sure if she should try. Maybe it would be simpler just to bolt for the door and call to Michael. Maybe they could get away. Maybe they couldn't. The cops had helicopters these days, didn't they? She shuddered.

"Okay." She turned to her uncle, all business. "This is it. Michael's been accused of a crime he didn't commit and he's looking for the man who can clear his name. I tried to kidnap him down home, but he kidnapped me, instead, and now I'm trying to help him look for this man."

Fred shook his head, his face stern. "This is all craziness,

Jessica. I think it's time to put a stop to it. Before you get hurt.''

"No, Uncle Fred…''

"Harley is my brother. We've had our differences, but I've got to look after his daughter, same as I'd expect him to look after mine.''

She got up, that fierce sense of protectiveness alive in her again. "What are you going to do, Uncle Fred?'' she asked evenly.

He rose, too, and faced her, his hands balled into fists. "Call the sheriff.'' he started for the telephone.

She stepped in his way. "Please don't do this,'' she said firmly. "I can't let you.''

His eyebrows came together in a ferocious scowl. "Oh, you can't let me? We'll just see about that.'' He pushed her aside and reached for the phone.

For an older man he was still surprisingly strong. Jessie stumbled when he pushed her, but she quickly regained her balance and lunged forward, slamming her hand down on the hook of the old-fashioned phone and cutting off the call even as he was dialing it.

"Jessica!'' He grabbed her hand and they stood glaring at each other. "I've got to do this, girl. He's a criminal!''

"You can't do this, Uncle Fred,'' she stormed. "I'm in love with him.''

That stopped him for a moment. His face crumpled, and then he grimaced, as though in pain. "All the more reason, honey,'' he said sadly. "Don't you see?''

There was love in his face as he told her that. Could you really hurt someone so badly out of love? "I'll never forgive you if you do,'' she warned him, eyes flashing.

"And I'll never forgive myself if I don't,'' he cried back. "You're too blind to see—you're just like your father. Now you get away and let me do what I have to!''

Jessie blinked at him, licking her lips. She knew she could stop him now, but what good would that do? He'd just wait until she left the room and then telephone. Or wait, even, until she and Michael were off down the dirt road. The sheriff could be here in no time. Glancing outside, she saw Michael leaning over the front fender of the truck, working on the engine. Inside stood her uncle, his weathered face set with determination. What was she going to do?

CHAPTER FIFTEEN

"DADDY."

They both swung around to find Cerise standing in the middle of the room. Clad in a flowing dressing gown, she looked like a blond princess awakened from a refreshing sleep and looking forward to a day of entertaining activities.

"Put the phone down." Her tone of command suggested she was used to telling her father what to do and he was used to obeying.

Fred frowned at his daughter. "I've got to call the sheriff, Cerise. That Michael's an escaped criminal."

"Put the phone down, Daddy. We're not calling any cops."

"But we've got to. He's no good."

Cerise looked from her father to her cousin. "He's Jessie's man, Daddy. You know how that is."

To Jessie's relief, Fred slowly lowered the receiver into the hook. "Do I?" he asked a bit plaintively.

Cerise smiled and came up to pat his cheek. "Sure you do. You've been through the mill with all us girls, but you know how it is when love strikes. You've got to follow your dream and take your chance." Her voice rose dramatically. "You've got to lean out and try for that big brass ring, Daddy. That's all Jessie's trying to do. You can't stop her. You can't protect her." She turned and smiled at her cousin, tears shining in her eyes. "Go ahead and nag her to death if you want to, but don't go calling any cops. It's not fair."

Jessie stood stock-still, numb. "Thanks, Cerise," she managed to get out.

Cerise nodded. "Daddy told me about Aunt Jessica's money.

That you all don't have any either, never did." She shrugged.
"Sorry I was so mean to you, Jessie. Can we be friends?"

She held out her hand and Jessie took it gladly. "Friends
and cousins," she amended.

Meanwhile Fred turned and looked at her sadly. "Jessie,
honey, I only want to do what's best for you."

"I know that, Uncle Fred." She reached out and took his
hand, too, her eyes beseeching understanding. "He's really not
guilty."

"How do you know that, honey?"

She shrugged, smiling, half-embarrassed. "I know him. And
I believe him."

Uncle Fred didn't believe him. Cynicism born out of a lifetime of disappointment shone in his eyes. But he nodded.
"Okay, honey. Okay."

She went to the bedroom to cool down, lying on the bed
and going over what had happened. Too much had happened,
too fast. She was beginning to have difficulty keeping everything straight. Her hand went automatically to twist her bracelet, then she remembered.

Joey. No, she didn't want to think about that. She didn't
want to think about what her uncle had said, either. She needed
to see Michael.

She knew he was shifting his things from the Firebird to the
truck, because she'd seen him pull his car up beside the Ford.
Suddenly she thought of something. Her bracelet. Maybe it had
fallen down behind the seat somewhere—maybe Joey hadn't
stolen it after all. If only that were true, then everything else
would be so much clearer for her. She got up quickly from the
bed and ran out to tell Michael to check carefully, but when
she rounded the corner of the house, the first thing that caught
her eye was the flash of fire in his hands.

His back was to her and he was doing something furtively.
But there was a second when his hand slipped to the side and
she saw them. Diamonds. A row of exquisite diamonds.

"What's that?" Her voice didn't even shake. She was proud
of herself for that.

He whirled, his hands cupped tightly, his face wary, his silver-blue eyes blank. They stared at each other for what seemed like a lifetime, each shocked.

"Listen, Jessie, this isn't how it looks," he began, but she'd been through enough and she was cold as ice.

"Looks like diamonds to me. Are you going to tell me I'm seeing things?"

He hesitated, then sighed and opened his hands. The jewels glittered like evil things. "Of course these are diamonds, and yes, they are the ones on the warrant, but listen, Jessie..."

Pain sliced into her head, shooting behind her eyes. For some reason she was short of breath. A lie. It was all a lie. Everyone was right. Her uncle was right. She was the one who was wrong.

Michael was speaking, saying something, but she couldn't hear the words. The pain was all through her now. He'd lied about the diamonds. He'd lied about everything.

It was all a lie. She'd been tricked, cheated. And worst of all, she had to face the fact that he wasn't what she'd been so sure he was.

To Michael she looked almost normal, her face stony, but quiet. He didn't realize how stunned and uncomprehending she was. He was working hard at explaining to a woman who didn't hear a word he said.

"Listen, Jessie. It's not the way it seems. I didn't steal these. They didn't belong to Sky Matthews at all. I just took back what belonged in my family to begin with. They were my mother's and Vanessa had them there in her safe, so I took them. I told her why at the time. They didn't belong to her."

But Jessie didn't hear the words. All she saw was his face, his eyes intense, his mouth moving, and the diamonds still sparkling in his hand.

"You lied to me," she said with seeming calm. "A convenient lie at a very convenient time."

That stopped him in his tracks. "Oh, God, Jessie, you don't think—"

"You lied to me," she repeated, and now fury was building in her eyes. "You lied to me when I trusted you most."

She started to back away, and he stepped forward as though to stop her. "Jessie, wait."

"Don't touch me. You just fix that pickup truck and get on out of here. I'll find my own way home."

He stopped, his eyes emotionless. "You're not coming with me?"

"No."

He reached for her. "Jessie…"

She jerked away from him. "Go on, get out of here, Mr. Innocent as the Driven Snow. Go tell your stories to someone else." Whirling, she stalked off.

She'll get over it, Michael thought as she disappeared into the house. Sure. She would go and think things over, then she would come back out and smile and…

He clenched the jewels, not even noticing how they cut into his palms. It was all baloney. She wouldn't do that at all. He'd hurt her. Cut her to the quick. How was he ever going to do anything to change that?

He swore viciously as he hid the diamonds in the driver's door panel so that he could get back to work on the engine again. He didn't have time to make up with her. He didn't have time for anything. He had to get to Las Vegas, find Kerry and clear his name. There was no time for anything else, especially not sitting around and thinking about what some damn woman thought she needed to make her happy.

He looked up. She was walking across the yard toward the stables, her head held high. He watched her go, and something twisted inside him. Making love to her had been one of the best, one of the cleanest things he'd ever done. She disappeared into the stables and he went back to work, but the imagine of her proud walk stayed with him.

JESSIE KEPT HERSELF BUSY with the horses, brushing down the dray gelding and getting fresh oats for the bay mare. She'd been a fool. For some insane reason she'd let her guard down the past few days. She'd let people get close, and sure enough, she'd been hurt.

There had been something about Joey that had touched her

heart. She hated to remember the rest—the bracelet. Or the fact that there was something about Michael that had touched more than her heart. First the boy and now this. Wasn't there a man in the entire world who was true to his word?

With sudden perception she saw the past two days as a circle, from suspicion to doubt to caring to risking—and back to suspicion again.

Cerise arrived after she'd been working for a few minutes. She sat and watched Jessie for a while, then finally spoke. "From the look on your face, I'd say you're mad at something. Is it him?"

Jessie didn't turn. "I'm not going with him."

Cerise looked out at the man leaning over the engine of the pickup truck and her eyes narrowed. "Hmm. Maybe I'll go with him. I could use a little vacation."

Jessie's heart flip-flopped and she looked up at her cousin, her feelings in her eyes.

"Oh, Jessie." Cerise laughed, shaking her head. "You're crazy about the guy. Go with him. Take a chance."

Jessie frowned. She hadn't told Fred and Cerise why she'd changed her mind and she wasn't going to.

She went into the house and tried to decide what she wanted to do. She could call Harley and ask him to come and get her. Or she could get Fred to take her to the nearest bus stop. She started to dial Harley twice, but put down the phone before she'd finished the number each time, sitting on the couch in indecision.

Uncle Fred came in. "He's going."

She looked up listlessly. "I've already said goodbye."

Fred stepped out on the porch and began waving. "Come again, young fellow," he called out, seeming to have forgotten that Michael was supposed to be a criminal. She could hear the engine of the truck come to life with a roar. She snuck a look out the window. The truck was off down the road, kicking up dust behind it.

He was gone. As she watched the dust settle, a huge emptiness yawned inside her. He was really gone.

Cerise looked at her with pity for once. "Now what?" she asked.

Jessie shook her head, refusing to meet the other woman's eyes. "I'll have to call Harley and see if he can come up here and give me a ride home," she said evenly, not about to let Cerise see her pain.

Cerise made a sound of disgust. "Boy, are you ever a fool," she said vehemently. "I don't know what you got so all fired mad at, but nothing could be worth throwing a good one like that back in. You just gave away the rights to a gold mine, honey. You're going to regret this for the rest of your days."

She probably was, but she wasn't going to admit it to Cerise. Retreating into the bedroom, she found a radio and turned it on loud so she wouldn't have to hear Fred and Cerise discussing her foolishness. There wasn't anything to pack and the bed was made. She threw herself down on the length of it.

She'd lost him. He'd lied to her. But she'd lost him. The two sentences kept echoing through her head until the room seemed to spin. She'd been a fool to trust him. But had she been even a bigger fool to let him go?

If she closed her eyes she could feel his touch on her skin, feel a shadow of the ecstasy he'd created for her the night before. Never to experience that again…. The pain sliced through her. She'd been a fool to let him go without her, a stubborn fool.

"Jessie?" Fred was at the door of the bedroom. "Turn that radio down, would you? There's some little boy here to see you."

"Boy?" She blinked at him, then gasped, coming back to life. "A boy? What's his name?"

Fred shook his head. "He didn't say. Nice looking kid, about eleven…"

"Joey!"

She leaped from the bed and ran to the living room, rounding the corner and looking straight into Joey's big brown eyes.

"Joey." Joy welled up in her chest despite everything. It was so good to see him again. Joey was a link to her time with

Michael. If she could see Joey again, maybe, just maybe...
"Oh, Joey, I'm so glad to see you! Did you find your mother?"

"My mother?" His huge, unsmiling eyes reminded her of a whipped dog. "No."

"What is it?" Frightened for him, she took him by the hand and led him to the couch. "Here, sit down and tell me what's happened."

"Nothing." He sat down and avoided her eyes.

"What happened to your mother?"

He shrugged. "Uh, she went on ahead. I've got to go find her."

She took his hand in hers, still confused. "Something's wrong, Joey. Tell me what it is."

"Nothing. I mean...well, here." Reaching into his pocket, he pulled out her silver bracelet. "I...I must have put it in my pocket by mistake," he mumbled, his eyes still avoiding hers. "I thought you might need it."

Jessie took the bracelet and stared at it, and suddenly her eyes filled with tears. "Joey," she whispered. She longed to hug him, but his stiff shoulders told her that wasn't what he wanted at all. So she touched his hair, patted his shoulder and contented herself with repeating his name a few times. She'd known he wasn't a thief. At least, she'd known he wouldn't stay one. Joy filled her. If Joey could be reformed, if affection and caring could turn him around, what did that say about Michael?

"How did you get here?" she asked him at last.

"I hitched from Bullhead City. I got pretty close. Then he found me on the highway." He gestured toward the front door and Jessie turned, her heart in her throat.

Michael stood leaning against the doorjamb, watching her carefully. Her gaze locked with his and her heart seemed to melt inside her.

"You coming?" he asked softly.

She glanced from Michael to Joey and back again. "I..."

"Someone's got to take care of the boy," he said, giving Joey a half smile.

She looked at Joey in surprise. "You're going with Michael?"

He nodded, eyes huge as saucers and full of hope.

"Yes," Michael confirmed. "His mother seems to be right on our path once again. So I guess we can take him along."

Jessie noted the use of the word *we*. She looked into Michael's silver-blue eyes. Did she love this man? She wasn't sure. Whatever she was feeling was bittersweet, and as wild as a flash flood, but right now she wouldn't trade it for any other feeling.

"Let's go," she said, her voice cracking only slightly.

CHAPTER SIXTEEN

MICHAEL SWORE SILENTLY as he drove along the bumpy road, the old Ford truck bouncing and groaning with every mile. He would never have uttered such words in front of a woman and a child, but he sure as hell said them to himself.

He was a first-class idiot, and probably had a death wish besides. Suicidal, that's what a shrink would probably call it. Flirting with danger just for thrills. Or was he just plain dumb?

He glanced across Joey's dark head and his gaze met Jessie's. Soft brown eyes stared at him from beneath the brim of that crazy hat. He wanted to step on the brakes, turn off the road and take her in his arms right then and there. His hands tightened on the wheel. What was wrong with him? He'd never felt this way about a woman—especially a cowgirl—before.

He should never have let her come along from the start. He'd been pretty much a loner all his life. Now he practically had a ready-made family on his hands. This was not the way he'd planned it.

A few more miles and they'd be in Las Vegas. He hoped to find Kerry right away and persuade him to return to San Francisco with him to testify. And that would be that.

And then, what on earth was he going to do with these two?

Joey would supposedly hook up with his mother somewhere on the Strip. All well and good, if it actually happened. That left Jessie. And that was the question. Could he leave Jessie?

It seemed incredible that he'd known her only a short time. He felt as if he'd known her forever. It was more than the lovemaking, although that had been great. There was something about her that seemed to fit with him, the way the pieces of a jigsaw puzzle interlocked. And that was about as philosophical as he was going to get about it. Bottom line—he liked being with her.

But she belonged on her ranch and he belonged behind a desk in San Francisco. So why had he come back for her? That was a question he couldn't answer.

They'd left the ranch with Fred and Cerise waving from the porch and promising to call Harley right away. Once on the main road, he and Jessie had talked about the diamonds and why he'd lied to her.

"The diamonds were an issue I didn't want to get into," he began. "The whole thing is confusing and charged with emotions. I wanted to avoid having to explain it all to you. But now I'm going to have to."

"You don't have to tell me anything," she said stiffly. "I'll take your word for it."

"No." He shook his head. "No, you won't. Not after you think I lied. I've got to tell you the whole story, then maybe you'll see."

He took a deep breath and gazed at the distant horizon. "My family was always good friends with the Matthews, but sometimes it was rather a strange relationship. Sky Matthews was ambitious and enterprising and successful, all the things my father was not. But Sky came from a poor background, and he always resented that my family's money went back generations. Whenever he could, he would belittle our heritage, yet when my aunt had to auction off her estate, he was right there in the front row, buying up everything, as though he could buy himself an old money background if he just paid enough." He turned and looked at Jessie. "Do you understand what I'm talking about?" he asked, mainly because he wasn't sure if he did himself. This sort of speculating on Sky Matthews's motives was new to him. He only wished he'd started it years earlier.

Jessie's eyes flashed. "I may be nothing but a simple cowgirl, Michael, but I do understand ambition and greed. People are people, no matter where you go."

"Of course." He liked the way she spoke her mind. "Sky and his daughter were always hot to have the Drayton diamonds. They tried to buy them from my father years ago, but he would never let them go, no matter how tight money was. It was a point of honor with him.'' He took a deep breath. ''But not with my mother, it seems. Once my father was dead, she handed them over to Sky Matthews without a qualm.''

''How do you know that? Maybe she didn't have any choice....''

His face was dark with anger. ''She could have come to me. But she didn't, because she would have risked having to listen to a lecture. So when she accrued an overwhelming gambling debt, she went to Sky Matthews and handed over a family heirloom for cash.''

''Have you asked her for her side of the story?''

''No. She's in Europe. I haven't seen her for six months.''

''Well, maybe she did give the diamonds away, but how could you take them back?''

''Those weren't her diamonds to give away,'' he said harshly. ''Those are the Drayton diamonds. They were my grandmother's, and her grandmother's before that. My mother had no right to give those diamonds away.''

Seeing the pain in his face, Jessie tried to find a way to comfort him. ''Maybe she didn't. You don't have any real solid proof. What if he stole them from her?''

''No. My mother doesn't deserve your standing up for her, Jessie. She's basically a very selfish woman. Sky's daughter Vanessa is like her in some ways. Vanessa showed me the diamonds in order to convince me that turning in her father would bring out ugly stories about my mother. Little did she realize that by showing the evidence of my mother's wrongdoing, she made me lose the last bit of respect I had for her. I don't really care what scandals arise. I grabbed the diamonds, promising to pay Sky back for the gambling debts, and left. They called that stealing. I don't.''

Jessie nodded quietly. She understood why he'd taken the jewels. That wasn't a problem for her any longer. But something about this woman he had mentioned sent warning signals down her spine.

''Vanessa...?''

He glanced at her, then away. "We were engaged," he said abruptly. "We're finished now."

"Oh."

And that was the end of that.

LAS VEGAS WAS LIKE a big, gaudy brooch someone had pinned on the wide expanse of a burlap sack. One moment they were in the dry, golden desert, the next they were riding down a boulevard of neon lights and shimmering signs. Joey's head whipped back and forth as though he were afraid he might miss something. "Wow" was all he said, and then he was quiet, taking in all the sights.

Jessie smiled and tousled his hair, then turned to Michael. "Where are we going?" she asked.

Michael hesitated, glancing at Joey. "We'll look for your mother later on, okay?" he said. "I want to stop at the Samarkand to see a guy first thing. I'm hoping he can help me find the man I'm looking for."

Jessie felt the tension in the air. They'd reached their destination now and things would begin to get real serious. "The man you're looking for...tell me about him. I want to be on the lookout, too."

Michael pulled the car to a stop at a red light and came to a decision. She might as well know everything. "Kerry Carter is his name. He was a pilot with Matthews Aviation. He tried to tell me Sky was running an illegal operation a few months ago and I refused to believe him. He said he'd been Sky's main coordinator with his underground connections, that he was mad at Sky and was thinking about turning him in. I thought he was a disgruntled fired employee. I told him to get lost." He shook his head as the light turned green and eased the truck out into traffic. "I traced him to Bisbee a couple of days ago, but he'd already left for Phoenix, and now he's in Las Vegas."

Underground connections. That sounded dangerous, Jessie thought. "How do you plan to find him here?"

"I've got a contact. I'll go from there."

Despite his tension he looked very sure of himself. Jessie sat back in the seat, but the Strip was a blur to her now. She was beginning to worry. Michael could be in a lot of danger once he started poking around the back rooms of the Las Vegas gambling world.

Michael drove the aging truck into the parking lot at the Samarkand and slipped it right in between a Rolls Royce and a silver Mercedes.

"You two want to go get something to eat while I—?"

"No," Jessie broke in quickly, looking around at the milling crowd. "We'll go with you."

"Suit yourself."

The hotel was shaped like a gilded replica of the Taj Mahal, with fountains everywhere. They walked through the casino to get to the main desk. Flashing lights and the sound of coins hitting bottom in slot machines made Jessie slightly dizzy. She was about as far away from the ranch as she could get.

"Jessie." Joey tugged on her sleeve, his eyes full of wonder. "Can I play the slot machine?"

"No, Joey. You're too young. It's illegal."

He couldn't have looked more disappointed if she'd told him he'd never be allowed to eat ice cream again. Then he had an idea. "Could I watch you play? Could I?"

She hesitated. Michael was already way ahead of them, and she didn't want to lose him in the crowd. "On our way out, okay?" she offered. "I'll play one quarter on our way out." she smiled to cheer him up. "I promise."

Only partly mollified, he joined her as she raced to catch up to Michael, who was already approaching the check-in desk.

"I'd like to see Mr. Ted Nargeant," Michael was telling the pretty girl behind the counter as they came up behind him.

The girl favored Michael with a smile a little less artificial than it had been for the previous customer. "Do you have an appointment?"

"No, but I must see him. It's crucial."

"Then I'm sorry." There was real regret in her eyes. "He's unavailable."

Michael took a deep breath. "How do I make an appointment?"

"You'll have to call his office." She reached into a drawer

and drew out a business card. "Here's his number. Good luck."

Jessie and Joey followed Michael to the bank of telephone booths and waited while he dialed. He emerged shortly, his face set. Jessie didn't have to ask what had happened. Mr. Nargeant obviously was not an easy man to get to see.

"You stay right here," he told them. "I'm going to take care of this."

While the two of them watched, he went back to the girl at the desk. He talked to her for a few minutes, laughing, teasing her, flirting a little. She blossomed under his attention, batting her eyes and pretending embarrassment. He leaned farther over the counter toward her, touching her arm. She giggled and pulled away, turning to answer the telephone. Jessie could see Michael reaching across the counter, but she couldn't see what he was after.

And then he was on his way back, talking to Jessie and Joey out of the corner of his mouth as he passed them. "Come on," he said. "This way."

He let them past the elevators and down a corridor, then made a quick turn and stopped them, looking around the corner to see if the way was clear before leading them right onto the employees' elevator.

"Don't you have to have a special key to operate something like this?" Jessie asked. Excitement was tingling in her veins. She felt very cloak-and-dagger.

Michael reached into his pocket and presented a key in the shape of a harem girl.

Jessie gasped. "How did you get that?" she cried in appreciation.

His grin was little-boy proud. "Flattery. It works every time. That, and a bit of sleight of hand."

He put the key in the slot on the wall and the doors slid closed. "Nargeant's got to be in the penthouse suite," he said, punching that button. "Let's just hope he's home."

The elevator zoomed noiselessly to the top of the building and the door opened to reveal an enchanted world. Tiled pools filled with sparkling water were connected to one another by a series of waterfalls, against a backdrop of caged birds, exotic plants and mirrored walls. The sounds of a sitar could be heard in the distance.

And two hulking bodyguards stood scowling at them.

"What do you think you're doing here?" one of them demanded.

"I've come to see Mr. Nargeant," Michael said. "I've got to see him. Where is he?"

"Wherever you ain't," the other sneered, advancing on Michael. "Beat it, buster, before we give you a sample of how we punish trespassers around here."

Michael squared his shoulders and Jessie set her feet, looking from one tough to the other. He wasn't going to try to fight them, was he? Michael was a strong man, but these guys were monsters. She pushed Joey behind her and hoped the dizziness she felt was only from hyperventilating.

"I have to see him," Michael was insisting. "If you'll just tell him…"

"We ain't gonna tell you nothin' but how to get out of here," the larger answered, his eyes alight, as though he were looking forward to the coming confrontation. "You're askin' for it, buddy."

Jessie felt a scream rise in her throat. This was no time to go into hysterics. She looked around quickly for a weapon, something she could use to help defend Michael.

But the guard wasn't going to wait for that. He had one hand on Michael's shoulder and the other poised all too near his face, when someone called out Jessie's name.

"Jessie MacAllister? Is that you?"

Everything stopped and everyone turned to stare at her. Bewildered, Jessie looked around, her heart still pounding. A figure materialized out of the mirrors, a thin blond man who seemed to be in his late twenties. He looked vaguely familiar, but Jessie couldn't place him.

"Jessie MacAllister," he repeated wonderingly. "You haven't changed a bit since high school, have you?"

He stopped right in front of her, grinning. "You don't remember me, do you? Lenny. Lenny Morton. I was a few years behind you at good old Fremont High. You went out with my brother a couple of times. Bernie.''

Bernie Morton. She remembered him. A skinny, wimpy looking boy who wanted to be an astronaut. She smiled uncertainly, still thrown for a loop by the circumstances of this meeting.

''So what's going on here?'' Lenny asked, looking first at the two goons, then at Michael.

Jessie quickly took the initiative. ''Lenny, this is Michael. He's got to get in to see Mr. Nargeant. It's practically a matter of life or death.''

Lenny's boyish grin faded and a sharp look took its place. ''Michael Drayton, is it?'' he said softly. ''Well, fancy meeting you here.''

Jessie assumed he'd seen the newspaper reports about them and that made her nervous. But there didn't seem to be a remedy available, so she decided to muddle on through.

''Do you work for Mr. Nargeant, Lenny?'' she asked anxiously. ''Could you get him in?''

Lenny's face fell back into a smile when he looked at her. ''Jessie, Jessie,'' he said softly. ''I had such a crush on you when I was in ninth grade. You were the coolest girl. Tough as a guy on the outside, but all female underneath.'' His grin broadened. ''For a long time you were my fantasy, you know that?'' He looked her up and down. ''God, it sure does bring back memories.''

Jessie glanced at Michael. His jaw was tight, his eyes hard, but the bodyguard's hand was still on his shoulder and he didn't say a thing.

''How…how's Bernie?'' she asked.

Lenny frowned. ''Ah, the guy's gone and become some kind of astrophysicist or something. Works for NASA in Florida. He never did know how to have a good time. I lost all respect for him when he took you out, had you right there in the palm of his hand and never even kissed you.'' He nodded at her knowingly. ''Oh, yes, he told me all about it. Told me how you sucker-punched him when he tried to put an arm around you.'' He shook his head. ''The wimp. No guts, no glory, I always say.'' His smile came back. "Now if I'd had you alone in that car..."

Jessie was blushing scarlet. She could hardly believe Lenny had the right girl here. She'd never been popular in school. She'd been too much of a tomboy for that. Beau was the only male who'd ever gotten to her in those days, and she had married him. To think of someone like this slightly sleazy Lenny having a crush on her was hard to believe.

"Can you get Michael in to see Mr. Nargeant?'' she asked again.

Lenny looked at Michael. "Sure," he said casually. "In fact, Mr. Nargeant has been expecting you."

Jessie felt herself go limp. "Good," she murmured, then felt a flutter of unease at the last sentence. Expecting Michael? Why?

But there wasn't time to ask questions. Lenny called the two goons off with a jerk of his head and motioned for the rest of them to follow him into a lush waiting room. Jessie sighed at the beauty of the place. The walls were hung with pastel silks that flowed and billowed with every passing breeze, and mirrors were everywhere, along with the sound of running water.

"You two wait here," Lenny told Jessie and Joey. "I'll take Mr. Drayton in."

They sat down on plush sofas and Jessie looked around the room. The strange opulence was overwhelming. She felt as though she'd stepped into a twilight zone—another world. Her heart was still beating hard from the confrontation at the elevators. Not only was this place strange, it was dangerous. She hoped Michael would find out what he needed to know fast and they could get out of there.

There was a rustle in a nearby hallway and suddenly two women emerged from the silken streamers, both dressed in high-heeled gold slippers and see-through harem pants, and both stark naked from the waist up.

Jessie gaped, suddenly remembered Joey and pulled him around so that he was facing the wall behind her instead of the unusual sight in the middle of the room.

"Where are the men?" the blond intruder asked Jessie, fluffing her hair. "We heard there were visitors."

"Th-there are no men here," Jessie stammered, trying not to look below the woman's chin. "Uh, maybe you have the wrong room." She blinked rapidly.

The dark-haired woman looked at her in disgust. "This is the waiting room and it's our job to meet the men." She flopped down on the sofa opposite, yawning. Then she glanced at Jessie again and her gaze sharpened. "You're the one who's in the wrong place, honey. You don't apply for the job up here. You have to do that downstairs."

Jessie shook her head, still stunned by the casual nakedness of these women. She'd heard about things like this, about the *Playboy* mansion and other such establishments, but this was the first time she'd ever come this close. She felt like a child on her first trip to the circus. "I...I'm not..."

"Oh, honey." the blonde stepped forward and pulled aside Jessie's jacket to get a better look at her attributes. "I don't know. You're kind of borderline. Ted likes us really big, you know. Maybe you'd have better luck trying out for a casino job."

Jessie scrambled off the sofa, grabbing Joey with her as she went. "Right," she said, nodding. "That's a good idea. I'll just go on down and..." A strained smile plastered on her face, she backed away, holding Joey's head in a viselike grip as he tried to get a parting look.

Outside the room she stopped, caught between exasperation and laughter.

"What were those ladies doing?" Joey asked, his eyes still round as saucers.

"Uh..." She did laugh then. "I don't know, Joey. But whatever they were up to, we don't want to see. We're going to find someplace else to wait, okay?"

"Okay." But he gave a longing look to the silk room as they started down the hall.

There were other rooms, but one had voices coming from inside and another was locked. The third door Jessie found yielded to her touch and they slipped in. More voices, coming down the hall. Jessie looked around the room and found another door. They quickly went through it.

The room they ended up in was empty, but one wall was covered with monitoring screens, obviously surveillance on most of the rooms in the suite. Only two screens were on, the one covering the room they'd just left, where the two half-naked women were still lounging around on the sofas, waiting for men, and the room where Michael was talking to a plump, bald man with a cigar in his mouth.

CHAPTER SEVENTEEN

MICHAEL HAD A BAD FEELING about the interview from the moment he walked into the man's office and saw the framed pictures that filled the wall. Familiar looking pictures. Pictures very much like those Sky prized above all others.

"You were in Korea," he said to Ted Nargeant, who greeted him with a fairly cordial handshake.

"You bet I was," the man responded, waving for him to come around the desk and take a look. "I served with Sky Matthews. He was our squadron leader. There he is." He pointed him out in a picture of a group of men standing in front of a bomber. "There I am. And there's your father."

That was his father all right. Michael couldn't ever remember seeing him looking so young and carefree. But the identification was unmistakable. He'd had no idea there was going to be this tie-in between this casino owner and Sky—much less his own father. Fate was strange. He glanced from one picture to the next and his heart sank. He wasn't going to get anywhere here.

Turning, he met the older man's steady gaze. "You knew I was coming."

Ted Nargeant nodded. "I keep abreast of the news. I've heard about you, and when I heard Sky was after you, I got curious." He gestured at the visitor's chair. "Sit down. We'll talk."

There wasn't much choice but to do as the man suggested. He was deep in the heart of Nargeant territory. There was no way he could escape if Nargeant didn't want him to. He sank into the leather chair, but his gaze never left the man on the other side of the desk. "Are you and Sky still friends?" he asked bluntly.

Nargeant smiled. "We've done business over the years. He does a favor for me. I do a favor for him. You know how it is."

"I see."

He shrugged. "I kept in touch with your father, too. I knew all about the way you took the rap for him a few years ago, did his jail time. I liked that. You were a good son to him."

Michael flushed, anger fueling the rush of color to his face. "How did you know?"

Nargeant smiled. "I just know. I knew your father. I can read the signs. Anyway, I've kept track of you over the years, and I know now that you're running from Sky, but I'm not real sure why."

Michael's eyes narrowed. "I'll be glad to tell you why, Mr. Nargeant, if you tell me where Kerry Carter is."

Nargeant's eyes narrowed, too. "Why do you want to find Kerry Carter?"

"Because he can back my story and help keep me from going to jail again."

Nargeant leaned over his desk, his chin in his hand. "Mmm" was all he said.

"He's been to see you recently, hasn't he?" Michael challenged.

"Yes. He has."

Michael took a deep breath. There was no point in beating around the bush. Either he got help here or he was in big trouble. In any case, it was time to pull out all the stops. "Was he trying to get your help to fight Sky?"

"Yes." He nodded. "That's exactly why he came to me."

Michael felt relief and excitement at the same time. "Well?" he asked impatiently. "What did you tell him?"

"Sky Matthews is an old friend of mine. We went through a lot together during the Korean War. It wouldn't seem right to turn an old friend in for various illegal activities that never hurt me personally."

A dreadful coldness swept through Michael. "So you're a crook, too," he said angrily.

The man raised a hand. "Hold on there. I'm no crook. I run a legitimate operation here. I might have done a few things in my youth that I regret now, but this place is clean and so is everything else I do these days."

"But you won't help Kerry and me."

"I didn't say that." He sat back in his chair. "Tell me, what do you say Sky Matthews is up to these days?"

"Smuggling. Mainly arms."

Nargeant shrugged. "So what? He's been doing that for years, supplying this little country and that little country, anyone who was itching to start a little war. They were going to get the weapons somewhere, why not from Sky?"

So everyone else in the world had known about it all along. Michael felt sick to think he'd been so blind for years. "Because it's against the law."

Nargeant nodded. "But I'm not a cop. I'd say this matter is between him and the law. How does this affect me?"

Michael ignored that question. "What he's doing now is a lot worse than running guns," he told the man. "It has the potential to affect you and every other citizen of this country."

Nargeant was looking at him steadily, his gaze bright and watchful. "Go on."

"I've seen evidence that he's selling secret information on embargoed computers and computer systems to eastern bloc countries. He's supplying them with a technology they haven't been able to develop themselves, giving them a major boost in the ability to control weapons systems, missile launching operations, et cetera." Michael leaned forward. "And that's not just illegal, Mr. Nargeant. That's traitorous."

For a moment he thought Nargeant hadn't heard, but the man finally moved, nodding, his expression vacant, as though he were far away. "You've seen this with your own eyes?" he asked softly.

"Yes. I stumbled into a warehouse and saw the crates being prepared for shipping. When I confronted Sky, he didn't deny it. In fact, he seemed quite proud of himself."

Nargeant was silent again. "And these charges against you?" he asked quietly.

"Completely false. He's just trying to scare me, to keep me from going to the authorities."

Nargeant nodded. "Interesting."

Michael moved restlessly in his chair. "How about Kerry?" he asked. "Where is he? Where can I find him?"

"I don't know. He came to me for help. I turned him down. From what I've heard, he's been trying to contact others here in Las Vegas for help, and not having a whole lot of luck." He shrugged. "I don't know where he is."

"But surely you could find out."

The ghost of a smile flickered across his thin lips. "Possibly."

Michael waited, then made a sound of impatience. "Why won't you help me?"

"I'm not sure I want to help you." Nargeant looked him up and down. "You see, Michael, I'm a cautious man. I've known Sky for years. I loved the man once. He changed. I didn't love some of the things he was doing, but I didn't interfere. It was none of my business." He shook his head. "But I'll tell you, selling secrets to the other side is going a little far. I'm going to have to think about this. You're going to have to give me time."

"Time is exactly what I don't have."

"I know that. And I'm sorry. But you're going to have to wait."

Michael rose. It was obvious he wasn't going to get anywhere here. "If you won't tell me where Kerry is, I'll find him on my own."

Nargeant rose, too, nodding. "You'll do what you have to. And so will I." He stuck out his hand. Michael hesitated, but finally shook hands with the man. "Come see me later," Nargeant told him as he ushered him out of the office. "You look for Kerry Carter, then come back. We'll talk again." His face darkened. "And listen...be careful out there. Watch your back at all times. Okay?"

JESSIE WAS STILL in the room with the monitors, trying to figure out how to work the controls. She turned one knob, then another, but before she could find the one that would let her hear what was going on in Nargeant's office, Lenny appeared in the doorway.

"That's a no-no, Jessie," he admonished, coming forward and turning off both screens before her eyes. But he grinned. "I should have known you'd be in here."

Jessie was beginning to take it all in stride now. She felt as though she were living in a TV movie. Something strange and different was happening at every turn. Hoodlums who claimed to have had crushes on her in high school, women who made a living entertaining men in the altogether, threatening bodyguards, eavesdropping devices—nothing else could faze her now. Even Lenny.

So instead of trying to explain, trying to justify, she merely sighed. "We had to leave that place where you left us," she told him. "I didn't think Joey needed to be exposed—so to speak—to a bunch of naked women."

Lenny looked truly distressed. "Oh. Sorry about that. Those are the welcome girls. They're supposed to come in whenever there are visitors and make them feel at home."

"At home, huh?" She made a face at him. "I guess you all have a pretty hip home life around here."

"Hey." He snapped his fingers, obviously thinking she was impressed. "It's life in the fast lane, baby. You know what I mean? But I guess you're a little young for that, aren't you, kid?"

He mussed Joey's hair, and when he turned away, Joey very carefully brushed it right back to where it had been.

"Well, come on, I'll take you to your Michael Drayton again."

Leading them from the room, he pointed out the way and then let Joey go a bit ahead down the hall. "Listen, Jessie," he said, his eyes sharp as a bird's, "I don't want to bum you out or anything, but I got to warn you. I shouldn't be telling you this, but I got to for old times' sake, you know?" He shook his head. "Your boyfriend's a marked man."

Even this hardly surprised her. She'd been expecting it all along. "What do you mean?" she said calmly.

His fingers circled her arm, reminding her of a vulture's claw. "He's hot, honey. There's a contract out on him. In fact, I know a few guys with a case of the greeds that are looking for him right now. Better keep him under wraps as best you can. Let him out on the streets and he's going to wake up with an ice pick in his back."

Everything went white around her. She kept walking, but she couldn't feel the ground.

"Hey, here we are, just like I told you."

Michael swam into her view and she wanted to reach for him, but something kept her arms stiffly at her sides. She felt like a robot.

They were on the elevator again and she wasn't sure how they'd got there. Lenny was waving.

"Take care, Jessie. Hey, listen, call me someday. We'll do lunch."

"Sure, Lenny." That was her voice, sounding normal. She shook her head and turned to find Michael gazing at her, one eyebrow raised.

"You certainly do have some strange friends," he noted.

She was beginning to get her bearings again, but her brown eyes were filled with concern as she looked back at him. She couldn't fall in with his teasing right now. She was too worried. "Michael, he said some things…"

"Later," he warned, glancing at Joey. "We'll talk about it later."

Later might be too late. She felt panicked. Suddenly every face she saw might be the enemy. They started through the casino and Jessie felt Joey's hand slip into hers and give a tug. "You said you'd play the slot machines," he reminded her.

She glanced down at him distractedly. "Not now, Joey."

Outrage swept across his face. "Jessie, you promised!"

She'd promised. He was right. "Oh…" She pulled a quarter out of her pocket. "Just one," she said, leaving him behind in the viewing area while she ran down to put the coin into the slot. Turning away before the reels had even stopped spinning, she was already wording her regrets to Joey, when the look on his face stopped her.

She whirled. Lights were flashing. Sirens were going off. For a moment she stood dumbfounded as people began to yell all around her. She'd hit the jackpot.

Money. Jessie's eyes got big as she watched the quarters spilling into the tray, but the way the lights and sirens were going, she knew there was much more involved in this win. Money. Big money.

"Come on."

She looked up blankly as Michael grabbed her arm and began to pull her away.

"Jackpot," she murmured. "I hit the jackpot."

"We've got to get out of here," he told her, steering her away from the noise. "Don't look back."

But she couldn't help it. "My jackpot," she moaned as he led her quickly away from the casino and out to the pickup. "Michael, that's enough money to—"

"To hang us both," he growled, opening the door to the truck and shoving first Joey, then Jessie inside. "Come on. We've got work to do."

The truck careered out of the parking lot and turned quickly onto a quiet side street. Jessie curled up in the corner against the door and whimpered.

"Sorry about that," Michael said, watching the rearview mirror. "We couldn't risk it."

"I know," Jessie said sadly. "Just let me mourn a little."

"Wow," Joey said again, his black eyes sparkling. "That was neat."

Michael took another corner and gave Joey a quick grin. "How are you doing?" he asked the boy, realizing he must wonder what all the commotion was about.

Joey's wise eyes were alight with excitement. "Great," he said chattily. "You know what? While you were in talking to that guy, we saw naked ladies."

Michael's startled gaze rose to meet Jessie's, and she nodded.

"Naked ladies, huh?" Michael murmured, taking another

sudden turn and keeping track of what else might have turned behind him. "How come I missed out on that?"

Joey shrugged. "I don't know. They came out and talked to us. They were only naked on top. And they said that Jessie could get a job there, too, only then they looked at her and said she was borderline."

"Borderline?" Michael choked out, forcing back his laughter.

Joey's head spun and he frowned at Jessie, whose cheeks were scarlet. "What's that mean, borderline?" he asked in all innocence.

Michael sputtered, then got out, "It means Jessie's too good for that job, Joey." Across the boy's head he gave her the once-over and mouthed, *"Borderline?"*

Jessie scowled at him and refused to comment, preferring to stand on her dignity.

Michael pulled the truck into a parking space in front of a hamburger stand and gave Joey money to go up to the counter.

Once the boy was out of earshot, Jessie turned to him. "Okay," she said, her dark eyes examining his face, searching for clues. "What did you find out?"

He stretched his long body behind the wheel and grimaced. "Not a whole lot," he said at last. "He knew who I was. He knows Sky. He knows the whole situation. But he couldn't tell me where I could find Kerry. And that was all I really wanted to know."

They were both silent for a moment, then Michael turned to Jessie. "So what did the remarkable Lenny have to say?" he asked.

She swallowed hard before answering. "There's a contract out on you. People are looking to kill you for the money." Just saying the words brought the panic back again. How could this be? Things like this didn't really happen.

But Michael nodded, as though that didn't surprise him. "Okay. I'll have to be careful."

That didn't stop her panic, or even soothe it very much. "Why would this Sky person want you dead?"

"Why do any of these crooks do anything? To cover his

tracks. Sky's probably hoping I get eliminated before I get arrested, because he definitely doesn't want me to talk.''

She looked at him. His face was set, hard, but suddenly so precious to her. A wave of nausea came over her when she thought of what might happen to him. This was crazy. ''You've got to go to the police,'' she said. ''This is no game, Michael. This isn't just cat-and-mouse, cops and robbers. These people mean business.''

His eyes, when they met hers, were expressionless. ''The police don't believe me, Jessie,'' he said slowly, as though to a backward child. ''They want to lock me up. And if they do, I'll be even more vulnerable to the people who want to kill me.''

''I can't believe that.''

''The only hope I have is to find Kerry,'' he said as though it were his last word on the subject. ''Here's Joey. Let's eat.''

They did. Joey finished quickly and ran off again to play on the slide at the front of the restaurant. Jessie tried to think, but fear was clouding her mind. The thought of something hurting Michael was more than she could bear.

''What now?'' she asked him as they pushed their trash into one bag to throw out.

''I've got to go casino crawling, I guess.''

''You can't,'' she protested. ''After what Lenny said?''

''What else am I going to do, sit in a room and wait to get killed?''

The word plunged into her like a dagger. Closing her eyes, she turned away.

Michael hesitated, then touched her cheek. ''Hey, come on,'' he murmured. ''Be 'tough as a guy' for me, okay?''

She could feel tears threatening, but she refused to give in to them. She never cried. It was her hallmark. Turning to Michael, she lifted her chin and answered challengingly, ''If you'd ever listened to Janis Joplin, you'd know that a woman can be tough, too.''

His lopsided grin warmed her. ''I believe it,'' he said softly, his face lowering toward hers. ''I've seen the evidence myself.''

His lips touched hers so sweetly she felt tears surging again. She pulled away. "Dammit," she muttered, hiding her face from him. "Don't kiss me when I'm mad."

"What are you mad at, Jessie?"

"You. The world. Life." Once again she managed to hold back the flow. She turned to face him in triumph. "I'm going with you."

He shook his head. "No, you're not."

"Yes, I am. It would be better that way. I can keep an eye on—"

He took hold of her shoulders and shook her, his face harder than ever. "It's too dangerous. You're not coming with me," he ground out. "And that's final."

Joey was at the door of the truck, looking curiously at them. Jessie leaned over to let him in. Michael was not going to cooperate, that was certain. She was going to have to think of some other way to protect him.

She sighed and watched the little boy climb in. In the meantime, finding Joey's mother was a priority. "Okay, Joey," she said as he settled between them on the bench seat. "Where do we go to look for your mother?"

Joey avoided her eyes. "I...I don't know."

"What do you mean, you don't know? You must have some idea, some name, some address."

He shrugged his skinny little shoulders. "I can't remember." He sat for a moment, then looked up at her, his black eyes hopeful. "Can we go back to that casino again?"

The light began to dawn in Jessie's brain. "Joey, listen. I know it's been a really exciting day..."

"It's been neat."

"But it's not always 'neat' with us, you know? Life isn't always that much fun. I know you got to see gangsters and naked ladies and a winning jackpot, but that's not going to happen again. This day was special. It's time to find your family and go with them."

He nodded solemnly. "I'll think about it. Maybe I can remember the name of the place."

She shrugged, looking at Michael. "Well, when you remember, you let me know and we'll take you there. Okay?"

Joey nodded.

Michael looked at him and couldn't help but grin. If he were Joey, he'd want to stay where the action was, too. It was funny how nice it felt, the three of them together this way. Like a family. Like the sort of family he'd dreamed about most nights when he was a little boy and his father was still at the office at ten o'clock and his mother was at a party or traveling in Europe. He'd spent more time with nannies and tutors than he had with his family.

"Let him stay with us for now," Michael said, garnering a worshipful glance from Joey. "What we'd better do is go check ourselves into a motel."

"No way," Jessie said quickly. "I'm sure your cash is running low. What are you going to do, use a credit card?"

Michael's mouth set grimly. "I don't have much choice, do I?"

Jessie reached into her pants pocket and produced a key. "My cousin Sheri's house," she said. "Cerise gave me this before we left, just in case we needed a place to stay. Sheri and her husband are on a trip to Chicago to visit his family. We can have the house to ourselves."

Michael's eyes narrowed and he looked at the key suspiciously. "How did she know we were going to Las Vegas? I thought we told them California."

She nodded. "Cerise isn't as dumb as she looks. She knew we were headed here." They'd parted on far more friendly terms than they'd started on, with Cerise pressing the key into her hand and giving her a quick kiss on the cheek.

Michael looked into the distance, toward the dark hills. "If she knew it," he mused, "I wonder who else put two and two together and came up with the same answer."

Jessie turned and looked at the hills, too, as though she could find the answer there. She was afraid now. Afraid for Michael.

CHAPTER EIGHTEEN

THE HOUSE surprised her. A charming little two story in a neat neighborhood, it looked a more likely place to find Snow White and a few of the dwarfs than Jessie's cousin.

"This is it?" Michael asked as they pulled up in front of the well-trimmed lawn.

"Uh-huh." Jessie checked the address Cerise had given her, then stared at the house. "Do you suppose the neighbors will notice us?"

"Sure," he said cheerfully, opening the door and jumping out. "And they'll call the cops and we'll all go to jail. But let's go on in anyway."

She felt like a burglar. An interloper. Sheri wasn't going to be pleased to find out they'd been tramping through her house while she was gone. But there wasn't much choice. They went up to the door and Jessie took out the key—and then they were in.

On the inside the house was decorated just as cozily as the outside had promised, with country prints and ceramic geese and an antique butter churn.

"Cute," Jessie said, and for just a second she actually felt a pang of envy for her cousin. It was cute, and a far cry from the bunkhouse ambience she and Harley had lived in for years.

"Cute enough to OD on," was Michael's comment. "Let's hope she doesn't pick out her husband's wardrobe."

He went right upstairs to the master bedroom and Jessie followed him. Throwing open the walk-in closet, he quickly picked out a blue shirt and a worn brown leather aviator jacket. Jessie leaned against the wall and watched as he pulled off his plaid shirt and put on the blue one, then the jacket.

"You look like a World War II bomber pilot." The smile died on her lips as she realized how appropriate that was. She was like a woman sending her man off to war. What kind of craziness was this? How had this happened?

But Michael seemed more excited than afraid. Striding to the dresser, he found a pair of dark glasses. Waving them at her, he disappeared into the bathroom. When he emerged, his hair was slicked back and the dark glasses were firmly in place.

She nodded, impressed. "Your own mother wouldn't recognize you."

"Are you kidding?" He looked into the mirror and preened a little. "My own mother doesn't usually recognize me. I'm lucky if she remembers she has a son."

"I don't believe it." How could any mother not be proud as punch to have a son like that, Jessie thought, her gaze slipping over his wide shoulders, his slim hips. He was handsome, smart, sharp and kind to boot. It made her shiver all over to think about how wonderful he was. Did that mean she was in love, as she'd told Uncle Fred?

"Okay." He turned and grinned at her, his eyes hidden by the glasses. "I've got to go."

She jammed her hands down into the pockets of her jeans, fear prickling along her spine. "Can't you just use the telephone first?" she suggested. "Wouldn't that be easier...and safer?"

"Sure. And also less effective." He touched her cheek with a lingering finger. "I've got to go out and mill around at the casinos, Jessie. It's the only way I'll have a chance of finding anyone who knows anything."

"But Lenny said—"

His voice was harsh as he cut in. "I know what Lenny said."

She bit back the rest, the begging and pleading, because she knew it was no use. He left her still leaning against the wall, and a few seconds later she heard the front door bang, then the truck start up. She'd never felt so all alone in her life.

THE LOUNGE SINGER was particularly repulsive, a middle-aged man with his shirt open to the navel who sported gold chains hung like Christmas ornaments around his neck. His voice sounded like Vic Damone's through a foghorn. Michael looked down at his drink and winced with distaste.

This was the sixth lounge in the sixth casino. The sixth lousy drink. The sixth lousy lounge act. And finally, despite all his efforts to avoid it, the liquor was beginning to get to him.

"Hello, handsome."

Make that the sixth woman cadging drinks, as well, he thought fuzzily. Not looking up, he raised one eyebrow. "Hark. Do I hear the call of yet another lovely lady?" he murmured, more to himself than to her.

She slid into the chair beside him without waiting for an invitation. "You shouldn't drink alone, honey," she purred. "You need someone here to protect you. Someone like me."

He made a gallant gesture, wishing he were more sober. That was it. No more drinks, not even to preserve the authentic look of the average tourist. "By all means. Be my guest." Peering at her, he decided she was indeed beautiful. That was nice. "What is it you've decided I need protection from?" He took off the dark glasses.

She seemed to ignore his question. "I'm Taffy. Who are you?"

"Who am I?" He frowned and searched his memory. "Let's see. I had a name when I came in here. What was it?"

Finally she giggled and patted his shoulder in a familiar manner. "Never mind, honey. I'll just call you 'John,' okay?"

He sighed. "I suppose that's appropriate."

"Buy me a drink, honey, and I'll tell you what you need protection from."

"But of course." He signaled the waiter. "Now tell me."

She gave him a seductive look he knew she must have practiced again and again in front of her own mirror. "Boredom, honey. That's my function in life. Protecting good-looking men like you from boredom."

Michael blinked, impressed with her expertise. The waiter arrived and he looked up. "Anything the lady desires. In fact, make that two of anything the lady desires."

The waiter nodded wearily. "How about you, mister? Want a refill on that Scotch?"

Michael looked at the glass regretfully. Another drink and he'd be out like a light. "No, thanks," he said. "I'll just chew on my ice cubes for a while."

"Tell you what, honey." She leaned closer, drawing circles around his ear with her forefinger. "Come on up to my room and I'll give you all the Scotch you want."

"My very own bottle?"

She nodded, pouting attractively. "With my blessing."

He stared at her for a moment, then gave her a crooked grin. Amazing. He wasn't even tempted. "Once you've sipped from the fresh mountain spring," he told her wisely, "it's hard to go back to plain old tap water."

She frowned, not sure what he meant but intelligent enough to know it didn't compliment her. "Listen, bud, I'm offering to do you a favor here. You can say yes or no, but you don't have to get smart with me."

Jamming the sunglasses back on his nose, he slumped in his chair. "I'm sorry, Miss Taffy," he muttered. "Please don't take umbrage. I do want a favor from you. But not the sort you're talking about."

She looked guarded. "I don't do any funny stuff," she began.

He laughed shortly, then sobered and leaned closer to her. "What I want, lovely Taffy, is information. Do you have any of that?"

Still wary, she shrugged. "Maybe. What kind of information?"

"I'm trying to find a man named Kerry Carter. Ever heard of him?"

She thought for a moment, her brows furrowed, then shook her head. "I don't think so. What's his line?"

Michael sighed. "He's a pilot. He's here in town looking for backing on a dangerous undertaking and I have to find him."

She wiggled in her seat. "Ooooh, I love pilots. What's he look like?"

"Blond with blue eyes. Six-foot-four. Laughs real loud."

She frowned. "I wish I'd seen him, honey, but I can't say I have."

Michael nodded. "Okay." His head was finally beginning to clear. "But let's move on. You know your way around this casino, I'm sure. Who can I talk to who might know Kerry? Who knows everything around here?"

She hesitated. "Danny, I guess. The pit boss. Do you want me to introduce you to him?"

Michael smiled. "You're a smart girl." He tucked a twenty-dollar bill into her hand. "Where is he?"

They found him going over receipts in a change booth. Taffy called him out and introduced him. "This is John, Danny. He wants to ask you some questions." She gave them both quick, tentative smiles and withdrew from the scene.

Danny was large and tough looking, like a retired professional wrestler. "I don't like questions," he said shortly, his beady eyes glancing here and there.

"Mine are painless." Michael tried a warm smile, but it met with no visible signs of a thaw. "I'm looking for a man named Kerry Carter. Have you by any chance—"

"Listen, mister." Danny's face came toward him, belligerently. "I don't see anyone. I don't hear any names. I just do my job and go home and play with my little two-year-old son. You get me? That's how I keep my job." He turned back toward the change booth.

Michael tried to stop him. "I can pay for the information—"

"Pay?" Danny wheeled on him, his face dark and angry. "Will you pay enough to make up for the salary I'll lose if I get fired here? Huh? I don't think so, mister. And anyway, I never heard of this Kerry guy. So leave me alone." Steeling himself to be more polite to a casino guest, he said stiffly, "I'm sorry I can't help you. Goodbye."

Michael watched him go back to work and sighed. This was getting to be a long, long day. Turning away from the casino floor, he hunched his shoulders and started for the back rooms.

There was always the kitchen help, the maids, the bellboys. Tracking Kerry down was getting to be a very tedious operation.

EVENING BROUGHT MELANCHOLY to Jessie. She and Joey had played every board game they could find in the house. She'd read a magazine while Joey watched television. Finally she'd fixed the boy a sandwich and settled down to watch the news, but it was hard to keep her attention on the television.

Michael should have been back by now. She kept thinking that if anything happened to him, she would never hear about it, because no one would know to call Sheri's house. Waiting was pure hell. She was tempted to run out to try to find Michael, but she didn't want to leave Joey. If only Michael would call or something.

"Look!" Joey was jumping up in excitement. "Look, on the TV. It's us!"

Jessie glanced at the screen and sure enough, there they were.

"The mystery woman who won the fifty-thousand-dollar jackpot at the Samarkand Casino and then simply walked away has been identified tonight," the newscaster was saying. "Seen in this videotape made by the security cameras in the casino, the woman has been identified as Jessica MacAllister, kidnap victim of fugitive Michael Drayton, who can be seen in the bottom right-hand corner of the picture, pulling her away. A police spokesman told this reporter they were very close to an arrest in this case. And what will happen to that jackpot? Nobody knows."

That did it. Now everyone knew Michael was in town. And everyone knew what both of them looked like. Even the neighbors might have noticed. She glanced around quickly, making sure all the shades were drawn tight.

Joey was at her feet, his eyes huge and searching as he stared up at her. "Did Michael kidnap you?"

She frowned, feeling cornered. Catching hold of herself, she stopped, took a deep breath, then relaxed with a short laugh. "Do I look like I'm kidnapped?" she asked.

He studied her hard. If there had been any evidence of foul

play, he surely would have seen it. "They're wrong," he said solemnly.

She tired to smile at him, her mind racing a million miles a minute. "Yes, honey, they're wrong. I'm with Michael because I want to be."

He nodded. "Me, too."

She laughed softly, drawing him up close, and for once he let her hug him. "But you don't belong here, Joey," she told him. "We've got to find your mother tomorrow. Or the next thing you know, they'll be accusing Michael of kidnapping you, too."

Involved in a thousand thoughts at once, she didn't notice how his little body stiffened, how he drew away, his face stricken.

"It's about time you got to bed," she said, getting up from her chair and leading him away. "You can sleep in the downstairs den. Okay?"

He nodded, his eyes sad. "Will you read to me? Like the moms do on TV?"

"Sure." She was beginning to feel like an old hand at this mothering business. It seemed easy with a kid as sweet and agreeable as Joey. "You wash up and get into bed and I'll be there." She watched him run off. She was going to miss him. What kind of crazy mother would let her child run wild?

The only thing she could find to read to him was *Aesop's Fables*, but he seemed to like them just fine. When she finally closed the book and turned off the light by the sofa bed he was sleeping on, he was still wide-awake.

"We're going to find your mother first thing in the morning," she promised.

There was a slight hesitation before he said, "Okay."

"Where do you suppose she is, Joey? Do you have any relatives here in Las Vegas?"

"No."

"There are no crops to harvest around here. What was she going to do here if not visit friends or relatives?"

"Probably she'll be getting a job at one of the big hotels," he said quickly.

Jessie was silent for a long moment, thinking that over, and when she didn't answer, Joey got a bit anxious. He rose and leaned on one elbow. "I could get a job in one of those hotels," he said wistfully. "One of the big ones with lots of lights and mirrors."

Jessie laughed at his tone. "You're much too young to work in one of those places," she told him. "We need to find your mother and get you back into school, where you belong."

"I don't go to school," he pointed out.

"That is all too apparent. And it's also something I'm going to have to talk to your mother about when we finally do find her." She was getting more and more angry at the woman. If she couldn't keep better track of her son than this, she didn't deserve to keep him. Jessie took better care of her horses than this woman did her child. Migrant work was hard and debilitating, and you had to get to the crops fast or you lost out. Jessie could understand that the mother might have had to leave Joey behind at some point. But why couldn't she have made better provisions for his travel? And why wasn't she moving heaven and earth and the highway patrol to find him now? It was very strange.

She stood and looked down at him. "Good night, Joey," she said softly, longing to lean down and kiss him. There was something prickly about him again, and she wasn't sure if he would like it. "Does your mama kiss you good-night?" she whispered.

Joey turned and she could see his eyes glowing in the darkness. "Sometimes," he whispered back.

"Will you let me kiss you, since she's not here?"

There was silence—then his small voice said, "Okay."

She leaned down and brushed his round cheek with her lips, then smoothed back his hair.

"Good night, Jessie," he said solemnly. "You read stories really good."

There was a lump threatening in her throat and she didn't dare to try to speak. Straightening, she beat a hasty retreat.

"Don't let the bedbugs bite," she said from the door, then closed it, leaning against it for a moment before moving on. There was just something about that kid that tugged at her heartstrings.

CHAPTER NINETEEN

THE BATH—last resort of the anxious and the bored. In Sheri's house it was also an event, for her bathtub was huge, with water jets and an atrium all around the back. Jessie poured in bubble powder and filled it to the brim, lowering herself in and sighing with pleasure.

The water was running and she didn't hear the bathroom door opening. When she saw Michael standing in the doorway, she jumped and gasped aloud.

"Oh!"

"Hi." His hair was still slicked back, but the dark glasses had disappeared. He had the leather jacket slung over one shoulder and his sleeves were rolled up to the elbows.

She resisted the impulse to leap from the bath and throw her arms around him. "You're back," she said simply, instead, and it felt as though some awful pain had been lifted from her. "Thank God."

He closed the bathroom door and came toward the tub, draping his jacket on the chair in front of the dressing table.

"Did you find him?" she asked anxiously, though she could see from the tired look on his face that he wasn't satisfied with his day's work.

"No. I must have hit every casino on the Strip, and most of the downtown places, too. I talked to a lot of people, got a few leads, but so far none of them has panned out."

She swished the bubbles that were stacked up high around her. "We were on television. The casino had us on tape."

He nodded. "I saw it in a bar downtown. Crazy, isn't it?"

Her smile was fleeting. "Yes," she murmured. "Crazy."

She put her head back and sighed aloud. "Fifty thousand dollars, they said. Fifty thousand dollars."

"Didn't anyone ever tell you that too much money is a corrupting influence? Look at it this way. I saved you from a life of conspicuous consumption. You should be grateful."

She closed her eyes and moaned. He dropped down beside the tub. "I'm sorry, Jessie," he said quietly. "Once we get this all straightened out…"

She opened her eyes and reached out, touching him with one soap-drenched hand. "Don't say another word about it," she told him. "Just let me enjoy my misery every now and then."

"Right." As she began to draw back her hand, he caught hold of it, a smile dancing in his silver-blue eyes. "Well, since I'm here, I might as well find out the truth," he said teasingly.

She gazed up at him, a little alarmed. "What truth?"

"About this borderline business," he said, glancing down at her bubble-hidden body.

With her free hand, she clutched a washcloth to her chest. "Michael!"

He pretended to be quite serious. "I think it's time I made my own judgment on the matter." Trailing his free hand in the frothy bubbles, he began herding them casually to the side and out of his way.

"Michael!" she warned, watching her comforting bubbles go.

But he ignored her, frowning his concentration. "I don't know. This is going to require careful analysis." He pushed away a final clot of bubbles and her breasts were revealed just beneath the soapy surface of the water. "Measurements must be made," he muttered as his hand entered the water and cupped her.

She giggled, trying without success to twist away, but her fingers curled around his.

"Samples must be taken," he went on. Bending down, with his tongue he touched one dark tip that just broke the surface. She sighed and leaned back against the porcelain tile as her body flooded with a tingling sense of relief. This was what she had been waiting for all day. All her life.

"Tell us, Ms MacAllister," he continued to tease, gazing deeply into her eyes. "In fifty words or less, what makes you think you'd be a good Samarkand welcome girl?"

She batted her lashes and pretended to think hard. "Let me see. Well, my biggest ambition in life has always been to help people."

"Real good. I need some help right now."

He leaned forward and brushed her mouth with his, moving urgently, hungrily, as though searching for something he hadn't found yet. She rose partway out of the water to meet him, her nakedness forgotten. His hands slid down her wet back, going beneath the water to take hold of her bottom. "That's just what I needed," he told her as he gently dropped her back to the water. Standing, he began to work on the buttons of his shirt. "That tub's big enough for two people, don't you think?"

She didn't answer. Her attention was completely captured by the bare chest he was exposing. She'd seen every kind of man in her time. It got hot riding fences and men took off their shirts. Some even took off everything to jump into a neighbor's reservoir, and Jessie had laughed and joined them. But this was different, so different. Just watching, she felt as though she could feel every curve, every angle, every line of his body. When he looked at her, his gaze burned so, that she caught her breath. There was something as natural as rainfall in the way she felt when she watched him. Natural as rainfall and wild as a stormy wind. This sort of desire was new to her. It consumed her like a flame, warming and singeing at the same time.

The shirt was tossed aside and the slacks slid down his muscled hips, followed by his briefs. The soft light in the room turned his body a creamy gold. She sighed aloud when he turned and came toward the tub. He was so beautiful, so male. Waves washed against her as he sank into the water. And then he was with her, his long body sliding against hers, his arms holding her, his face nuzzling her neck.

The water was their medium, almost another partner in their sensual rendezvous. It lapped against her cheek, splashed against his muscular back, drained from his hands as he lifted them, poured like a waterfall down over her breasts. Parts of their bodies emerged dreamlike from the sudsy water, now his hard, hair-darkened thigh, her slender, chiseled shoulder, now his sinewed buttocks, her long, golden legs. They were all movement and touch, splash and sigh—a ballet of seduction.

She didn't allow herself to think. Thinking brought on an awareness of the risk and the certain knowledge that this man was not really hers, not in the long run. That he would be gone soon.

But a part of her still knew, and that was painful. Pleasure and pain merged, so that the lovemaking had a bittersweet tinge that only heightened the intensity with which she clung to each beautiful moment.

The bedroom they were using was beside the bathroom. They wrapped each other in thick, fluffy towels and made their way to it, tumbling down on the bed in a tangle, towels and bodies, softness and love.

And then there was no time for play. Jessie was all urgency, whispering for Michael to hurry, and Michael was hard and sure and thrusting inside her, his hips coming against hers in rhythmic mastery, his breath hot on her face, rasping in his throat, and her legs curled around him and held him tighter still.

She wanted desperately to give him what he was searching for, to be what he was searching for. She didn't know if she succeeded, but she knew what they had was good. They were magic together. Ecstasy had never been so fine.

They lay very still when it was over. Neither of them spoke, but Michael's body still covered hers, and his breath tickled her ear.

"Jessie," he whispered after a while. "Tell me about the incident with the shotgun."

She didn't open her eyes, but her face froze. "You don't want to hear about that."

His hands slid along the pillow, framing her face. "I want to know everything about you. Everything there is to know."

She opened her eyes and stared at him, a spark of anger in her dark gaze. "Why? What possible difference can it make in your life?"

Startled, he pulled back a little, giving her breathing room. "I care about you."

"Sure." Her mouth formed a bitter line. Now that the love-making was over, she couldn't hold back reality any longer. The thoughts she'd suppressed came flooding to the surface. "You're going to be gone soon. You're going to find Kerry and get Sky arrested. And then you'll go back to San Francisco and I'll go back to my ranch. And then what difference will it make if you know all about me?"

His hand captured her wrist and held it tightly. "You're right, Jessie. I could be gone tomorrow," he said, the features of his face hard and jagged in the muted light. "Or I could be dead tomorrow. We don't know. All we have is right now. Right now I care. And I want to know."

She stared at him, wishing he hadn't put it so bluntly. But why not, after all? If she was going to be blunt, he should be allowed that himself.

"Have you ever been married, Jessie?"

She didn't want to tell him about Beau, or about the shotgun thing. But maybe it was time. He wanted to know all about her.

"Yes. I was married once." She shifted her position. "Not for very long. It was a teenage thing. I got married thinking I would live something out of a fairy tale. And instead it ended up like something off the funny papers." She shook her head. "What he wanted and what I wanted were such different things. Funny how hard that was to see before we got married…and how impossible to ignore once we were." Good old Beau. She wondered what he was doing these days. "We parted ways pretty quickly."

"And after that? Have there been many men in your life?"

"There've been almost no men in my life. Oh, there have been plenty of men who've tried. I've had a lot of men working for me over the years, some thinking it might be nice to marry themselves into a ranch, others just fancying a roll in the hay. I managed to avoid most of that sort of thing."

A viselike pain twisted inside him. He knew what it was and he despised himself for it. He didn't want to hear about her having other men. Maybe it was because he was old-fashioned; maybe it was because he was a chauvinist. He didn't know which. But he did know he didn't want to hear about it. He knew how old she was, that she was a healthy, vibrant woman, knew she wouldn't be normal if there hadn't been someone. But some irrational side of him wanted her to be all his, to have never touched another man. Stupid. That was what he was. But he couldn't help it.

Now he was not about to ask for a blow-by-blow account of every cowboy who'd ever stumbled into her life. That history was better left unspoken. But he did want to know about the shotgun affair. For one thing, something about the way she spoke of it told him it had been important.

His hand began to play with her tangled hair. "Except for the shotgun incident," he reminded her.

"Yeah, there was the shotgun incident."

"Tell me."

She took a deep breath. "It began over a year ago, at the Halloween dance. I wasn't going to go, but Annie, my best friend, talked me into it and even loaned me a dress. And I was feeling, I don't know, really alone. So I went. I curled my hair, I put on makeup."

She turned on her side and looked at him. The rest wasn't going to be so easy to tell. "And I had a real good time. The punch was spiked and I drank a lot of it. There was this one guy who kept dancing with me. His name was Bud Harvey."

She dropped her gaze to the bedspread. "It...it was bad what I did, flirting with him. I knew he was married. But I hadn't flirted like that in ever so long, and it felt so good." She glanced up to see what he thought, but she couldn't tell for sure, and she looked away again. "He was a good-looking guy, and I guess I'd have to admit I was flattered that he was paying me so much attention. I wasn't used to that. He was treating me like a princess or something."

She had to stop and steady herself. She'd never told anyone about this before. "But a little later, when I went outside to get some fresh air, he came out, too, and he started trying to kiss me. When I resisted him, he just laughed. He said he liked

wildcats.'' She swallowed hard. ''I started to realize I'd made
a big mistake. I knew he was married. There was no way I
was going to…to do anything with him. But he pulled so hard
and he…he tore my dress…'' Her voice cracked and she
stopped, embarrassed. If she was going to start crying or something sappy like that, she would just give up, that was all. She
waited. The tears seemed under control. She glanced at Michael. He was lying very still, waiting.

''You forget how strong men are,'' she continued. ''I work
with men every day and I can ride as hard and do everything
the roughest man I hire can do. But when a man tries to force
you…you forget, that's all.'' Her voice was rising and she
wished it wouldn't do that, but she didn't know how to to stop
it. ''I…he tore that dress. I couldn't even give it back to Annie
like that.''

Michael's hands balled into fists and a nerve began to twitch
at his temple. ''Did he…?''

''No. But he tried hard enough, laughing the whole time,
like he thought I was just playing hard to get. I finally got
away from him and ran.''

''Did you go to the police?''

She laughed harshly. ''The police? What for? It wasn't like
I was blameless. I mean, I did flirt with a married man and
everyone saw me.''

A man from a city environment, Michael didn't quite understand what difference that made. ''But that didn't give him
the right…''

''No. It sure didn't.''

His face was carved from stone. ''What did you do?''

Now she was on firm ground again. Her voice was clear and
steady as she went on. She did what any self-respecting rancher
would have done when insulted the way she had been. ''I went
home, loaded up my shotgun and drove over to Pine Creek,
where he lived. I got behind a tree and waited for him to arrive.
It wasn't long before his car came up the driveway. I cocked
the gun and waited, ready to blow him away.''

Michael leaned on one elbow and stared at her. ''You're
kidding.''

"No, I am not kidding." She shoved together pillows and leaned back, half-sitting. "What did you expect me to do? I don't have a man to fight my battles for me. I have to take care of myself."

He nodded slowly. "Go on. What happened next?"

"He got out of the car. I aimed, got him right in my sights." She pantomimed the shotgun on her shoulder. "That felt so good, knowing I could get back at him so easily. I remember the feeling, the satisfaction." Her smile was wistful. "And then there was this creak. I can still here it. The front door opened and out on the porch came—" she sighed "—his wife, carrying their little baby." She laughed softly, dropping her arms and the imaginary shotgun. "I took one look at them, and it was all over. I knew who I'd be hurting if I killed the bastard. And it wouldn't be him."

Michael studied her solemn face. "So you didn't get your revenge."

"Not yet." Her soft brown eyes regarded him serenely. "But he's not going anywhere. And neither am I."

Michael's eyes glittered in the soft lamplight. He admired this woman who took matters into her own hands without complaining to others. He also admired the fact that she had second thoughts. Killing a man would only have made matters worse, of course. But getting even—that was a concept he could understand.

"What was his name again?"

"Bud Harvey."

"Bud Harvey," Michael repeated slowly. "Right. You want to get even with him the way I want to get even with Sky Matthews."

"I guess so."

They both lay still, thinking their own thoughts. Somewhere down the street a church bell chimed the midnight hour.

"Where's Joey?" Michael asked.

"He went to bed long ago."

"No word from his elusive mother?"

"No. Tomorrow he's going to look. He promised." She turned and gazed at him. He'd listened to her story and he

hadn't ranted at her or blamed her or told her she was stupid.
Was this man real? Emotion filled her and she reached for him,
sinking her fingers into his thick hair and kissing his mouth
with short, loving kisses.

He took her in his arms. "Funny," he murmured near her
ear. "The more I get of you, the more I want."

She sighed happily, and then her mind wandered back to the
subject of Joey again. "Poor Joey," she said softly, playing
with Michael's fingers. "If I were that boy's mother, I'd be
going out of my mind with worry. I'd have his name on every
television station, on the radio, everywhere. I don't understand
it. Do you?"

Michael shrugged. "Joey's probably never lived the kind of
life you and I know, with parents together and a real house."
He paused, realizing how ridiculous his words were. He was
talking about the middle-class ideal, the suburban dream, not
his own reality—or even Jessie's, for all he knew.

But Jessie had taken his statement to heart. "Poor baby.
From what he's told me, he hasn't had a whole lot of schooling.
He's spent most of his life with the migrant workers, following
the harvests."

Michael nodded and leaned his head back, eyes closed. He
was tired. Her heart went out to him. She hadn't stopped to
think of the emotional toll this was taking on him. A pang of
conscience shook her.

But before she could act upon it, he opened his eyes and sat
up. "I've got to go out again," he said.

"No!"

"Yes." He swung his legs around until his feet hit the floor.

She came up on her knees on the bed. "Michael, you can't.
It's too dangerous."

His mouth twisted in annoyance. "Don't you see that we're
in the middle of a nightmare? It's got to end. We can't go on
like this."

He was right. They couldn't go on like this. Something awful
was going to happen if they did.

She lay back down, lying very still as he got up and went

into the bathroom to find his clothes. Their lovemaking had been so sweet, she'd hoped...

But he hadn't found what he was searching for. Not Kerry, something else. He hadn't found it in the love they'd made together. She wished she knew what it was. She wished it were her.

Slipping off the bed, she put on a robe she found in the closet, once again wondering just what Sheri was going to think when she came home and found she'd had visitors while she was gone. Jessie knew she herself wouldn't be too happy about strangers coming in and using her clothes.

Running down the stairs, she reached the front door just as Michael was going out. The leather jacket was back, and so were the sunglasses, despite the late hour.

"Be careful," she called to him.

He turned and looked back at her, the ghost of a smile hovering on his lips. "You, too," he answered, and then he was gone.

Gone. She was numb. He was gone again and she felt as though life had stopped again. Everything was suspended as she waited to see if he would survive. She knew she wouldn't be able to sleep.

Joey. She would check on him and that would make her feel better. Almost like a mother. She caught sight of herself in the hall mirror and smiled at her reflection. Almost like a mother? Funny. She'd never wanted to be one before, but it felt so right with Joey.

Opening his door a crack, she looked in. He didn't stir. All was quiet. Too quiet. Alarmed, she opened the door all the way and went quickly to the bed, pulling back the covers. It was empty.

"Joey?" she called, whirling and making a dash for the adjoining bathroom, only to find another empty room.

He was gone. She could feel the emptiness of the house all around her. Had he gone to look for his mother, after all? Possibly. But she remembered his wistful talk of getting a job in a casino. Somehow she had a feeling the Strip was a likely place to look.

Michael was gone. Joey was gone. There was no way she was staying.

Racing back up the stairs, she spun into the master bedroom and began to rifle through Sheri's dresses. She couldn't go out on the town in jeans any longer, not after the television clip. Silk dresses, wool jerseys, nothing looked right to her, until she came upon a homespun cotton peasant dress with embroidery around the hem and neckline. Dropping the robe, she slipped into the dress and rummaged around in the bottom of the closet for shoes that would go with it, then ran to the dressing table and pulled a brush through her hair, letting it drape about her shoulders like a cape. Golden bracelets, golden hoop earrings, and she was set. No one would recognize her now.

She paused and stared at herself in the mirror. It felt good to wear this sort of dress. A part of her was looking forward to Michael's reaction. How very strange. She couldn't remember ever feeling quite this way before.

In another moment, she was out the front door. Stars sparkled in the black sky, so bright she could have reached up and grabbed a handful. There was no traffic. No lights on in the neighborhood. She felt very much alone as she made her way quickly down the silent street.

The Strip was only a few blocks away. She got there in no time, and it was like stepping into another world. The traffic was almost as heavy as it had been during the day. The neon lit the sky. You couldn't see the stars from the Strip.

She had no idea where to begin looking for Joey, but the Strip seemed logical. Where else would a boy go in the middle of the night? She began glancing at faces, looking quickly up and down in every crowd, hoping to spot one small child among the milling adults. The need to find him was beating like a drum in her chest. It was her new obsession.

CHAPTER TWENTY

THE NEON LIGHTS cast a garish wash of color over the midnight scene. Faces looked distorted as she hurried past them. Laughter seemed leering; stares seemed threatening. The sound of slot machines, of money hitting metal, of lounge bands playing discordant notes, echoed in her head as she searched the streets and corridors for Joey.

He had to be somewhere. How could you lose a little boy in the middle of the Strip? He should stand out. Most little boys were in bed, safe, sound asleep. Where was he?

Should she go to the police? No, that would be a crazy move. She had to find him herself. If only she knew how.

Finally she stopped her headlong flight into the night, found an empty chair at a keno game and sank into it, buying a drink from the waitress just to have something in her hand. And she gave herself a moment to think.

Joey had left under his own power. He was a sharp, canny child, obviously well equipped to fend for himself. He'd been doing it when they'd met him. He'd be doing it after they all split up. What was the panic here? Was she afraid the world would hurt him—or that she wouldn't see him again?

Maybe he wasn't on the Strip at all, but in one of the many bedroom communities that spread out from the gambling area. There was no way she could search all over town.

Okay, Jessie, she told herself. *Calm down. Take a deep breath. Start over.*

The only way she could possibly hope to find the boy was to get hold of someone who knew what was going on in this town—someone in the know.

Lenny Morton. Why hadn't she thought of him in the first place? Of course! Lenny.

Leaving her drink unsipped and her keno card unplayed, she slipped out of the casino and hurried toward the Samarkand, only a few blocks away. The casino lobby was crowded. A floor show was just letting out and she had to fight her way against the tide to reach the house phone. She asked for Mr. Nargeant's rooms, and to her surprise, the switchboard operator patched her right through. The telephone rang three times and finally a sleepy voice answered.

"Hello? What is it?"

"Hi, can I speak to Lenny Morton?"

There was an outraged silence. "What the devil, do you think he lives here or somethin'? He only works for me, lady. He doesn't sleep with me." The line went dead with a crash.

Jessie hung up quickly. It had never occurred to her that Mr. Nargeant would pick up his own calls. It had also never entered her mind that Lenny might have an existence apart from what she'd seen.

"Idiot," she chastised herself as she walked away from the telephone. Now what?

After wandering aimlessly up a winding walkway that circled the open interior of the building, she stepped out onto a balcony that overlooked the casino floor. Leaning against the railing, she looked down at the people at the slot machines, the quick hands at the green felt blackjack tables, the slouched shoulders at the poker tables, the tuxedoed men and formally gowned women at baccarat. The excitement in the air was palpable, but what drove all these people was anticipation, hope, eagerness. Jessie was driven by a sort of panicked despair. She didn't know where Joey was. She didn't know where Michael was. And worst of all, she didn't know how she could help either one of them.

"Hey." A hand touched her arm. "Jessie, is that really you?"

She turned into Lenny's delighted gaze. He looked her up and down and whistled softly. "It really is you. God, you're gorgeous."

She breathed a sigh of relief. "Oh, Lenny, I've been looking all over for you!"

His grin was cocksure. "I guess it's true what they say. I just lost a bundle at the tables. And then you fall into my lap." He laughed, chucking her under the chin. "Lucky at love, unlucky at cards."

Grabbing his hand, she pulled it away from her face and stared up at him earnestly. "This has nothing to do with love, Lenny. I need your help."

"You need me." Turning to look back at his friends who'd been hanging around, waiting for him, he said, "You hear that, guys? She needs me. You'll have to go on without me."

She clutched his arm as his friends wandered off, laughing. "Do they know who I am?" she asked nervously.

"How would anybody know who you are, the way you look? You're a goddess, baby. I can't take my eyes off you."

She was glad he thought she looked good, but that was hardly the pertinent issue. "I had to change my appearance after I was all over the news and everything."

He took a step back, hand in the air. "Hey, you didn't just come back to get that jackpot, did you? Because that's out of my hands. There's nothing I can do. You should have stayed and collected...."

She frowned in exasperation. "No, it's nothing like that."

"I couldn't believe it when I saw you on that videotape. You and that kid and—"

She grabbed him by the arm. "Listen to me. That's the first thing I want your help with. The kid is gone. The boy who was with us, his name is Joey and he's disappeared. I want to make sure he's all right. I need help to track him down."

Lenny appeared taken aback. "What, a kid? Don't look at me. Go to the police. Oh, I guess you can't do that, can you? Well, go to a child care center or something. We don't handle kids here. They're not in my area of expertise."

"I just thought that maybe if you heard something or saw him somewhere...you might hear of a little boy hanging around the Strip."

"Okay, okay. I'll keep my ears open. I'll ask around. Now, what else can I do for you?"

She hesitated, wondering how to put it. "The other thing's a biggie."

Lenny could swagger even when he was standing still. "Yeah? Shoot."

She leaned a little closer, not wanting to be overheard by any passerby. "You know that Michael is looking for Kerry Carter."

"Sure."

She licked her lips and then blurted it out. "Where is he?"

Lenny looked confused. "Where is who? Michael?"

"No. Kerry Carter."

He laughed. "Oh, honey. You think I know that?"

"You're the only person I know who might know."

"Am I?" He took that as a compliment and reached out to touch her cheek with one rough finger, his eyes narrowing as he gazed at her. "You know, you turned out so pretty, Jessie. You're making me all shivery inside, just looking at you."

"Lenny…" She tried to push away his hand again, but this time he caught hold of her shoulders and wouldn't let go.

"Tell you what," he said, his eyes gleaming. "I might be able to find out where this Kerry guy is. I could make some calls. But we can't do it here. You come with me to one of the back rooms and we'll put our heads together. We'll see what we can do."

"One of the back rooms?" she asked suspiciously.

"Sure. They're set up real comfortable, with telephones and everything."

Jessie had a feeling that Lenny was up to no good. But she'd do just about anything to help Michael. She was sick of sitting around and waiting. "Okay," she said quickly, deciding to pretend to go along with him. "I'll come with you. If you really think you can find Kerry."

"Oh, baby." He sighed, his fingers digging into her shoulders, his face much too close. "With you by my side, I can do most anything. I know I can." He drew back and glanced around them. "You wait right here. I'll go check if the way is clear. Okay?"

He walked quickly toward an unobtrusive door and pulled it open, looking back at her. "Don't go away now." His face was half leering, half anxious.

She waved at him, an artificial smile on her face. "I won't go anywhere."

The door closed behind him and suddenly Michael was beside her, his mouth a set line of white fury. "I'm getting you out of here," he muttered, taking her roughly by the arm.

Her relief at seeing Michael was overcome by the need to explain to him quickly what she was accomplishing here. She put a hand on his chest, stopping him. "Wait. Wait, Lenny's going to—"

He covered her hand with his own. "I heard what he said, Jessie. Lenny's not going to do anything but try to make a pass."

"I know, but he knows where Kerry is. He said he'd tell me."

"Yeah?" He searched her eyes. "Jessie, listen. I won't let you pay a price like that for information. Besides, I don't believe he even knows." His large hands framed her face and he stared down at her, his silver-blue eyes clouded with questions. "Why are you doing this?"

She faced him bravely. "Why do you think I'm doing it?"

He stared at her. Her love was in her eyes, but he couldn't accept that. Not yet. What if he believed and she turned out to be like all the rest?

"I don't know. I don't understand. You're ready to throw your entire life away to help me. I've never known a woman like you, Jessie. I keep looking for your angle, but there doesn't seem to be any. What makes you tick?"

She could have told him, but he wouldn't have wanted to hear it. So she just shrugged and smiled at him. "Just crazy I guess," she murmured.

And then he was kissing her, his hands still holding her face, deep, lingering kisses that made her want to close her eyes and float away.

"Hey, man, what is this?" Lenny's shrill voice intruded on her dream. "Get your hands off my girl."

Michael swung toward the man. "She's my girl, Lenny," he said icily. "Not your girl." He moved quickly, taking Lenny's shirtfront in his hand and twisting it up into a choke hold, jamming the man against the wall. "Now tell me everything you know about Kerry."

Lenny flailed ineffectually at the air. "I don't know nothing!"

Michael twisted the shirt more tightly. "You told Jessie you knew something. You were going to let her buy it off you, weren't you, slimeball? You were going to get your pound of flesh...."

"I told her I'd try to find him, I never said I knew!"

"You know anything, you'd better spill it now, Lenny. I'll come back and find you later if you're holding out on me."

"Get your hands off me, man! I...I just wanted—"

"You just wanted Jessie." He slammed him back against the wall. "I'll tell you something, you little weasel. You'll never have Jessie. She's out of your league." He watched for a moment as Lenny sagged toward the floor. "Come on," he said to Jessie. "Let's get out of here."

With an arm around Jessie's shoulders, he started away. Jessie looked back, feeling worried. "I don't know if it's such a good idea to make an enemy out of Lenny."

"My patience is about used up," Michael replied. "At this point I don't care who I make an enemy out of. All I want to do is find that damn Kerry."

They hurried down the winding corridor and out through the casino where she'd won the jackpot earlier. She looked longingly at the slot machine as they passed, then turned and gazed up into his face.

"Michael, Joey left."

He stopped in the middle of the lobby. "What do you mean?"

"After you went out, I looked in on him. He was gone."

Michael nodded slowly and resumed walking. "It's probably

for the best," he said. "He'll find his mother. That's where he belongs."

But what if he didn't find his mother? She wanted to shout it out, but she held back. Michael had enough to worry about right now. Joey was her problem. She would bear the worry alone.

He led her out of the Samarkand and across the street, heading toward the Farouk Casino. In another moment they were in the lounge, sitting in a shadowed booth, with tall, icy drinks on tiny napkins in front of them.

"What if Kerry's not in Las Vegas anymore?" Jessie suggested.

Michael shook his head. "He's here, all right. I've picked up bits and pieces that lead me to believe that firmly. I've talked to people who've seen him, one as recently as yesterday afternoon. But no one seems to know how to get in touch with him. I keep looking around in every crowd, expecting to see his face." He shrugged. "And I just might."

She brought up the next thing hesitantly, knowing how he felt about the matter. "The police might be able to find him better than you can. They've got the resources, the connections. If we just told them, maybe anonymously or something..."

"Jessie, you know how I feel about the police. I went to them in the first place and all I got was the threat of being arrested. No police. No matter what."

She nodded quickly, staring at her drink. No police. That meant he was going after these crooks alone, even after he found Kerry. She didn't see how he could possibly have a chance.

"Hey," he said, his eyes shining as he looked at her. "What happened to my cowgirl?"

Her mouth turned up at the corners. "It's dangerous being a cowgirl in this town. I thought I'd try being something different." She shook out her long hair, enjoying the way it felt as it swayed across her back. "How'd I do?" she asked shyly.

"You look delicious," he said softly. His hand swept up under her hair and he leaned close to kiss behind her ear. "Do you think anyone would notice if we made love right here in the booth?'' he whispered.

She glanced around at the inhabitants of the lounge, most of whom seemed to be falling asleep over their drinks. ''Not really,'' she whispered back. ''But I still don't think it's a very good idea.''

''Then don't think,'' he teased, kissing her neck and breathing in her fresh scent. ''Let me do the thinking for you.''

She laughed softly, but a waiter passed at that moment, glancing at them curiously, and she pushed Michael away. ''We really shouldn't do anything to draw attention to ourselves,'' she reminded him.

He sighed and stretched his long, strong body beneath the table, leaning back and looking at her. ''Have you ever been to San Francisco, Jessie?'' he asked. He was trying to picture her at Top of the Mark, having cocktails, and somehow the image didn't jell for him.

Her smile was fleeting. She had a feeling she knew what he was thinking. ''No. But I've been to L.A.''

''L.A.'s not San Francisco.''

''No. But they've got just as many people per square mile up there, don't they?'' She shrugged. ''Even Las Vegas is too crowded for me.''

That wasn't quite it, and they both knew it. The truth was, she wouldn't know how to operate in a city. She'd been born and bred to the wide-open spaces. Try as he might, Michael would never make a city person out of her. She glanced at him, wondering if he was even thinking seriously of any such thing. Perhaps he thought it would be fun to take her back to the city with him, to watch her gape at the big buildings and use the wrong fork at dinner and try to pretend she knew who Nietzsche was when his friends discussed philosophy. A flush rose on her cheeks. Never. She'd do a lot for Michael, but she would never ever risk that.

''Michael, I'm a rancher. A ranch is where I belong. Right now I'm itching to get back into jeans and I'm wondering how Smoke, my horse, is doing without me and I'm making little mental notes on some fencing material I saw advertised.'' She took a long sip of her drink. "That's me, Michael. Take it or leave it."

He didn't say a word, and after a long, silent moment her heart began to break a little. There was no use fooling herself. This romance was fated to be short-lived no matter what happened in the next twenty-four hours.

Suddenly Michael's hand was on her arm, squeezing hard. "Don't look up," he warned. "Don't turn around. But get ready to move fast when I say."

Her heart leaped to her throat. "What is it?" she whispered.

His hand tightened on her arm, signaling her to silence. She waited, wishing she could see behind her. Michael's face was tense, but excitement flowed in his eyes. Jessie made a sudden discovery. He was enjoying this!

Working with one hand, he pulled out the dark glasses and put them on. "Now," he said urgently, pulling her to her feet. "Out the side exit."

She moved with him around the corner, where he flattened himself against the wall and stopped her beside him. "I want you to look back," he told her. "I want you to see him so you'll know him the next time."

Carefully they both peeked around the edge of the wall back into the room.

"There he is, talking to the waiter. See him? He's starting to go bald."

"I see him." A moment later they hurried out into the casino and on out into the street. "Who is he?" she asked, short of breath by the time they'd reached a safe distance away.

"His name's Bob Taylor. He and I went to school together. Now he's a cop."

"He didn't see you, did he?"

"No. Not yet. But if he does, he's going to work hard to put me away for a good long time."

"But if you're not guilty..."

His face was almost fierce and the effect was heightened by the flat dark lenses of the glasses he wore, which completely veiled his eyes. "Do you really think guilt or innocence matters, Jessie? My experience has been otherwise."

Her head went back, reacting to his tone, and his face softened immediately. "You go on home," he said, taking her in his arms and hugging her tightly. "You need some sleep."

"What about you?"

"I'll be back when it gets light and things wind down around here. I'll get plenty of sleep then."

She laid the flat of her hand against his rough cheek. "Be careful," she said. "I'll be waiting."

CHAPTER TWENTY-ONE

SHE LET HERSELF into the silent house and went right to the den to check if Joey had come back. The bed was as empty as ever. She climbed the stairs wearily, going into the bedroom and dropping her clothes to the floor where she took them off. The bed felt good. She'd thought she'd never be able to sleep, but in a moment she was out, and she didn't wake until morning, when voices roused her.

She was alert in a second, her eyes open, every nerve on edge. She jumped up and went to the bedroom door, then held her breath and listened.

"I just know someone's been in here," a woman's voice was saying, getting higher and higher all the time. "I can just feel it...and look! Look here! Someone's moved my chairs. I swear it, Sam, I know when someone's been in my house...and Sam! Oh, my God, look at the bed in the den. Someone's been sleeping in it! Oh, my God, call the police!"

Jessie shrank back into the room. Sheri and her husband were home. Now what? Obviously the first order of business was to make sure they didn't call the police. Moving fast, she picked up the robe from where she'd slung it across the bed and slipped into it, tying the sash as she went down the stairs.

"Hi, Sheri," she called cheerfully. "It's me, Jessie."

A slim, blond woman stared up at her. "Jessie MacAllister! What on earth are you doing in my house?"

"Cerise gave me your key."

"I can't believe that." A short man with dark curly hair stepped into the entry hall. "Look, Sam, it's my cousin Jessie. Cerise gave her the key. Can you believe that?" She tried to smile, but it was obviously an effort. "It's good to see you, Jessie, but I wish you'd let me know."

"I know, I feel terrible about this. I would hate it if someone just came barging in and used my house when I was gone. But this was kind of an emergency and Cerise said why didn't I just use your house since you were going to be in Chicago, anyway."

"You were asleep upstairs, right?" Sheri looked confused. "Then who's been sleeping in the den?"

"Uh, Joey."

"Joey?"

"Yes, he's this boy who's been traveling with me. He ran away during the night and I've been really upset, trying to find him." She felt as though she were spouting nonsense, but she had to keep talking to cover for the furious thinking she was doing. Glancing at Sheri's husband, Sam, she remembered what Uncle Fred had said about his being in the Mob. He certainly looked the part.

Should she tell them about Michael? After all, Uncle Fred and Cerise knew all about him. But what about Sam? If he had criminal connections or anything else, he might be on the wrong side. What if he worked with the people who were trying to kill Michael? She couldn't take the chance.

"Did you call the police?" Sheri asked.

"What?" She paled and clutched the banister.

Sheri appeared puzzled by her reaction. "About Joey. Don't you think the police would—"

"No!" She smiled quickly to cover the vehemence of her response. "I mean, I don't really want to get the police involved." She looked from one to the other of them. They were still staring at her. She smiled nervously.

"I...I'm kind of in trouble. I can't tell you about it right now. I'm sorry, I feel like such a hypocrite, coming into your house, then telling you I can't say why, but it just wouldn't be safe."

"Hey." Sam shrugged grandly. "No sweat. You're family, right? You tell us when you're good and ready."

She nodded brightly. Good old Sam. He seemed to understand these things just fine. "If you could just let me stay a little, just to rest."

Sam gestured wide. "Take all the time you need."

She smiled her gratitude and turned to go up the stairs, then looked back. "What brought you home so early?" she asked.

"Oh." That changed the subject beautifully. Sheri threw up her hands. "We were having a perfectly nice visit in Chicago and then Sam got into a fight with his mother and we had to leave on the next flight." She leaned closer to Jessie, as though speaking confidentially. "You would not believe these Italian families. All they do is scream at one another all day long. I've got the worst headache."

"Yeah, we may scream a lot," Sam said, grabbing his wife for a bear hug, "but we also love a lot, and that's what you love about me, isn't it, honey?"

The way Sheri giggled, Jessie knew Sam had hit the nail right on the head. She studied the man. He looked illegal, but he also looked like a warm, caring individual, and Sheri sure seemed to like him. She decided to take a chance.

"Sam, maybe you could help me with something. I'm trying to find someone. It's really important. His name is Kerry Carter." She watched closely, but there was nothing in Sam's dark eyes to indicate he recognized the name. "If there's any way you could find out for me where he is, it would probably save a life."

Sam's eyes sharpened as though he could read her mind, or at least was a darn good guesser. "Who's he working for?" he asked.

"I…I don't really know. He worked for an aviation executive named Sky Matthews in San Francisco. He was a pilot. Supposedly he's been looking for someone to help him go against Sky Matthews now. If you know anyone who might know something, I'd sure appreciate it if you could find out where he's staying." She watched him carefully, wondering if what she'd done had been stupid or brilliant.

Sam nodded slowly. "Kerry Carter? It's kind of early, but I know a few people I can call. I'll see what I can do."

She sighed. For some reason she believed and trusted him.

"Thanks. Listen, I'll take care of cleaning up the den in a minute."

Sheri waved her offer away. "You go on up and get some more sleep," she told her. "It's barely dawn. Sam and I are going to be getting some rest, too, aren't we, honey?"

Sam didn't answer in words. He merely growled lustily as he attacked her neck. Jessie beat a hasty retreat up the stairs and into the bedroom.

Relief surged through her as she closed the door. Things were looking up now. She could feel it. Taking off her robe and lying down on the bed, she let her mind go over all that had happened to her in the past few days. She felt as though she'd been on a crazy carnival ride, sometimes up and racing through the clouds, sometimes down in the scary darkness, rushing toward danger. All in all, she'd probably done a year's worth of living in this short space of time. *Crazy* was a good word for it.

It wasn't long before she felt sleep coming quickly. Drowsiness had just about overtaken her, when she heard a sound and realized someone else was in her room.

SKY MATTHEWS SAT staring at the morning fog. He hadn't moved from his leather chair all night. This was what it felt like when your back was to the wall, he thought groggily. This was what it felt like when everything you loved, everything you lived for, deserted you.

Memories had been fluttering through his mind all night, memories of Korea and the camaraderie he'd had with his men, of his wife the day before she'd died in that car crash, of Winslow Drayton, of Michael. Memories of Vanessa when she was a little girl, of Pamela Drayton when she'd come to him one night during a windstorm. He'd thought that by possessing her he would somehow take on the Drayton mystique. But he'd been wrong. It hadn't meant a thing, and Pamela had laughed at him. And so he'd found a way to get the Drayton diamonds from her. But that hadn't been completely satisfying, either.

There had to be something, some way to have it all. He'd thought Michael's marrying Vanessa might do it. But now that dream was smashed. Nothing was going the way he'd planned it.

On the whole, he'd done what he'd set out to do with his life. He'd made a lot of money. He'd become rich and powerful. He had everything a man could possibly want.

"Everything," he muttered aloud, "except the respect class brings with it."

And he'd tried to buy that, taking over the Drayton aunt's estate, controlling Winslow, manipulating Winslow's wife, taking possession of the Drayton diamonds, trying to control Michael, first through Vanessa and finally right up front. If only Michael had married Vanessa before he'd come face-to-face with the smuggling. Surely Sky would have been able to keep him under his thumb.

It had all worked so well. Until Michael. Because of Michael he could lose everything. It was time he faced it. Michael was the fly in the ointment. Michael had to go.

He reached for the telephone, his hand shaking. Pressing the buttons with effort, he made his long distance call to Las Vegas. "Ernie?" he rasped out to the man who answered. "I've made up my mind. Do what you have to do. Do it now."

"MICHAEL!" Jessie gasped as he stepped out of the shadows and dropped down to sit on the bed, taking her in his arms.

"Hush," he warned her, kissing her lips, her cheeks, her eyebrows. "They're back. I saw." He kissed her again, hungrily, as though he were drawing something from her that he needed badly. "I won't stay long," he whispered.

"How did you get in here?"

"I climbed up the drainpipe. As long as no neighbors saw me, we're home free."

"The truck…?"

"I parked a block away."

"I didn't tell them about you. I thought it would be better."

"Tell them anything you want after I've gone," he said, his mouth brushing hers as he spoke, nibbling at the corners of her smile. "It won't matter anymore."

His tone frightened her. "What is it, Michael?"

"Hush," he said softly, his hand cupping her cheek, and his lips touched hers again. His kisses were exquisitely tender, his affection overwhelming her and bringing tears stinging to her eyes. "Just let me hold you for a moment more."

An inarticulate dread began to build in her. She felt as though they were clinging together at the edge of an abyss she didn't dare look down into. She turned into his caress, let him drown her in his touch, his kisses, just to keep from facing what was surely coming next.

"Jessie." The voice calling her name wasn't Michael's. She froze.

Sheri was at the door, knocking softly. "Jessie, do you need any clean sheets or anything?"

The first time she tried to speak, nothing came out. She tried again. "No, thanks, Sheri. I'm fine." Then she held her breath, praying her cousin would go away.

"Jessie, I just want you to know that it's nice to see you. I know our families have had their differences, but you and I have always been friends. At least I always thought we were."

"Oh, yes," she cried out in answer to her cousin. "Definitely."

"Good. When you get up we'll have a nice long talk."

"Sure. See you a little later."

The footsteps retreated down the hall. Jessie looked at Michael. His face was hard, closed to her. "What's wrong?" she said. "What's happening?"

He touched her cheek. "It's over for you, Jessie. I want you out of here. I want you to go back to the ranch." He pulled out some bills and put them on the bed. "There you go. That's what you've wanted all along. Bus fare home."

That hadn't been what she wanted for a very long time. Didn't he know that? Didn't he understand anything? She stared at the money, repelled by it. "I don't want to go."

"But, Jessie, you have to. I don't want to have to worry about you any longer. I want you safe." He moved impatiently. "I've been selfish to keep you with me this long as it is." He hesitated. "Look, I met a man just a little while ago who knows something about Sky and his operation. He's a dealer at one of the casinos downtown and he's been around for years, seems to know everything. He told me there was a move to oust Sky about ten years ago. Two of the leaders of the movement were shot to death. The third disappeared and his body was never found.''

She hated hearing this, but it didn't weaken her resolve. ''I don't have anything to do with Sky Matthews. What would anyone do to me?''

''I don't know. And I don't want to find out.''

She was shaking her head, her long hair flying around her. ''I won't leave you. I can't.''

He took her shoulders in his hands and forced her to look into his face. ''Listen, Jessie. These are rough boys we're dealing with. I'm getting close and I don't know how they're going to react when I do get there.''

Her eyes widened anxiously. ''You heard something about where Kerry is?''

He hesitated. ''I've got some stronger leads,'' he said. ''This same contact has promised to take me to someone who might help me find Kerry a little later today. I'm going to have to leave in a minute to meet him. But I had to come back and warn you to get out of town. I want you to go home.''

He wanted to protect her. He wanted her out of the way when the shooting started. That meant he expected danger and, very possibly, a tragic end to this journey of theirs. Didn't he see that those very elements made it mandatory that she be here with him?

There was only one way out of this nightmare that she could see. She put a hand on his arm. ''What is this all really for?'' she asked him. ''How long can you go on combing the streets for clues, just asking to get victimized? Don't you think it's time you went to the authorities and tried to reason with them? They may throw you in jail, but at least they won't kill you.''

The warmth in his face drained away and his eyes hardened to steely silver. ''No,'' he said fiercely. ''I'll never go back to jail. Understand that, Jessie. I'll die first.'' He rose from the bed and moved away from her, and at the same time she could feel a wall coming between them, as though he'd closed down the side of his emotions that had been open for her. He looked at her as though she were a stranger. "Go home, Jessie," he said again. "Go as fast as you can."

They both heard the car pulling up in front of the house. Michael went to the window and drew back the curtain a crack so that he could see down into the front yard.

"It's the cops," he said with certainty. "Only cops drive such mediocre, nondescript cars." She rose from the bed, reaching for her robe. "It's Bob Taylor," he said, turning back from the window. "And he's got backup."

She stared at him. There it was again, that charged excitement. He was living on the edge, and he was enjoying himself. Anger sizzled through her. She wanted to scream at him. Didn't he see what he was doing? He was in the midst of a dangerous game, a game that might just kill him.

"Damn you," she whispered, tears threatening to spill over.

But Michael didn't notice. Pressed against the wall, he was watching the progress in the front yard. "Okay, I'm going out the window," he told her. "The backup will go around the house and check the yard as Bob rings the front bell." He caught her to him and kissed her hard. "You go down and talk to the man. Tell him everything, anything, that will let you off the hook. I'll go back the way I came. You'll be covering for me. Okay?"

She nodded, but the lump in her threat meant she couldn't say anything. He was out the window in one smooth movement, and she turned and left the bedroom, going quickly down the stairs. There at the bottom stood Bob Taylor, the man Michael had pointed out to her the night before.

"You're Jessie MacAllister, aren't you?" he said wonderingly as she came toward him. "I've found you at last. Are you all right?"

She held her head proudly. Michael was escaping right now. Michael was running out of her life. But she would do this one last thing for him. She would cover.

"Do I look damaged to you?" she asked the detective.

"No." He surveyed her, walking around her in a circle and

noting especially the defiant light in her eyes. "You don't look damaged. But you do look conned."

She glanced into the hallway, where Sheri and Sam were hovering, watching this confrontation. She stared at them for just a moment, and they, taking a hint, retreated into the kitchen. "What's that supposed to mean?" she asked Bob Taylor, turning to meet his gaze.

"I mean that it appears to me, from all the evidence I've seen, and now, by looking at you, that you ended up falling for your kidnapper, and now you'll do just about anything to keep him out of my hands. Am I right?"

She glared at him, and he thought, bingo. There were a number of ways he could attack this problem. He could tell her she wasn't the first, that women fell all over Michael Drayton every time he turned around and gave them his famous smile. That he used women and discarded them like last year's trendy clothing.

But this one knew that already. She had a sharp intelligent look to her. She was in love, but she was aware of the pitfalls of being in love with a man like Michael. The pall of cynicism was no stranger to her.

He could tell her about Michael's conviction and jail term. She might not be aware of that, and it might put a new light on her rapture. But that would be an unpleasant thing to do and he wouldn't like himself for it.

He could threaten her with prosecution for aiding and abetting, or for collusion even. But she'd see right through that.

That left only one avenue. The truth.

"Well, listen, Jessie MacAllister. If I am right, if you did fall for the guy, you'll want to do what's best for him. And I've got to tell you, if Michael doesn't give himself up, he's going to get killed."

She didn't look surprised. She'd already known it.

"Are you going to arrest me?" she asked, her dark eyes level and clear.

"Arrest you? What for?"

"He didn't kidnap me. I went with him willingly. I helped him. I'm still helping him."

"Yes, that much is obvious." He smiled as he looked at her. What was it about a man like Michael that inspired such loyalty? This woman would do anything for him. Was it his looks? His warmth? Or did he have some fatal charisma that knocked women cold and took over their minds? Whatever it was, he'd seen it work time and time again. He felt sorry for Jessica MacAllister. As far as he could see, she was just another of the victims.

"I'm not going to arrest you." He sighed. "We've been following your trail, you know. We talked to your uncle just this morning, and when we found out you had a cousin living right here in Las Vegas, it took no more than a routine call to arrange things with the Vegas police. I had a feeling you'd be here. The only thing I want to know now is, where is Michael? When did you last see him? Where did he say he was going? And all those other questions you're going to refuse to answer."

He waited. She didn't say anything, and he nodded. "Eventually I would like you to come down to the station and give us a statement. For now, I just wanted to make sure you were all right. My main objective is to find Michael. You could help me do that."

"Maybe I could," she replied. "But I wouldn't hold my breath if I were you."

Bob paced slowly back and forth in the entryway, nodding slowly, thinking. Then he turned and faced her. "You're a bright lady, Jessie. I can see that by looking at you. Surely you can read the odds as well as anyone. If Michael stays out there on the run, he's going to get himself killed."

Her dark eyes flashed. "If you know that, why don't you go after the men who are threatening him?"

He nodded, half smiling, conceding that one to her. "Good point. However, my knowing it and proving it—in other words, my superiors knowing it—are two different things. I am here in my capacity as a law enforcement officer, and my assignment is to take Michael Drayton into custody and arrange extradition to California. Period."

He waited, but she didn't say anything. "If you could tell

me what he's doing to disguise himself, what kind of clothes he's wearing, where he's hanging out—you could make my job a whole lot easier. I guarantee I'll do everything possible to keep Michael from getting hurt in any way.''

Still she didn't speak. He stared into her clear eyes and knew she wasn't ready yet. It would take time. Time, and a bit of mulling over her options. He would give her the time. He only hoped the thugs who were after Michael wouldn't make the issue a moot one.

Finally he turned to leave. "Okay, Jessie. Have it your way. But just remember." He put his card down on the hall table. "If you want to get in touch with me, I'll be waiting." He gave her one long last look. "Do yourself and Michael a favor, Jessie," he said softly. "Call me soon."

The door closed behind him, and Sheri and Sam came out of the kitchen. Jessie felt drained. Reaching out, she leaned against the stair railing, wishing Michael were here, wishing she could lean on him. She looked at Sheri and Sam and wondered what she should tell them.

"We know all about it now, Jessie," Sheri told her quickly. "We've just been reading the paper."

That was a relief. Better they should know, especially when she was using their house this way. "I can't believe he didn't take me in," she said, sagging against the banister. "I was sure they'd take me in for questioning."

"You know what that means?" Sam told her. "Come on over here." He pulled back the drapes. "Look down the street. What do you see?"

Another nondescript car. With a man in the driver's seat, just sitting there.

"They want to tail you," Sam said. "They're hoping you'll lead them right to this guy—what's his name? Michael Drayton?"

"Oh, Lord," she moaned. "How do I let Michael know? What if he comes back?"

Sam looked out at the car again. "You go on upstairs and get dressed, Jessie," he said. "Then we'll toss this thing around and think of something."

She looked at Sheri, grateful that they were taking this situation so calmly. Sheri gave her a hug. "I bet you don't have any clothes with you, do you? Go ahead and use anything you like from the closet in that room." She giggled. "It's mostly Cerise's stuff, anyway."

"Thanks," she said, hugging her cousin back. "I don't know what I'd do without you."

"No problem. Just go on up and get dressed."

Jessie took a long, steamy shower, then dried herself with a big fluffy towel and used the blow-dryer she'd found in the bathroom on her hair. Pulling open the closet, she stared at all the clothes. Another decision to make. This time she reached for a pink cotton sweater and a gray wool skirt. That was a change. She slipped into the clothes quickly and looked in the mirror.

And did a double take. For just a second, she wasn't sure who that was. Her cheeks were flushed, her hair curling softly about her face, and in the pink sweater, she looked so feminine. So…pretty. She put a hand over her heart and thought of Michael. It was true. Love did change your life.

Downstairs she found Sam and Sheri sitting around the table in the breakfast nook. Pulling up a chair, she joined them, and Sheri poured her a steaming cup of coffee. The newspaper with the article about her and Michael was sitting on the table. She glanced at it and looked away, suddenly embarrassed.

"You're famous," Sheri said. "You've had a wild few days, huh?"

Jessie tried to smile. "He's not a crook. He's innocent."

"Sure, honey. Sure he is."

They didn't believe it for a minute, she could tell. She started to explain, then stopped herself. What was the use? They'd never believe her. The important thing was, they seemed ready to help her, anyway.

"Okay, listen now, Jessie," Sam said, his forehead creased, his eyes somber. "I've been calling around, talking to some of my acquaintances in the business, and I think I found out where this Kerry guy is. In fact, he seems to be staying in an apartment building I own part of. How's that for a coincidence?"

Jessie's jaw dropped. "You're kidding!" She leaned forward eagerly. "Kerry can clear Michael. We've been searching for him since we got here and no one knew where he was."

"Yeah, that's cuz the guy went into hiding and he didn't want anyone to know. But like I say, I own part of this apartment house. Anyway, the point is, I think this Kerry's got an apartment there. I wrote down the address for you." He slipped a piece of yellow paper in front of her. "And the apartment number. Why don't you give it a try?"

Jessie couldn't believe it. "Oh!" she breathed, staring at the paper. "Oh, I've got to get this to Michael right away." She leaped up and started for the door.

Only Sam's quick move to get between her and the outside world stopped her. "Aren't you forgetting something?" he said archly. "Our little friend down the street."

"You're right." She looked out. Sure enough, the car was still there. "What will I do? I can't just stay here when Michael could be in trouble. I've got to get out of here!"

"You can't go now. They'll be on you like a burr on a field horse. You just stick one little toe out the door and they'll be popping up all over to watch every move you make."

She turned slowly, thinking. "You and Sheri could get out. Then you could find Michael...."

"Do you know where he is?"

"Not exactly, but..."

Sam shook his head. "I don't think that will work. If the police can't find him, how do you think Sheri and I are supposed to do it?"

"Jessie has to go," Sheri said quietly. "Only she won't be Jessie. She'll be me."

"Huh?" They both turned and stared at her. "What are you talking about?"

Sheri smiled sunnily at her husband. "Remember that blond wig I got when I dyed my hair that champagne color and didn't like it? We'll put it on Jessie. You drive the car up close to the door, she'll jump in, they'll think it's me. You can drive her to wherever she thinks she can start looking for Michael. And I'll stay here, doing my nails, pretending to be Jessie.''

Jessie whirled and stared at Sam, full of hope. Sam looked at her and shrugged his wide Italian shrug. ''Why not? You're family.''

CHAPTER TWENTY-TWO

THE RUSE seemed to work. Sam dodged up and down streets to test whether they were being followed, and it appeared not. Jessie's head felt hot and scratchy under the blond wig, but her spirit soared.

"Thanks, Sam," she said, getting out in front of Caesar's Palace.

Sam's face scrunched with concern. "What are you going to do, kid? He's going to be hard to find. Like a needle in a haystack."

"I've got to try. And if I can't find him, I know someone I can ask to help me." Lenny. A real last resort, but one she couldn't ignore.

Three hours later she knew she had to give Lenny a try. She'd been up and down the Strip, stopped in every casino, every lounge, and there hadn't been a sign of Michael. Time was passing much too fast and she was running out of hope. When she'd planned her search it had seemed inevitable that she would run into him somewhere. But as the day wore on, she began to see how foolhardy her assumption had been.

Finally she stumbled wearily into the Samarkand and sat down on a couch in the lobby. Lenny was going to have to help her. He was the only one she knew who might be able to pull some strings. But she needed a moment to think over what she was going to say.

Thinking didn't do her much good. She still didn't know how she was going to approach him after what had happened the night before. The best thing to do was hold her nose and jump in. She went to the house phone and called Mr. Nargeant's suite. This time a girl answered, and got Lenny for her right away.

"Hi. It's me, Jessie," she said.

"Oh, no," Lenny said quickly. "No, you don't. I'm not messing with you anymore, baby. You keep that gorilla away from me. He ought to be registered with the SPCA. The man's an animal!"

"Lenny, I'm sorry he hurt you, but you did ask for it. Anyway, I can't find him. The police have been after me and I've got to find him. If you know where he is, or where I might go to look…"

"Jessie, baby, are you crazy?" he hissed in a conspiratorial tone. "You can't call me about this here." He paused, speaking to someone else in the room, then came back on the line. "Listen, meet me in the Sandstorm Bar, behind the blackjack tables. Go ahead and get a table and order two drinks. I'll be there." The receiver clicked off in her ear.

She did as he said, finding the Sandstorm Bar with no problem, but the ice in his Scotch and soda was almost melted by the time he finally appeared.

"Sorry," he said. "Got tied up with the big boss." He slid into the booth beside her, looked her full in the face and grimaced. "Pitch the blond wig, baby. It's not your style."

She'd forgotten all about it. Reaching up, she touched it gingerly. "I have to wear it. The police…"

He waved her explanation away. "I know, I know. We all do what we have to." He looked at his drink, then glanced at her suspiciously. "You didn't slip me a Mickey, did you?"

She sighed in exasperation. "I don't want you knocked out, you idiot," she grumbled. "I need you fully alert. I've got to find Michael."

He gulped down half his drink, then faced her, his eyes sparking. "Why should I help you, after the way you treated me last night? I mean, I was ready to go out of my way to help you, and you let your boyfriend rough me up. I'm not exactly feeling kindly toward you and yours at the present time, sweetie. Friends help friends, you know. Not the other way around."

She couldn't blame him for feeling that way, but she wasn't about to apologize. "Look, Lenny, I don't have time to make amends." She put a hand on his arm and gazed at him be-seechingly, her eyes luminous. "I've got to find Michael."

His face softened a bit. "Got a one-track mind, don't ya?"

"Uh-huh."

He took a long sip of his drink, then nodded. "Where have you been looking?"

"In every casino, every club..."

He shook his head vehemently. "No good. Last I heard he was visiting boardrooms and corporate offices."

She stared at him, at a loss. "How do I go about looking for him in those?"

"You don't."

"Then what can I do?"

"Nothing."

"No way." She shook her head, her eyes flashing. "Unac-ceptable."

A half-dressed showgirl walked by and waved to Lenny. He grinned and waved back. "Look there," he said to Jessie, poking her with his elbow. "That's Velma Wright. *She* loves me." He turned to look at Jessie. "Now why can't you?"

Jessie sighed. "Lenny, do you think you could stick to the subject for once? What am I going to do?"

Lenny looked uncomfortable. "What you should do is forget all about this loser and concentrate on me," he grumbled. "But I guess you're not going to do that, are you?" He didn't wait for an answer. "Okay, tell you what I'll do. I've got people who know these things, and some of them owe me favors. I'll see what I can do about finding out where Michael is for you. But it might take a while."

She closed her eyes. "Please do it, Lenny," she said after a moment of silent prayer. "Anything. I've got to find him."

He nodded, looking a bit abashed by her intensity. "You really go for the guy, don't you?"

She met his gaze and tried to smile. "Yes. I really do."

His affectionate grin almost disarmed her. "I always did like your style, Jessie," he said. "I knew you'd be a tiger under the right circumstances.'' He sighed his regret that he would never know more firsthand. Suddenly his expression changed. "Say, I almost forgot. I've got something to show you."

"What?"

"Come on." He took her hand and pulled her from the booth. "Just don't say old Uncle Lenny never did anything for you, luv."

He led her up and down corridors, then into the kitchen and beyond, into the supply rooms for the casino. Jessie couldn't imagine what he might have to show her, and she began to wonder if he was up to his old tricks. Finally they came upon a section where produce was being sorted for the cooks.

A small, dark figure was bending over the boxes and her heart gave a lurch. She didn't have to look twice to know it was Joey.

"Joey!" she cried, rushing forward.

He looked up, startled at first to see this blond lady running at him, but once he recognized her face, he broke into a smile and let her hug him.

She laughed with happiness. "Joey, are you all right?"

She had to feel him all over, his arms, his legs, his hands, as though checking for broken bones, before she was satisfied that he was okay. "Oh, Joey, I was so scared for you!"

Joey's grin was shy but pleased. "I'm okay," he said gruffly.

"He came around early this morning, looking for a job," Lenny said. "I heard about him and came down to take a look-see, after what you'd told me, and sure enough, it was him. So I got him a job."

"A job?" She rose, turning to glare at Lenny. "He's eleven years old!"

"So?" Lenny was hurt that his good deed was getting short shrift here. "It's good to get that old work ethic boiling in them early, I always say."

Her hands went to her hips as she faced him, anger evident in every word, every gesture. "But a job with a casino?"

"Look, he's not working for the casino, because that would be illegal, even though he claims to be sixteen." Lenny wagged a finger at the boy. "He's working for a man we contract some of this work to. So we can't be held responsible now."

She rolled her eyes heavenward. "Even though you got him the job."

Lenny didn't seem to understand why she was criticizing him. He'd been expecting praise. "Well, you asked me to take care of him! What else was I supposed to do?"

Jessie's glare slowly dissolved into a grin. She wasn't really angry with Lenny, but he sure was easy to rile. Her grin faded as she looked down at Joey. "Did you find your mother?" she asked anxiously.

He avoided her eyes and shook his head. She stared at him, then turned to Lenny. "Could you give us a few minutes alone?" she asked. "I've got to talk seriously to this boy. He needs to make some plans."

"Sure," Lenny allowed obligingly. "I'll be in the next room. Come on in when you're finished."

When Lenny was gone, Jessie sat down beside Joey on a cardboard box. She looked at his dark hair, much in need of a haircut, at his pug nose and his long black eyelashes. "I've missed you," she said. "I ran all over the Strip looking for you last night."

He appeared surprised. "I thought you'd be glad I was gone."

"What? Why would you think a thing like that?"

He hesitated. "You said…"

She waited, but he didn't finish the sentence. "What is it, Joey? What did I say?"

He squared his shoulders and stared at the gray wall before them. "That I'd better go before they thought Michael kidnapped me, too."

"Oh, Joey." She couldn't believe such an offhand remark could have sparked his running away. She touched his hair. "No, honey, that wasn't what I meant. I never meant for you to run off. We both loved having you with us. Don't you know that?"

He hung his head and didn't answer.

"Only, your mother has to be so worried about you. Joey,

we've got to find her. Do you have any idea how we could get in touch with her?''

Joey didn't move, didn't say a thing.

A horrible thought came to Jessie. ''You didn't run away from home, did you, or anything like that?''

He shook his head, but he still wouldn't look her in the eye.

Her heart ached for him. She wanted desperately to help him, but she couldn't do anything until she knew what the problem was. Reaching out, she stroked his hair lightly. ''What is it, honey? Please tell me.''

He looked at her, started to speak, then turned away again.

''Joey,'' she said softly, putting an arm around his thin shoulders. ''Where's your mother?''

His face was hard as stone. ''In heaven,'' he said shortly. ''She's been dead for two years.''

White agony shot through Jessie. She closed her eyes. This was something that had never occurred to her. ''But Joey, you said…''

His little body was stiff now, as though he didn't want her arm around his shoulders or her hand in his hair. He wanted to be left alone. His posture, his face, said, *Don't touch me.* ''I told you I had a mother like I tell everyone. I didn't want you to turn me in to a government agency or something.'' He looked at her bravely, his lower lip protruding. ''I can take care of myself. I move with the migrant workers. There are some families that let me stay with them. Nobody asks where my parents are. I do the work and nobody asks.''

''Your father…?''

''I never knew my father. I don't even know his name.''

The pain, the vulnerability were clear behind the mask of toughness. He was still a little boy. A little boy in trouble.

''Oh, Joey.'' She pulled him to her and held him tight, despite his resistance. His little body lost some of its stiffness. *He's going to learn to hug,* Jessie thought, determination steeling her will. *I'm going to teach him.* She drew back and stared at him. ''You don't have anyone? No brothers, no sisters, no aunts, no uncles?''

''No one.''

She took his hand in hers. "Will you come with me?" she asked. "Will you come and try living on my ranch with me? Just to see how you like it."

Hope leaped in his eyes, but he quickly suppressed it. It was obvious he'd been disappointed before and he was wary of investing too much of himself in anyone. He shrugged. "I guess I could try it," he said. Then he looked up into her eyes. "Do you have a dog?" he asked.

She felt a welling up of emotion, but she held it back, smiling at him. "We've got dogs and horses and cows and chickens. You're going to like it."

His little face was still under tight control. "I'll do work to pay for my keep," he said firmly. "I'm a good worker."

"I'm sure you are." Her voice was starting to shake, and she knew it was time to get out of there before she fell apart. "Come on." She got up, blinking back tears and hoping no one would notice, and took his hand. "Let's go find Lenny."

"Jessie." Joey's hand curled inside hers, snuggling comfortably. "When we get to the ranch, will you bake me chocolate chip cookies like the moms do on TV?"

That did it. To think that he had no mother to do those simple things, that he watched television and dreamed of having a home like those he saw portrayed—she had to turn her face away so he wouldn't see the tears. "Sure, Joey. Sure I will," she answered while digging for a handkerchief and walking rapidly away.

They found Lenny in the next room, flirting with a waitress. Jessie didn't hesitate a moment before barging up and ruining his fun. "You've got to take care of Joey for me," she said sternly, leading him away.

"What?" His thin face expressed raw horror. He looked from Joey to Jessie and back again. "But I—"

"And no 'jobs.' You take him to a room with a television and books to read and keep him there until I get back."

"Aw, come on, Jessie…"

"You've got to do it. I'll be back as quickly as I can." There was no time left to wait for Lenny's contacts to come through, or anything else. Now that she'd found Joey, she had to make sure Michael made it alive through another day.

She looked down at Joey and touched his cheek, smiling at him. She'd never felt this sort of tenderness toward another human being. Toward newborn foals, maybe. But never toward a human. Joey was special and she was going to make sure nothing ever hurt him again. Tearing herself away, she started for the door.

"Come on, buddy," Lenny was saying. "God, did you ever think she'd turn out to be such a pushy broad?"

Jessie remembered something and whipped back, calling, "And Lenny, no naked ladies!"

The disappointment on Joey's face was comical to see, but Jessie didn't feel like laughing. Too many things were happening too fast.

Hurrying outside, she hailed a cab, adjusting her wig as she sank into the back seat. She showed the driver the address on the yellow paper Sam had given her. If she couldn't find Michael, at least she could try to find Kerry.

The apartment building was new and very modern, southwestern cream-colored adobe against blue tiles and tinted glass. Kerry Carter's apartment was on the second floor. Jessie climbed the wrought-iron stairway and tried to still the hammering of her heart.

She would knock on the door, she told herself. Kerry would answer. She would say, "Hi, I'm Jessie MacAllister. Michael Drayton is a friend of mine. He needs your help." And they would go on from there.

Simple. Clean. To the point. How could the man refuse? Together they would call the police and get this whole thing straightened out, Michael could stop running and...?

That was the black hole, the terror she refused to look in the face. There was not a doubt in her mind that Michael would eventually convince everyone of his innocence. But what then? What would happen once Michael was free to go back to his life in San Francisco? The knot twisted inside her and she winced at the pain.

Number 242. She checked the paper, then walked up to the

door. It was slightly ajar. "Hello?" she called, rapping lightly with her knuckles. The door swung in another foot. No one answered. "Is anyone home?" she called again, pushing the door a bit more and leaning inside to get a look around. "Hello!"

The apartment was starkly furnished and the drapes were partly closed, leaving the room dark and gloomy looking. There was only a chair and a small table in sight. And a body lying on the floor.

All the air went out of Jessie's lungs and she couldn't seem to get it back. A body. A man. She had to go closer. She had to look. What if it was…?

No, it wasn't. She'd never seen this man before, and that was good, because he was very dead. There was blood. She didn't want to look again; she only wanted to breathe. She backed away, her hands to her face. Suddenly there were arms around her from behind. "Michael," she gasped, turning, but it wasn't Michael. It was Bob Taylor, and he was holding her tightly, but looking over her head at the body in the middle of the floor.

"Is this the guy Michael thought would help clear him?" he asked her dispassionately.

She nodded, still gasping for breath. "I think so," she managed to say.

"Let's get you out of here." He led her out onto the corridor. Other policemen were coming up the stairs and he motioned for them to go on into the apartment. Gently he pulled off the blond wig, taking out the pins that held it in place. Her own hair tumbled free around her shoulders.

She looked up at him, her pale face anxious. "Where's Michael?"

"I was hoping you knew that."

She shook her head, shuddering.

"That's too bad. We've been following you all over town and I figured you wouldn't have been wandering around that way if you actually knew where you were going."

She gazed at him foggily. "You knew?"

"That you were wearing the blond wig? Sure we knew. We counted on it."

She nodded. She should have known. She only wished it had worked out as he'd planned, and that she'd led him right to Michael. At least he would be safe. The way things stood, she had no idea where he was.

"I have to go," she said, pulling away from Bob.

He held on to her arm. "You can't go. You're in no condition—"

"I have to. I have to find Michael."

He slowly released her. Assessing the situation and the look in her eyes, he decided it was the best way. Reaching into his pocket, he took out another of his cards and quickly scribbled a telephone number on it. "Call me when you find him," he said. "Okay?"

She accepted the card and stared at it for a long moment. Then she looked up into his eyes. "Okay," she said. "That's what I'll do."

She turned and went down the stairs. He watched her go, shaking his head. She would call. He could read the signs. He only hoped she would find Michael before it was too late.

CHAPTER TWENTY-THREE

"Perfect timing," Lenny said when she arrived back at the Nargeant suite. "Michael's here."

"Oh!" She swayed and Lenny caught hold of her shoulders. "He's all right then."

"Sure. Hey, baby, what's the matter, anyway?"

She swallowed and leaned against Lenny for support. "Kerry Carter is dead," she said. "I just came from his apartment. He's dead, and I was so worried about Michael...."

"No sweat." Lenny pushed her down into a chair and called out to a passing employee for some water. "Michael's in talking to Mr. Nargeant." He leaned close and whispered, "I think he's working on the old man to help him fight Sky Matthews. At least, that's what I've heard."

"No." She shook her head. "No more fighting. I've got to talk to him."

Lenny looked concerned. Somehow this didn't sound like the cowgirl he knew. The girl arrived with the water and he offered it to Jessie.

"Here, drink some of this and calm down a little. That was rough, I'll bet, seeing that guy dead and all." He hesitated, watching her sip the water. "Do you want to go lie down or something?"

She looked up and tried to smile. "You're being very sweet, Lenny," she said. "I really appreciate all you've done for me over the past two days. I never would have thought..." Her voice trailed off and her eyes took on a vacant look.

Lenny watched for a moment, frowning, then left the room. When he came back he had Michael with him.

Jessie rose quickly when she saw him. He erased the distance between them in a heartbeat and then he was holding her hard against his chest.

"Michael, Kerry…"

"I heard. I'm so sorry you had to see that."

"Michael." She looked around the room, glad to see Lenny had left them alone. "Michael, there's no time to lose. You've got to turn yourself in now."

He let her go as though she'd suddenly become repugnant to him. "Jessie, I've explained to you again and again that I can't do that."

She shook her head vehemently. "There's no longer any choice, Michael. People are getting killed."

"I know what I'm doing."

"Do you? I'm not so sure about that."

"Sit down, Jessie."

"Michael…"

"I said sit down. I'm going to explain something to you."

She sank to the edge of the chair, hardly listening. She had to find a way to convince him. There was no turning back.

"Jessie, this isn't just a case of clearing my own name. Surely you know that by now. Sky Matthews hurt me, hurt my family beyond repair. You remember how Bud Harvey hurt you, and how you needed to get revenge? That's the way I feel about Sky Matthews. I realize now that he was the worm eating away at the heart of my family from the beginning. He used my father to launder his dirty money. He used my mother to get at Drayton heirlooms. God knows what else he did to make us miserable right from the start. And he tried to destroy me." He took her shoulders in his strong hands. "I can't let this pass, Jessie. I can't sit around and wait for trials and tell my story and have no one believe it. And most of all, I can't spend any more time in jail. That's a sort of death in itself. I'd rather die fighting than be locked up again."

He stared into her empty eyes. "You don't understand, do you?" he said softly. "You aren't even listening to what I'm saying." His hands slid down her arms and back again. "Jessie, Jessie, what can I do to make you see? I talk and talk and you just won't understand."

Michael was wrong. She understood only too well. It was ironic, really. She'd waited all these years for the man she could love, and when he came along, she thought he was a city slicker. Only she'd been sorely mistaken. Michael might think of himself as an urban sophisticate, but he was a cowboy at heart. Just an old dumb cowboy who let his instincts of right and wrong and a man's duty rule his brain and common sense. What a laugh.

"Michael," she said evenly. "When I went to Bud Harvey's house with my shotgun, I was doing something awful. Something even worse than what he did to me. I thank God I saw him with his wife and baby girl. If I'd shot that man, I would have regretted it for the rest of my life. And I would have paid. I would have spent time in prison myself." She touched his face and spoke passionately. "Don't you see? That's what will happen if you go on with this. If by some miracle you come out alive, you'll have done things you can never take back. Hurt people." She shook her head. "It won't bring you peace. It will only bring you sorrow."

"Do you have peace over the Bud Harvey business?" he demanded. "Do you?"

She hesitated. He knew she didn't. She still smarted, still yearned for some form of revenge. "Some things you just have to live with," she said shakily.

"Not me." He rose and stood over her. "Not me, Jessie. I don't have to live with this and I won't. You should have gone back to the ranch when I told you to. Maybe now you will. Now that you know there's nothing left for you here."

He half turned, then looked back for a moment uncertainly. "Goodbye, Jessie," he said. "I've got work to do."

"Goodbye, Michael," she whispered, but he'd already left the room. "I've got work to do, too."

MICHAEL STEPPED BACK into Nargeant's office and sank into the chair across the desk from the man. "Sorry about that," he said gruffly. "I had to make sure Jessie was all right."

"Of course." Mr. Nargeant smiled, folding his hands before him. "I think we've covered the preliminaries. You've told me all you know. I've told you all I know. And I've made up my mind."

Michael looked at him expectantly. "Well?" he said, not bothering to hide his impatience.

"I've loved Sky Matthews in my time. I've admired him. I've envied him. And now I'm going to help you put him away. Because above all, there's nothing I despise so much as a man who sells out his country."

Michael's shoulders sagged with relief, but his face was still dark with anger. "I wish you'd come to this conclusion a little more quickly," he said pointedly. "We might have save a man's life."

Ted Nargeant shrugged. "I'm sorry, but I could not make the decision to turn on an old friend lightly. I had to consider every angle. I had to go over every memory and savor all the good times." He sighed, looking older than his years. "Sky won't forgive this one, I'm afraid. I'm losing a part of my past. Have a little respect."

"Oh, I'm just full of respect," Michael said sarcastically. "But I want to get moving on this before another one of us has to bite the dust in order to support your lengthy thought processes."

Nargeant's smile was humorless. "Yes, if we don't hurry, he'll get us before we get him."

Michael grimaced. "Let's get down to business," he said. "How are we going to do this?"

Nargeant leaned forward across the desk. "That is exactly what you and I are going to map out right now."

IT SEEMED FOREVER between the time Jessie phoned Bob Taylor and the time he and the Las Vegas police arrived in the Samarkand. She stood when she saw them coming in the lobby.

"Upstairs?" he asked her.

She nodded. "In Mr. Nargeant's suite."

He hesitated. "Would you like me to have someone take you home?"

"No. I'll wait right here."

His gaze swept over her and she could see he thought that

was a mistake, but she didn't care. She knew what she was doing and she knew what Michael would think about it. She had to stay. She had to see his face.

So she waited, standing in the lobby, and finally they came down, Michael in handcuffs between Bob and another man. He saw her standing there and his silver-blue eyes glittered like those of a wolf cornered in the wilderness.

He paused in front of her and held up the handcuffs so she wouldn't miss them. He didn't say a word. She licked her lips and waited.

"Congratulations, Jessica MacAllister," he spit out at last. "You finally got that reward money you wanted so badly. I hope you choke on it."

She stood very still, as though paralyzed, and they left through the huge glass doors. Her face didn't give a hint at the emotion that raged within her. He hated her. She'd known he would. But what could she do? She loved him and she had to save him from himself. Even if that meant she would never have him for her own.

She felt hard and cold and tired. She ached inside. But she couldn't cry. There was a tremendous, burning lump in her throat, but other than that she felt hollow. A dry, dead thing that might blow away with the next big wind. At the moment, it seemed as though her life were over. Who could ever bring her the joy Michael had? How could she live knowing she would never feel his touch again, see his smile, join in with his laughter?

She stood for a long time. People glanced at her curiously as they passed, but she didn't notice.

Something bumped gently against her. She glanced down. Joey had found her. He curled his little warm hand into her cold one. She looked at it, the immature fingers, and suddenly violent sobs wracked her body. She pulled him to her tightly, and finally she cried.

They walked back together, first down the neon boulevard, then through the quiet residential streets, and Joey's hand never left hers. When they got to the house, Sheri and Sam were solicitous, making her take a long hot bath and feeding Joey.

Bob Taylor called and asked if she would come in the next day to make her statement, and she agreed to, speaking normally. Looking at her, most people wouldn't know she was one of the walking wounded. But Joey knew. And he was never far away, always ready with that comforting little hand in hers.

Sam drove her to the police station the next day. Bob Taylor watched her walk in, and he wondered what was going through her mind. She looked so calm, so cool. Maybe he'd been wrong about her. Maybe she hadn't been as taken with Michael as he'd thought.

"Good morning," he said, offering her a chair. "I'm going to record what you have to say, if you don't mind."

She sank into the chair and shook her head. He began questioning her, going over everything that had happened from the time she first saw Michael in her father's café. She told him about the night in the desert, the scorpion sting, the ride to her uncle's, the diamonds. Everything. It all came out. She spoke in a clear, unemotional voice. This was just another chore, something to get out of the way.

When it was over, he turned off the tape machine and looked at her, chewing on his lip. She seemed calm, but something told him the appearance was deceiving. He wanted to help her, if he could. But he didn't know how.

"Will you be needing me to testify?" she asked.

He shook his head. "I doubt it. Your relationship with Michael has a lot to do with his flight from justice, but that's not what he's being charged with. You have nothing to do with the original crime."

"The alleged crime," she corrected him.

He smiled. "Right. The alleged crime."

"What's going to happen to him?"

"We'll be leaving for California this afternoon. He'll be arraigned there. I have no idea when he'll be tried." He looked at her kindly. "Would you like me to keep you posted?" he asked.

She looked relieved. "Yes. Please." Taking a pen from his box, she quickly wrote out the address of the ranch on a piece of paper for him. "I'd appreciate it."

"No problem." He paused. She sat very still. "That's all I need right now. Will you be going home?"

"Yes. If you don't need me, I think I'll start back in the morning."

He stood, shaking hands with her as she got up from her chair. "Good luck. And thank you."

Her smile was cool. She turned to go. But when she reached the door she stopped and stood very still for a moment, then turned back.

"Can I see him?" she asked dully.

He'd been afraid of that question from the beginning. He hated to tell her, but he had no choice. "I'm sorry. He has specifically said he doesn't want to see you."

She nodded, not surprised. The emotions were boiling inside her again. One little slip like that and they all came surging to the surface. She bit her lip, holding her feelings back.

But there was just one more thing. "I don't suppose you could arrest me," she said, her eyes deep and troubled, her voice trembling. "I don't suppose you could put me in jail." She knew she was being irrational, but she felt that was where she belonged. She wished she could somehow take Michael's place there.

"No, Jessie. I'm afraid not."

"No." Her heart had done the asking. Her head knew better. "Well, goodbye." She even managed a smile. And then she was gone.

SKY GLANCED OUT at the men sitting in his waiting room. The best lawyers money could buy. It was too bad it had come to this, but he'd been in fights before. He'd weather this storm just as he'd weathered others before it.

He closed the door and sank into the chair behind his desk, procrastinating. He wasn't really ready to face the legal eagles yet. There was one more thing he had to do.

"Betty," he asked his secretary over the telephone, "get me Vanessa in Paris."

It took almost ten minutes to get through. He spent most of the time staring out the window at the city below. San Francisco. His home for all this time. Surely it wouldn't turn on him now?

No. A fierce anger swept through him. No, dammit! They weren't going to get him. He would fight the government and the district attorney and every other man, woman and agency that tried to ruin him and the business he'd built up over the years.

To do that he needed to gather his forces. And he needed his family around him. Vanessa would have to come home and help her old man, now that he needed her. She'd pout and beg to stay in Paris. He knew his girl. And usually he'd give in to her. But not this time. He needed her. She had to come.

"Mr. Matthews, I have your daughter on the line."

He picked up the telephone. "Vanessa, baby."

"Daddy!" Her voice sounded wonderful above the crackle of the overseas line.

"Sweetheart, how are you? Are you having a good time in Paris?"

"Oh, Daddy, I was going to call you. Guess what? Daddy, I think I'm in love."

He couldn't keep the exasperation from his tone. "Again?"

"No." Her voice got very soft and confidential. "This time it's for real, Daddy. His name is Mark Beaumont. He's an artist. He does the most beautiful work in watercolor." She laughed. "Oh, Daddy, it's so amazing. I think he loves me, too."

Sky frowned. "Well, of course he does."

"No." Her voice was solemn. "Haven't you ever noticed, Daddy? They never love me. All the men in my life, it's always been me crazy in love. Never them. Just look at Michael and how he acted. And this time…" Her voice got very soft and warm. "Oh, this time, Daddy, I think it's true. I think he loves me back."

Sky made a helpless gesture no one saw. "Well, what about Michael? Have you forgotten all about him?"

Vanessa sighed. "Michael is in my past, Daddy. He said when he left he would never marry me. I didn't want to believe him, but now I see he was right to cut me free like that. Mark is my future. I can't ever leave him.''

Sky hesitated. "Sugar…'' It was breaking his heart. "Honey, I'd like you to come home. I…I've got sort of a problem here.…''

Her voice was all tragedy. "Oh, no, Daddy, please don't make me. If I leave now, I don't know what will happen. I can't go. If I do, I'll be throwing away my only chance at happiness!''

Sky felt something choking his throat. He was facing jail and his daughter was still looking for happiness. "Honey, this is serious. I'd feel stronger if I had you here beside me.''

"Stronger?'' She laughed. "You're kidding, aren't you? Oh, you old kidder! Honestly, Daddy, I'd come if I could. But we both know you can handle anything. You're still Superman in my book. You'll get along just fine without me.''

What could he do? He loved her. His shaking hand went to his forehead and he closed his eyes. "Okay, honey,'' he said, his voice raw. "You just have a wonderful time. I…I'll call you later in the week.''

He hung up the phone and looked around the office. He really was all alone. Everyone he'd ever loved was gone. Suddenly he felt very old and very tired. Leaning over the intercom, he said, "Betty, send my lawyers in. I'm ready now.''

CHAPTER TWENTY-FOUR

RANCHING WAS A GOOD SCHOOL for life, Jessie decided one morning as she and Smoke were out riding across her land. You worked so damn hard at it, trying again and again, and it gave you a lot of joy, and then it turned around and kicked you in the teeth, just for the fun of it. And you had to pick yourself up and dust off the seat of your pants and start all over again. Just like life.

A ranch was also a good place to raise a child. She gave a yell as she saw a rider appear on the crest of the hill, and the rider answered and rode hell-bent for leather toward her, reining to a stop in a cloud of choking dust.

"Joey! You do that one more time, I'll have Harley tan your hide!"

The boy laughed. They both knew she was bluffing. She loved to watch him ride. He'd taken to it as though he'd been born in the saddle. He seemed to have grown a foot in the six months since they'd been back from Las Vegas. His little body was thickening nicely, and the smile on his face couldn't be beat.

"I'll race you home," he challenged. "Bet I win."

"That'll be the day." But she grinned at him. "Actually, I've got to go and check the back lot. Mike said he thought there might be some strays hiding out there. There's been rumors of cougars lately. I don't want to leave them so far out. You go on back, though, cuz Harley could use your help with the lunch crowd."

Joey groaned. "I hate that old café," he complained, and Jessie had to grin again, because she knew he was just voicing her opinion.

"But you don't hate Harley," she reminded him. "So go on back and give him a hand."

"Okay." Despite his complaining, he wore a cheerful expression as he rode off.

Jessie continued on her way, riding slow. It was a crisp November day and she was feeling good. Feeling thankful. Counting her blessings.

First and foremost was Joey, of course. She'd brought him back with her, moved him into the house as though he were her adopted child. Harley had taken to him right away, but friends, neighbors, even the ranch hands had said it wouldn't work.

"A runaway like that? He'll be gone in a week" was the general opinion. "And he'll rob you blind in the meantime. Don't set yourself up for a broken heart."

Well, he was sort of a runaway, but he'd been a runaway searching desperately for the middle-class life he mostly saw on television. Jessie and Harley couldn't quite provide that, and most of the TV stuff was a fantasy, anyway. But they could give Joey things he'd never had, the security he craved, the love that made him strong. And he'd blossomed in their care. Jessie was looking into adopting him legally, and the lawyer said there should be no problem, as soon as it was proven both his parents were deceased.

The boy was a joy to have around. Jessie often told herself that all the pain and suffering were worth it, because of Joey. He was her reason to live.

Another good thing was the money. Jessie had been in no mood to think about it that last day before she'd left Las Vegas, but Sheri and Sam had taken matters into their own hands and made sure she got the money from the jackpot. She was on videotape. The proof was there. All she had to do was show up to collect it.

Of course, a good part of the fifty thousand dollars disappeared fast once commissions and taxes were paid, but there'd been enough left to do some good around the ranch, to fix up the house a little, to improve Harley's café, to buy a few head of better stock.

Harley and Fred had patched up their quarrel. They went together to the registrar of wills and took a look at what Aunt Jessica had left. It turned out there hadn't been much of a fortune at all, and what there was had been willed to the Arizona Historical Society. They'd laughed over that. The ten years wasted were a shame, but they were making up for lost time now.

About a week after she returned home, someone called about the reward for capturing Michael. All he wanted to do was advise her of her right to apply for it, but she hung up on him and never looked into it. That was one bit of money she would starve to death before she'd take.

Michael. Her heart still ached when she thought of him, but she'd survived. Bob Taylor had sent her updates on his condition, as he'd promised, and sure enough, the authorities had clamped down on Sky Matthews and found enough evidence of Michael's innocence that he had never even had to stand trial. She didn't know how long Michael had been forced to spend in jail. She was sure his hatred of her had grown with every passing hour he was behind bars.

But she knew he was out now, had been for months. At first a part of her had hoped he would get in touch with her. But as the weeks slipped by, that hope had died. It had been six long months since Las Vegas. She didn't have time to live on memories. There was too much work to do for that.

It was usually at night when the ghosts of that insane journey across the countryside came back to haunt her. She'd fall asleep quickly, as any woman who did the sort of physical labor she did would have done, and then at about two in the morning she would find herself wide-awake, staring at the ceiling, and Michael's face would be floating there, his smile, his laugh, his passion. And she would have to go over every single detail of their time together once again before she could sleep.

It was crazy really how four days could have changed her life so drastically. But they had.

She found the strays and turned them over to one of the hands to get back to the main herd, then rode over to Harley's café to see how the lunch take had been. She swung down and tied Smoke out back, stomping hard on the back steps as she came into the little restaurant.

Joey was doing dishes. The only customer was the sheriff, and Harley was leaning across the counter, talking to him. Jessie tossed her hat like a Frisbee and it landed on top of the hat rack, then bounced down to occupy a handy chair.

"Hi, Sheriff," she said cheerfully, leaning next to Harley, placing her chin in her hands and smiling at the man. "What's new?"

The sheriff looked up from the piece of cherry pie he was attacking with relish and stared at her. Putting down his fork, he took off his dark glasses and stared again. Finally he spoke. "I was just telling your father here about a strange thing that happened. It seems to have something to do with you. Maybe you can help me figure it out."

She shrugged. "I'm always ready to cooperate with the law. You know that."

The sheriff grunted, but he didn't return her teasing grin. "It seems someone went out to Bud Harvey's ranch, called the man out into the yard and beat him up." He fixed her with a stern eye. "You know anything about this?"

Jessie had blanched on hearing Bud Harvey's name. She knew the sheriff had noticed. Avoiding his eyes, she shook her head. "No...no, I don't know anything about it." The initial shock passed and her courage came back. She looked him straight in the eye and lifted her chin. "I can't claim to have any great love for Bud Harvey, but I don't believe that makes me unique. What makes you think I had anything to do with this?"

"Well, you just listen, and I'll tell you." He had another bite of pie and took his own sweet time chewing it before a serious swallow. "Harvey's wife called me. Said some guy in a suit, some city fella, was out in the yard beating her husband up and would I come quick and stop it. I said sure. I got in my car and drove on out there. The fella was long gone by the time I arrived. But one of Harvey's hands, young stinker by the name of Petey, saw the whole thing. Told me the man called Bud out and just started beatin' on him, then, when he had Bud down in the dust, said…'' He brought a napkin to his mouth and cleared his throat before continuing. "He said, 'This is for Jessie MacAllister. Touch her again and you'll die for it.'" The sheriff paused and squinted at Jessie. "You got anything to say?"

Jessie was trembling. There was only one man who knew what had happened between Bud Harvey and her. But…it couldn't be. It just couldn't be.

"No, sir," she said as firmly as possible. "I haven't got anything at all to say about this matter." She looked the sheriff in the eye. "I guess it was just some Good Samaritan who knew Bud Harvey had done me an injury once and figured to make sure he didn't do it again. I hope you can leave it at that."

She stared at the sheriff and he stared back. Finally a smile began to tug at the corners of his mouth. "For someone who's got nothing to say, you said plenty, Jessie." He pushed the pie dish away. "I reckon I'll take what you said under advisement. See y'all." He stomped out of the café to his car.

Jessie swallowed hard. "He didn't pay," she complained to Harley.

"He never does," Harley returned, looking curiously at his daughter. But he knew better than to question her. All in good time. She'd tell him when she was good and ready.

Jessie opened the freezer, just to have somewhere to look that faces weren't watching at her. It couldn't be. Could it? Her mind was in state of panic and she stared into the freezer until frostbite threatened her nose. Just as she was closing it again, she heard a sports car pull up outside.

Jessie didn't move, but her hand went to her hair. It was in those awful braids. She heard the screen door slam, but she didn't turn around.

"Howdy," Harley was saying. "Pick any place you want, mister."

From the creaking sound, she could tell the man had taken a seat at the corner. She waited, holding her breath.

"What'll it be?" her father was asking.

"Actually, I came in to see about a job," the man said. "But I'll take a cup of coffee."

"A job. You mean on the ranch? You'll have to talk to my daughter about that. Jessie? This here fella's looking for work. Weren't you saying your wrangler is going home to Montana next week?"

Jessie turned slowly. Michael's silver-blue eyes met hers from under the brim of a gray Stetson, sending an exquisite shiver down her spine, sending her heart into a race that threatened to take her breath away. He was dressed Western, but everything was brand-new, from the hat to the shiny new cowboy boots. The picture he presented might have been comical if it hadn't been for his strong, tall body and handsome face. There was nothing funny about that.

"Yeah, Larry's leaving," she said slowly, coming up to the counter. Michael gave no sign of knowing her. She could feel the bright spots of color in her cheeks, but she couldn't do anything about that. "But it'll take a damn good man to replace him."

She waited, wanting a cue from him, something that would tell her why he was here. For all she knew, he'd come back to yell at her again, to let her know just how miserable she'd made him by turning him in. But nothing changed in his eyes. For all any onlooker knew, he was a stranger. Just a drifter looking for a job.

Harley had no idea who this was. He was poking her with his elbow, saying out of the corner of his mouth, "Come on, Jessie. He looks like a pretty good fella to me. Don't cut him off at the knees before you've given him a chance."

But Michael didn't need Harley to plead his case. "Tell me, Miss Jessie, just what does it take to be a 'damn good man'?" he asked pointedly.

She leaned on the counter, fascinated that he would ask. "Well, I'll tell you what Larry can do. Larry can ride everything from a Brahma bull to a rattlesnake. He can shoe a horse in ten minutes flat, brand a calf in ten seconds. He knows where every head of stock is, no matter what time of day or night, and can smell a cougar coming two counties away." She raised an eyebrow. "Can you do all that?"

His silver-blue eyes were guileless. "I don't know. I've never tried."

Harley was sputtering in the background. He poured Michael's coffee and nearly spilled it all over the counter as he listened, agape, to the crazy things Jessie was saying.

"What have you tried, mister?" she challenged now. "Ever been on a horse at all?"

He nodded. "Now this will surprise you," he told her quite seriously. "When I was a teenager I got myself a part-time job giving riding lessons to little girls in Montgomery Park, near where I lived in the Bay Area. I can ride, Jessie. In fact, I'm pretty good."

Wonderful. *But why are you here?* This cat-and-mouse game was beginning to get on her nerves. It was just like Michael to throw her off guard this way.

"Riding is all well and good. But there are other things necessary to earn the 'damn good man' title."

Harley swallowed hard and looked from one to the other of them, wondering if his daughter had burned out too many light bulbs. She'd always been a tough employer, but she wasn't usually rude to people. And to such a good-looking fellow, too. It seemed a shame.

"Oh, yeah?" Michael was replying to Jessie's thrust. "Like what?"

Okay, Michael Drayton. This is where you get it with both barrels. She stared at him, her eyes full of all she was feeling. "Like kindness and consideration for other people. Like listening and trying to understand another point of view. Like forgiveness." Her voice shook on the last word and she cursed silently, wishing she could take it back.

Michael shoved the hat back away from his face and met her gaze with total candor. "I can do all those things, Jessie. I may not have done much to prove it lately, but I know I can. Will you give me a chance to show you?"

What was he asking? If only she were sure. She stood very still, waiting for a revelation, some sign...

Joey came banging out of the kitchen, swaggering in his cowboy boots. His eyes widened when he saw who was visiting. "Hey, Michael," he said with a nod, climbing up onto a stool beside him. "'Bout time you got here." He looked at Harley. "I finished the dishes. Can I have some pie?"

Michael's face dissolved into a grin. He looked at Jessie. He hadn't known she'd kept Joey with her. "Who is this smart-aleck kid?" he asked her. "Where'd he come from?"

Harley was staring at him, finally getting it. "Is this...?"

Jessie's joy was brimming over. "It sure is," she said, her voice choked. "It's Michael Drayton."

"Why, you look different, son." Harley stuck out his hand and gave Michael's a firm shake. "Glad to really meet you after all this time."

Jessie's eyes were full of tears. Thoroughly ashamed of herself, she tried to duck away to find a place to wipe them, but Michael was up off his stool and around the counter and holding her by the shoulders, forcing her to look up at him. She couldn't really see him. Through her tears all she saw was a blurry image. But she could feel his lips when they gently brushed hers, and the tears began to stream down her cheeks like small rivers.

"Oh, Michael," she cried out, and his arms were around her and he was holding her so tightly, so sweetly, she didn't want him ever to let her go.

"Does this mean I get the job?" he asked, his own voice husky with emotion.

"I don't know," she said, sniffing. "How long do you need it for?"

His arms tightened. "The rest of my life," he said. "What do you say?"

Jessie couldn't say anything. She was crying so hard the words wouldn't come.

EPILOGUE

JESSIE HEARD MICHAEL'S CAR roar into the driveway that evening and she gave a quick glance at the mirror. She looked okay. She'd tied her hair back with a pink velvet ribbon, and she was wearing a soft white dress that clung to her body. She couldn't have looked more feminine if she'd tried. And that made her grin.

It seemed so long that she'd been afraid to dress up, to be a woman. She'd actually felt that it was a sign of weakness, that men would walk all over her if she gave an inch. She didn't believe that anymore. Oh, she still lived in jeans most of the time. But it was fun to put on a dress now and then. Especially tonight. Michael was coming.

"Hi." She met him the door. "You're early."

He looked her up and down and smiled. "I couldn't stay away." Drawing her into his arms, he kissed her once, twice and then again. "God, you taste so good. I don't even need dinner."

"But dinner is what you'll get," she said primly. "Harley and Joey have gone into town to the movies and we're going to have a proper meal."

"You cooked just for me?" He gazed at her wonderingly. "When did you have time?"

A sheepish look passed over her face. "Well, if you want to know the truth, Harley cooked the dinner before he left." She perked up. "But I'm real good at heating things up, and I can pour wine into goblets like a champ. Just watch me."

As good as her word, she poured out a glass of wine and handed it to him, her gaze slipping over him as she did so. He was so wonderful. So handsome, so good. Her heart ached with love for him. What had she done to deserve this luck? She'd never know. He'd walked into the café that afternoon and the sun had come back into her life.

"Let's go into the living room and talk," she said once she'd poured some wine for herself. "I want to hear all about every-thing."

She'd worked hard at sprucing the living room up, getting herself some green plants and things, and she was proud of how it had turned out. Michael didn't comment, but that didn't surprise her. He didn't know how bad things had been before. Back when she didn't care.

They settled on opposite ends of the overstuffed couch. "You promised to fill me in," she said, loving the way the late-afternoon sun slanted in and made his silver streak gleam. "Though I do know some things. Bob Taylor kept me posted on how you were doing."

"Did he?" Michael's grin was rueful. "Good old Bob. He helped me out a lot in the end. Without his backing it would have taken me a lot longer to get an investigation going on Matthews Aviation."

"So Sky was a crook?"

"You'd better believe it. It seems he had his fingers in a lot of pies. But the worst was selling computer secrets to the east-ern bloc countries." He took a sip of wine and went on. "He'd hoped to scare me into coming back into the fold with the warrant for my arrest and the reward. When that didn't work, he wanted me shut up quick, before I did any more damage to his operation."

She nodded. "She'd already figured that out herself. What happened after Bob took you back to California?"

"The most important thing happened *before* I ever left Las Vegas. I talked to Nargeant and convinced him to do something about Sky." He set down his glass of wine on the coffee table. "You see, Nargeant may come close to the edge at times, but on the whole, he's an honest businessman. He'd had dealings with Sky and hadn't been pleased with the results. Kerry had contacted him and gone to Las Vegas to ask for his help in nailing Sky, but Nargeant had been reluctant to get involved.

Then when I backed up what Kerry had been telling him, he began to change his mind. After Kerry was murdered, he came in behind me all the way. But it took time to get that through the system. The FBI had to get involved first. In the meantime, I sat in jail.''

She nodded, her eyes clouded. ''But you're still alive. Kerry's not.''

He looked at her for a long moment. ''True,'' he said at last. ''But I can't pretend I wasn't furious with you for what you did.''

''I know.'' She tried to smile. ''And I paid for it.''

He leaned closer. ''I forgive you this time. But the next time you have me thrown in jail, there's going to be hell to pay.''

''I'll keep that in mind.'' She lifted her face for his kiss. ''Did you give the diamonds back to your mother?''

His face was stony. ''No. She's in Paris. I don't think we'll be seeing her very soon.'' His shoulders straightened. ''She proved a bad caretaker. I don't see any reason to give her another chance. So the diamonds will go to the next Mrs. Drayton. Don't you think that's appropriate?''

Jessie blinked and nodded. ''I guess so.''

His gaze skimmed over her, a glint of amusement in his eyes. ''They really are exquisite, you know. They deserve to be worn against flawless skin, around an elegant neck. Only a woman with that certain je ne sais quoi can carry that off. Don't you think?''

Jessie stared at him. Was he trying to tell her something? Like maybe they didn't belong on a ranch? She knew that. He didn't have to rub it in.

''I guess so,'' she muttered. ''Although I don't know what good a string of shiny rocks like that is to anyone, anyway.''

He raised one dark eyebrow. ''You don't want them?''

She stared at him. ''Me?''

His sigh was pure exasperation. ''Of course you. Who did you think I was talking about?''

She babbled, confused. ''But you said...''

His arms came around her and he gazed down into her puzzled face. ''What do you want, Jessie? Do you want me to go down on my knees and beg you to marry you? If that's what you want, I'll do it." He kissed her nose. "Just say the word."

She was still not sure. "But you can't marry me," she sputtered. "I'm a rancher. You belong in the city."

"I belong with you." His breath tickled her ear. "I've never known anyone like you. I can trust you, Jessie. I can always count on you to do the right thing, no matter how much it hurts. That's something I can bank on. I want that something in my life."

"Michael..."

"I love you, Jessie MacAllister. And I want to live out here on your damn old ranch, where the air is clean and people say what they mean and you can trust your neighbor." He kissed her hard. "I want to make love with you every night and have a dozen little brothers and sisters for Joey and watch Harley grow old. Will you let me do that?"

"Michael! Oh, Michael!" Her arms went around his neck and she clung to him, her heart overflowing. "I love you more than anything, anything."

His mouth on hers prevented any more talk for a long, long time. Finally Jessie stirred and managed to whisper just a little plaintively, "Dinner..."

Michael laughed softly against her cheek and his hands began to move over the white dress. "Throw it out," he growled. "We've got six months of lovemaking to fill in. Starting now."

That was all right with Jessie. She felt herself blossom at his touch. Ranching had always been her first love, but she had a feeling this new activity was going to take its place real soon.

A LETTER FROM THE AUTHOR

Dear Reader,

Got a yen for a long, tall cowboy? Got a hankering for hard, sinewy muscles and a cool stare, for jeans worn silver in the sun and spurs that jingle, for a day's growth of beard and hands that can punish wrongdoers and gentle a terrified horse? Things were clear-cut in the Old West. The good, the bad and the ugly each knew its place. Men and women both struggled for survival. But they had no doubts about what was wrong and what was right. They say men treated women better in those days, that even the most hard-bitten gunfighter held a woman in respect and treated her with courtesy. Maybe that's why we hold a special place in our hearts for the time and the place, and like stories set in the modern-day equivalent. Michael Drayton, the hero of *Desperado*, is originally a city man, but he has the instincts of a cowboy. And when he meets cowgirl Jessie MacAllister, he quickly becomes a Western man himself, and together they play out a drama of good versus evil, just as they do in any good Western.

That's one reason that I love this book, and why I'm so pleased it is appearing as part of the WESTERN LOVERS series. I hope you like it, too, and I hope it gives you the same Western feel it gave me to write it.

Sincerely yours,

Helen Conrad

HARLEQUIN *Presents*

The world's bestselling romance series...
The series that brings you your favorite authors,
month after month:

Helen Bianchin...Emma Darcy
Lynne Graham...Penny Jordan
Miranda Lee...Sandra Marton
Anne Mather...Carole Mortimer
Susan Napier...Michelle Reid

and many more uniquely talented authors!

Wealthy, powerful, gorgeous men...
Women who have feelings just like your own...
The stories you love, set in exotic, glamorous locations...

HARLEQUIN *Presents*

Seduction and passion guaranteed!

HARLEQUIN®
INTRIGUE

WE'LL LEAVE YOU BREATHLESS!

If you've been looking for thrilling tales of
contemporary passion and sensuous love stories
with taut, edge-of-the-seat suspense—then
you'll love Harlequin Intrigue!

Every month, you'll meet four new heroes
who are guaranteed to make your spine tingle
and your pulse pound. With them you'll enter
into the exciting world of Harlequin Intrigue—
where your life is on the line
and so is your heart!

THAT'S INTRIGUE—
ROMANTIC SUSPENSE
AT ITS BEST!

HARLEQUIN®
Makes any time special ®